MW01493436

BLOOD
AND
BONBONS

BLOOD
AND
BONBONS

MELISSA NICOLE

To Nicole,
Enjoy the ♡

Shattered Glass
PUBLISHING

The characters and events in this book are fictitious. Any similarities to real persons, living or dead, are coincidental and not intended by the author.

Published by Shattered Glass Publishing.

BLOOD AND BONBONS. Copyright © 2023 by Melissa Nicole. All rights reserved.

Cover design by Trif Designs
© Depositphotos.com
Proofread by The Proof Posse (Jackie, Dawn, Heather, Mirjam, and Roxanne)

ISBN 978-1-63869-033-7 (eBook Edition)
ISBN 978-1-63869-034-4 (Paperback Edition)

No part of this publication may be reproduced, stored in a retrieval system, or transmitted in any form or by any means electronic, mechanical, photocopying, recording, or otherwise without express written permission from the author.

Version 2023.10.10

To friendship, imagination, and laughing until you pee.

CHAPTER ONE

"YOU'RE FIRED."

Vena, my best friend and roommate, snorted at my comment and gestured at the wall.

"It's only twenty feet, Everly. Stop being a baby, and just do it."

I stubbornly crossed my arms across my ample chest.

"We could have done anything. Golfing. Bowling. Yoga. Why rock climbing?"

"Because it's close and takes care of the credit we needed for —"

"The credit you needed, not me. It should be Piper here. She's the mountain goat." Even as I complained, I turned my head to look up at the imposing indoor rock wall. The height didn't bother me. It was the damn cord attached to the uncomfortable harness buckled around my hips that did. While I wasn't a diva by any means, I did take care how I dressed. The rock climbing harness wasn't flattering.

"Look," I said, pointing at my downstairs. "I look like I'm packing. This is not okay."

1

Vena turned away from me to hide her laugh as if her shaking shoulders didn't give it away.

"Reach the top, and I'll buy you anything you want from the French bakery by the capitol," she said.

She knew my weakness. I had a love for all things found in a bakery.

"Don't toy with me, Vena."

She faced me with a wicked grin. "*Anything* you want."

I looked up at the wall and started bouncing side to side, psyching myself up for the most uncoordinated climb in history. "I'm going to *own* this wall."

"Yeah, you're going to need to get closer than that to own it."

I didn't bother shooting her a dirty look. Instead, I attacked the wall, grunting and sweating my way slowly up its length. My arms burned, and my legs shook before I even made it halfway.

"Come on, Everly. You got this," Vena said as she climbed past me.

Easy for her to say. Where I clung to the wall, she kind of just hovered there. She even let go with one hand to brush back a loose strand of her long, dark brown hair that she'd pulled back into a ponytail. Not a droplet of sweat misted her brow. I easily imagined my sweat-matted blonde hair clinging to my face, despite my attempts to tie it back.

I didn't hate Vena for her athleticism. She worked on it. A lot. And I didn't.

"You're going to need to talk dirty to me if you want me to finish this," I said, straining to maintain my handholds.

"All right. But remember you asked for this." She took a deep breath then, in her most sultry voice, murmured, "Opera cake. Macaron. Canelé. Beignets."

I laughed so hard that my grip almost slipped from my next handhold. But her teasing distraction had done the job, and I managed to find the willpower to keep going until I touched the buzzer at the top.

Pretending to faint, I free-fell backward, letting the mechanism slowly return me to the ground.

"Please tell me the first time's a charm. I don't think a fifteen-minute break is going to be enough to get me to go again."

"That's what he said," Vena said with a grin beside me.

"How are you almost twenty-two and still using that line?"

"Pfft. I heard your grandma say it to your mom. It's timeless."

With a playful groan, I started stripping from my harness on the way to the counter.

"We should rock climb outside once," she said. "I think you'd enjoy it more."

I paused in handing over the harness and shot her a suspicious look. "Voluntary outdoor activity? Why?"

"Because, if your skin was any pastier, people will start thinking you're a vampire."

The clerk made a choking noise.

"Don't even joke about that, Vena." I turned my exasperated look to the guy behind the counter. "It's the middle of the day. I'm obviously not a vampire."

He nodded and busied himself with straightening the harnesses while I dragged Vena out the door into the early summer sun to scold her.

"It's not funny when you do that. You might be comfortable tossing out that kind of stuff in a conversational tone, but not everyone is."

Three generations hadn't been enough time to erase the old

fears regarding the existence of otherworldly creatures like vampires. It was barely enough to make werewolves socially acceptable. Granted, it helped that werewolves didn't crave human blood like I craved desserts.

"People need to relax more. Fearing something won't make it go away," Vena said, walking beside me through the parking lot.

As if her smart remark summoned it, a small splash of blue flew in front of my face, startling me. Stumbling back a step, I batted a hand at the tiny creature and squealed.

"It's already gone, Everly. And stop with the swatting. Neither of us can afford the five-hundred-dollar fine if you hurt one."

I shuddered. "I hate fairies. How are they endangered if they're flying around in the city like this?"

"You need to overcome your fear," Vena said. "It's been five years."

"Fairies are my snakes. I don't tell you to get over your fear."

"That's different. It's natural to fear something that has fangs and wants to kill you."

"Fairies have sharp teeth."

"They're not out to kill a person. They're nothing more than trash diggers and thieves."

"Tell that to the one that tried to electrocute me," I said.

She snorted. "It wasn't trying to kill you. It wanted the curling iron. And Miles tossed the fairy out of the bathroom before anything happened."

Lies. Something had definitely happened that fateful day at her family's home. Her brother, in full-on hero mode, had burst into the bathroom and witnessed my naked flailing in the

4

shower. I'd been traumatized twice that day and wasn't sure I'd ever get over my fairy grudge.

"Whatever. I'm not a fan. Let's focus on what's important. You owe me bakery," I said as we headed to the car.

"You got it," Vena said too cheerfully for my comfort. "We'll have just enough time before Miles gets to our place."

"Why is Miles coming over?" I asked suspiciously.

"Can't a brother come and visit his only sister?"

"Sure, but the only time he seems to come over is when he has . . ."

Miles was an avid researcher of one particular thing: Treasure. And not just any treasure. Supernatural treasure.

"No. Absolutely not!"

"He's coming over to visit. That's all."

She was acting way too innocent.

"Spill it, or you're going to owe me so much bakery that I won't be able to squeeze into the rock climbing harness anymore."

She gave the slightest guilty shrug and quickly said, "Miles found a lead, and it's a solid one."

"No."

"Please. Let's hear him out."

Vena hadn't chosen a nice sedate occupation such as a researcher like her brother. Oh no. She wasn't one to sit still for hours at a time. She wanted to follow in her grandparents' footsteps as a treasure hunter.

"Not happening," I said. "The last time you went after something, you came home with a concussion and bruised ribs. You're officially grounded from hunting."

"What if I said this artifact could cover the tuition for both our fall semesters?"

"I'd say it's not worth the risk."

5

"Think about the math. Do you know how long it will take us to pay off our loans at an entry-level 'normal' job? Forever. And we're not the only ones who'd benefit from this. Miles has been working his butt off to establish connections in the trade. The only way anyone will ever pay him for his research information is if it proves viable to someone else. If you won't agree for our sakes, then do it for Miles," she said with a sweetness that only came out for coercion. "He really needs a win."

"This goes beyond bakery. We're talking high-end chocolate now."

She grinned, knowing she had won. I sulked a little on the way to the bakery and consoled myself with a beignet and a fancy eight-inch chocolate-layered cake to-go.

"I promise this won't be like the last time," Vena said as she drove us home. "I've been reading my grandparents' journals. Prepared will be my middle name."

Rolling my eyes, I swallowed a bite of my bribe so I could respond.

"It's impossible to prepare for the unexpected. So your promise is pointless and not appreciated. Why can't you be a dentist or something?"

"Could you seriously see me doing something that mundane?"

I couldn't. Hunting for treasure was in Vena's blood from her father's side. Her grandparents had been renowned for their finds, and both Vena and Miles sought the same notoriety within the Shadow Trade community. I didn't. Her grandparents had mysteriously disappeared on a hunting expedition ten years ago, and it wasn't a fate I wanted my best friend to share. Not that she ever listened to my warnings.

"I'm going to worry the entire time you're gone," I said instead.

"Unless you come with me."

"Ha! Not happening. If treasure hunting concusses you, it would kill me."

It was an old argument. While treasure hunting might call to her as a means to earn money, it didn't call to me. No matter how boring regular employment sounded, it was safe. I liked safe. And I liked knowing when and how much I would get paid.

Miles' empty car sat at the curb in front of our house when we arrived. Seeing it tweaked my anxiety. I knew there was nothing I could do to stop Vena from diving head-first into whatever hunt her brother's latest research lead would take her on, which only made me worry for her more.

She parked behind his car and got out.

Taking care with my cake, I did the same and looked at our old, one-story bungalow. A cheery yellow coated the wood siding, one of the few nice attributes of the place. The deafening noise of the train rattling behind our house was the biggest negative. However, our home's proximity to the still active track was one of the reasons we could afford the rent. The daily mini tremors were the reason we couldn't hang any pictures.

We climbed the weathered steps and crossed the slanted porch to the front door. Inside, the train was muted enough that Vena called out a greeting once the door was closed.

"In here," Miles called back.

We made our way through the small living room to the dining room. Papers were spread out over the table, along with a few maps. Miles' research, no doubt.

Shaking my head, I continued to the kitchen and found Miles bent at the waist, looking at the contents of our fridge.

In the month since we'd last seen him, he'd changed. Based on the way his jeans hugged his backside and thighs, he'd built muscle. It looked good. But then again, forbidden usually always looked good.

"Looking for something?" Vena asked, walking in behind me.

He straightened and flashed us a grin. His tousled light brown hair and the excitement dancing in his bespeckled blue eyes made my stomach dip.

As Vena's lifelong friend, I should have been immune to Miles' good looks and charm. Not a chance. He was smart, fun to be around, and had an athletic build that would make any straight girl's mouth water.

"Please tell me there's something in that bag for me," he begged, seeing the bakery bag I held.

I set it on our yellowed counter and gave him a hard look. "I'll let you have half of this cake if you promise that your sister's not going to get hurt hunting whatever little treasure you've found."

He made a face. "No cake for me, then. I only make promises I know I can keep."

I shot Vena a look. "More reason not to do this, Vena. Even Miles thinks you're going to get hurt."

"That's not what I said," he interjected quickly. "The cache should be an easy find, but we both know the nature of this business. The unexpected happens. Even a stubbed toe could count as an injury."

"You've been working with fae too much," Vena said. "Even they would have no reason to skirt around the truth. You know Everly means serious bodily harm."

He shook his head. "I'm not dumb enough to promise that either. You take risks you shouldn't take."

My stomach gave another sickening twist. "For the sake of my sanity, I'm going to shower while you two bicker and work out what kind of hellish mission you're sending your sister on."

Neither tried to stop my retreat.

After grabbing a change of clothes, I closed myself into our only bathroom. While the water ran, I stripped and thought of anything but what they were talking about in the kitchen.

Vena knocked on the door as the water started to cool.

"You can stop hiding in the shower and come out now," she called.

She knew me too well.

Five minutes later, I emerged dressed from the bathroom and saw half my cake on the dining room table. The other half was missing along with Miles and his stuff.

"He said it's as close to a promise as he'll give you," Vena said with a smirk.

"He just wanted half my cake."

"Yeah. Probably. What time are you heading in to work?"

I checked the time and grabbed the remainder of my cake.

"Four-thirty. What if you don't find what you're looking for, Vena? Why not have a 'day job' as a backup plan? It'd be a smart move for times when hunting jobs are sparse."

"Let me guess…there's an opening at Blur."

"No, but say the word, and I can get you in. Shepard loves me." He truly did. I never missed a shift, didn't need smoke breaks, and the customers loved me because I knew how to be cheerful.

"I'll make you a deal," she said. "Agree to come rock climbing with me tomorrow, outside in the wilds of nature, and I'll go in with you today to talk to Shepard about a job."

I paused with my fork halfway to my mouth and stared at her.

"Outside?"

"Yep." She smirked. "It won't be a vertical climb like we do indoors. More like a rocky hike. Nothing you can't handle."

"How long?" I asked.

"We'll be home before dark."

"Before dark? We'd be hiking all day?"

"No. I know you'll want to sleep until ten, minimum. Plus, it's an hour's drive to get there. So, not all day. We'll be home well before dark. A few hours in exchange for working some epic shifts at Blur with me at your side."

"Deal." Anything so she wasn't dependent on her hunting money. "So when are you going hunting?"

She grinned at me. "I thought you didn't like knowing the details."

"I need to know when you leave so I know how long to wait before I report you missing."

"Ha-ha. I promise to tell you before I leave your side. Until then, we both know you're happier when I keep you in the dark."

"Fine."

As I ate my cake, I flipped on the news for a bit then switched to our guilty pleasure. *The Other House*, a reality TV show that had held the highest ratings for thirteen years running. It followed a group of eight housemates that changed from season to season. What made this show stand out above and beyond all the others was that only seven of the housemates were human. It was like Jersey Shore meets Clue with everyone in the cast trying to figure out who wasn't human while the viewers heard the confessions of everyone, even the non-human.

It was a damn fine drama and one of the major reasons people were more accepting of werewolves. The guy from season one had been a knockout who fell hard for a human woman. Vena and I gobbled up the romance.

An hour before my shift, I stood with a stretch.

"Let's get ready so we can talk to Shepard before my shift starts."

Vena sighed and headed to her room.

While I couldn't see her working in most "normal" places, I could see her managing well at Blur. Serving drinks while listening to music wasn't bad.

As an upscale nightclub, Blur cultivated a clientele that didn't get rowdy, appreciated a smile served with their cocktails, and tipped well. Blur also openly welcomed patrons who identified as non-human, which made the place a novelty.

"You know," I called as I pulled on my black tights, "by working at Blur, you might even make a few connections that could help you and Miles." I smoothed my hands over my fitted skirt when I finished and inspected myself in my full-length mirror. Playing on my curves usually got me better tips. My naturally sunny blonde hair with a natural wave and thickly lashed dark grey eyes helped too.

"Or you could make those connections for us," she called back.

I rolled my eyes and fiddled with the black-silver medallion hanging around my neck, thankful for the protective charms etched into the delicate weave. While Blur's clientele was generally more refined than the average club, I was smart enough to know that didn't mean it was completely safe.

After smoothing the white, button-up shirt over my chest, I put on my loose black tie, which was part of the standard uniform. When I emerged from the room, I found Vena slipping on her low-heeled, black shoes. The top she wore showcased her medallion while mine was safely hidden under my shirt and tie.

"What do you think?" she asked as I gave her a once-over.

The black stretch pants hugged her lean figure and looked nice enough for a potential interview. The red top complemented her feisty personality. Vena's hair was down for a change, and she'd put on a little makeup to accentuate her deep blue eyes.

"You'll do," I said with a conspiratorial smile.

We drove separately since I knew she wouldn't want to hang around all night. She parked in front while I went to the back employee lot.

The aromas coming from the kitchen off the service entrance made my mouth water. Most nightclubs didn't offer food, but Blur wasn't most nightclubs. The pricey tapas Shepard put on his selective menu tempted any patron with a designer palate.

After placing my purse and keys in my locker, I hurried through the door to the main lounge. The extensive seating area offered a range of tables near the dance floor and stage. The svelte chairs upholstered in purple leather matched the purple accent lighting and table tops. The black ceiling and walls toned down the color and added a moody element Blur's patrons enjoyed.

I saw Vena already waiting at the bar. A sparkling water sat in front of her. She grinned at me as I approached.

"Who was at the door?"

"Army," she said. "He remembered me. And I thought for sure you were going to appear with a tie and tell me to get to work."

I laughed. "You're safe for the moment. Shepard's probably in his office. You okay hanging out here for a few minutes while I talk to him?"

"Don't worry," Buzz said from behind the bar. "I'll keep an eye on her."

Vena winked at the big blonde man, and I shook my head. This wasn't the first time Vena had visited Blur, so most of the staff knew she was a friend of mine. Vena also knew that Buzz liked to tease and flirt. He was harmless enough unless someone started causing trouble. The muscles he flexed when he mixed cocktails weren't for show. They also helped keep the peace if things got too rowdy.

I gave him a nod and headed toward the stairs.

"Hey, Ev," the muscled bouncer at the bottom of the steps greeted.

"Hey, Anchor. Shepard in his office?"

"Should be. Tell Buzz to stop gawking at Vena's cleavage."

I chuckled. "She'd be the first to say she doesn't have cleavage. But I'll let her know you're watching out for her."

Making my way up the steps, I scanned the empty VIP section. Everything was as neat as I'd left it the night before, and Detroit was already prepping the VIP bar.

With a nod to him, I made my way along the glass wall toward the offices.

As I reached Shepard's partially open door, I heard, "Get your shit together. Next time I catch you drinking on company time, you're fired."

I rarely heard Shepard use that tone. With shoulder-length dark-blonde hair, sun-kissed complexion, and muscles that had muscle babies, Shepard was the kind of guy people usually wanted to make happy. Including me.

Before I could decide if I should come back later, the door opened fully and Gunther, the dishwasher, blew past me, dark head down and shoulders hunched. He was the quiet sort, one who kept to himself. He'd always been friendly enough, though.

Shepard, who'd been watching Gunther's retreat, noticed me in the hallway. His hard, light grey gaze softened, and he leaned back in his office chair.

"Hey, Everly, I didn't know you were on the schedule tonight."

"That's funny since you do the schedule and I'm here every night," I said, stepping inside.

He gave a small smile.

"Is this a bad time?" I asked.

"Not for you."

"I brought Vena with me today. She's interested in adding 'cocktail concierge' to her list of life skills if there's still an opening."

"Where is she?"

"I left her with Buzz. Do you want me to bring her up here?"

"No, I'm on my way down anyway." He met me at the door and gestured for me to go first.

He followed me down to the main floor where Vena was sitting at the end of the bar. One of the beverage distributors hovered next to her, and warning alarms blared in my head.

He leaned in to say something to her and set his hand on her shoulder. Sparks of fury lit her eyes as she glared at him, and as she was about to latch onto his wrist, I called, "Vena!"

She glanced over and spotted Shepard behind me. Her expression lightened, and she stood, smoothly maneuvering away from the man.

I let out a breath of relief. It was better if Shepard didn't learn about Vena's temperament until after she was hired.

Shepard held out his hand to her. "Nice to meet you, Vena."

While her hand looked small in his, I knew how much damage she could inflict with that innocent-looking hand.

Shepard pulled away with a practiced smile and gave her an assessing look, his gaze taking in her form-fitting black pants and strong arms.

"You'll do. Come in on Monday to fill out paperwork."

"That's it?" Vena asked.

"Any friend of Everly's has a job with me. It's up to you to prove yourself."

After Shepard gave me a nod and headed over to the bar to speak to the distributor, Vena looked at me.

"Wow. You really do have a lot of pull with him." Her gaze swept over Shepard's broad shoulders. "He's a bit older than you. But so delicious. I think he'd be open to an invitation if you wanted to sample that."

"Please don't make this awkward," I said. "I have to work with him."

"Or maybe work up a sweat with him."

"Keep your voice down," I said, eyeing Shepard to make sure he didn't hear Vena.

He chose that moment to look over at me. His light grey gaze locked with mine and held for two pounding heartbeats before he turned back to the man, making me wonder if he had heard Vena.

CHAPTER TWO

VENA RECOGNIZED MY PANICKED LOOK AND CAUGHT MY FACE between her hands.

"Shepard didn't hear anything," she said. "The music is playing."

"Shepard has unnaturally good hearing."

She gave me a speculative look. "How good?"

"I don't know. But employees get into trouble even when they think he can't hear them."

"Is he a werewolf?"

I batted her hands away.

"I don't know. It never came up."

"Interesting."

That one word set off all the red flags. One of Vena's best and worst personality traits was her tenacity. She was like a dog with a bone for any information dealing with the shadow world.

"Don't," I warned.

Vena's curious expression turned innocent. "I just want to know who I'll be working for. That's all."

"You'll be working for Shepard, a man who is very private. Leave him alone. There are plenty of people here whose lives you can pry into. In fact, Anchor would love some of your attention."

Vena glanced up at the dark-haired bouncer at the bottom of the stairs. He was exactly the muscle-bound type she liked. "I wouldn't mind giving him some attention. But not tonight. I fulfilled my end of our arrangement, and now I need to head home and prepare so you can fulfill yours."

I wanted to question what tomorrow's hike would entail that she needed to prepare, but I feared the answer. Besides, if she left now, Shepard would be safe from questions. The last thing I needed was for Vena to poke around where she shouldn't.

"Fine. But remember, I faint at the sight of sweat."

She smirked. "Yours maybe, but I bet not his," she said with a side glance at Shepard.

I hadn't lied when I'd said Shepard was a private person. The only things I knew about him were that he ran the club, was a great boss, and was nice to look at. And that was the way I wanted to keep it.

"I have to get to work," I said.

"Oh yes, please do. Wouldn't want to get in trouble with the boss. He might spank you," Vena said with a wink.

As she left, I wondered if I'd made a mistake by getting her a job with me. But, Vena working at Blur was better than the alternative. I didn't want her hunting. If that meant making me slightly uncomfortable at work, then it was worth it.

As soon as the rest of the evening shift's servers were clocked in and waiting in the upstairs staff room, Shepard started assigning our sections. The DJ's sound check filtered heavy bass music through the building as he prepared for the night crowd that would be lining up at the door to pay the premium cover charge.

"If he gives Everly VIP again, I'm quitting," Sierra whispered in front of me.

"Maybe if you showed up for your shift on time as consistently as Everly, you'd earn that privilege more often," Shepard said without looking up from his tablet. "VIP is going to Adrian tonight." Shepard looked at the tall redhead. "If you need help, pull Everly."

I smiled, noting Sierra's flush. Had she really thought he wouldn't hear her?

"Sierra, you're on stage left, lower section. Everly, you're on stage left, upper section. Thomas, you're stage right lower. Pam, stage right upper. We're down one behind the bar tonight. So, I'll be filling in. Any questions?"

When no one spoke, Shepard let us go.

As soon as Doc, Shepard's second in command, saw we were ready, he nodded to Army to begin carding and taking cover charges as patrons arrived. It took another hour before the tables filled. The bartenders hustled to fill our orders, keeping us running at full swing.

I handed off an Effervescence, one of our signature cocktails, along with an extra napkin, to a full-bearded dwarf. He grinned at me as he accepted both.

"Thank you, *Vezrama*. The foam is fun but sticks everywhere."

I winked at him. "Sometimes that's the fun part, too."

He and his companions chuckled as I'd hoped, and I left them to enjoy their drinks and checked on my other tables.

While serving drinks at Blur wasn't my life's aspiration, I didn't mind the work. People were appreciative of a well-made drink delivered with a smile. The tips at the end of the night always proved that. But it never failed for there to be that one person every night who made me question my life choices.

Unfortunately for me, tonight's douche canoe sat in my section. His full black attire and slicked-back hair made me suspect he was trying to make himself appear tougher than he was. Judging from the friends who sat with him, he and his group wouldn't survive long here. They were all looks with nothing to back them.

"How can this be *the* club to go to in D.C. with all the trash you let in?" he asked me instead of answering my question, which had been a request for his drink order.

A table over, the nice dwarf slowly turned to glare at the guy. The stoutly built fellow might be a full foot and a half shorter than the butt monkey before me, but that wouldn't hinder him in a fight.

I'd witnessed it before due to the prejudices that still ran rampant against fae, dwarves, and werewolves. Which was why werewolves rarely publicly announced what they were. The fae and dwarves didn't have the luxury of ambiguity.

"I'll give you a minute to look over the drink menu and be right back," I said with a smile I didn't feel and moved over to the dwarf and his friends.

"Can I get you fine gentleman a refill on anything?" While speaking, I put my hand on the dwarf's shoulder and flashed him a genuine smile. "The kitchen has a new appi-teaser if you're feeling adventurous. Lamb skewers with—"

"You didn't even take my order. What the hell kind of service is this?" the asshat demanded.

"—an herb dipping sauce on the side." I could feel the dwarf's tension under my palm. Yet, he looked up at me without a hint of anger and nodded to my suggestion.

"The skewers sound tasty."

"Make it two orders," one of his companions said. "And another round of drinks."

"Perfect. I'll be right back."

The douche canoe stopped me from fleeing with a summoning wave of his fingers.

"Do I need to tell the manager you can't manage to take more than one order to the bar?" he asked.

"What would you like?" I asked, keeping my smile firmly in place.

"I'd like less trash in this place," he said, making his friends laugh.

"I'll let management know. Anything else?"

They finally gave me actual drink orders, and I hurried to the bar to talk to Shepard.

"I need Doc at table twelve," I said. "How do you feel about two skewers on the house for table thirteen?"

"If you think it's warranted, I'm fine with it." Shepard never stopped mixing as he spoke.

"Thanks."

Doc joined me as Shepard placed the last drink on my tray.

"The whole table or only the one?" Doc asked me.

Doc might have silver streaked through his brushed-back hair and trim beard, but even the younger bouncers built like armored trucks knew how much damage he could inflict on a person. Thankfully, most people knew not to test him.

"I think if you kick out the leader, they'll all go."

The douche canoe watched us approach. I hurried past and let Doc do his thing as I served the drinks to table thirteen. I couldn't help listening, though.

"Are you management?" the man asked.

"I'm Doc and management enough. I hear you have a problem."

"Doc?" The man laughed, and I internally cringed. "What kind of name is that? I don't need a doctor; I need someone to get rid of the sludgemuckers next to us."

Doc's low laugh was chilling. He set his hand on the man's shoulder and leaned in.

"I'm called Doc because that's the next person you'll see if you don't get up from this table and walk yourself out the door. Your invitation to Blur has been revoked indefinitely."

The man was about to argue, but his friends shoved him from the table and hurried him out the door. The troublemakers never stayed long after a visit from Doc. Friendlier people who'd tipped better sat in their place, and thanks to the skewers and a little kindness, I had two twenties in my pocket from the dwarf's table when I headed home after closing.

My college and dream bakery fund grew little by little every night I worked.

Sleeping until ten hadn't been enough to prepare me for Vena's enthusiasm for our "hike." As I followed Vena up the steep incline, my legs shook from exertion, and the sun beat down on my head. The backpack, which had initially seemed light, hung heavily against my sweat-drenched back.

This was no mere hike. We had veered off the well-traveled paths of Sugarloaf Mountain and were now in dense vegetation. Tripping on camouflaged roots and rocks had me stumbling as I tried to keep up with Vena. She didn't have the same issue as she bounded up the hill like a kangaroo on steroids.

The only thought that kept racing through my mind was how much tip money I'd have to earn to pay for emergency services to airlift me off this mountain.

"Almost there," Vena said.

"You said that five times already," I said, gasping for air as my foot slipped again. How high was this dumb mountain?

"I swear," she said.

"I'll be swearing soon if you're lying to me again. I have a shift tonight, and I'm exhausted. I'll have to crawl to the tables."

She laughed, but I wasn't entirely joking. If it wasn't for our deal, I'd have turned back the moment she left the marked paths. However, I was too worried Vena wouldn't show up Monday to fill out the paperwork if I bailed, which was the only reason I continued.

When Vena paused in a clearing, I looked down over the green landscape below us while I tried to catch my breath.

I grudgingly admitted the view from twelve hundred feet up was magnificent. A sparkling river wound along the valley floor, making me wish I was down there in the cool water.

"It's around here somewhere," Vena said.

"What's around here?" I perched on a boulder to give my legs a break and searched my pack for water.

"The entrance."

I looked up at her with growing trepidation. "What entrance?"

Her gaze scanned the glade's sparse vegetation and rocky terrain as a sick feeling settled into my stomach.

"Vena, what entrance? This was a hike. Remember?"

"A peek, that's all," she said. "It's for Miles."

"Are you hunting? Is this a hunt? The one you and Miles just talked about? You tricked me into coming with you? I agreed to hike up this stupid mountain, not go inside of it."

She gave me a sheepish look. "It wasn't a trick. I knew you would worry, and I wanted to prove that hunting isn't dangerous."

I stood, which hurt more than anticipated, hitched my pack up, and started my retreat.

"Where are you going?" she asked.

"Home."

"We're so close. Let me find the opening. Then we can go."

"No. I have to work tonight. I have to be a responsible adult so we can pay rent. I—"

I smashed my toe on a rock.

Cursing, I wobbled around as my toe throbbed in pain.

"Sit down before you hurt yourself again," she said.

It hurt too much to sit.

Just walk off the pain, I thought, hobbling in a circle. I was too afraid I'd trip again if I left the clearing before my toe stopped throbbing. When I limped close to Vena, she reached out to grab my arm. I dodged her attempt.

"Everly, stop!" She stood still, her wide gaze darting around us. "Did you feel something?"

"Yeah, I feel like my toe is busted."

"No, I mean the ground. Did you feel it shift?"

"I can't feel anything except my aching toe."

"Stop moving!" she yelled right before the ground gave way beneath our feet.

My stomach lurched as we fell. The scream that ripped from my lungs was cut short a second later when I landed on something that made a huge clatter of noise and hurt like the devil.

Rolling to my side with a groan, I sat up. My cheek stung like a bitch, and when I gingerly touched it, my fingertip came away red.

Turning my head to look for Vena, I saw where I'd landed instead.

Light reflected off hundreds of shiny things underneath me.

23

Confused, I picked up a bottlecap and squinted at it. My gaze slid to the metal pen under my hand and the aviator sunglasses beside it.

"Are you okay?" Vena asked with a cough.

"No, I'm not okay." I scrambled to my feet and looked up at the sunlit hole above us. "We landed in a fairy hoard, Vena. What the hell were you thinking?"

She slowly got to her feet.

"I thought we'd locate the opening, maybe peek inside for something valuable that we could pawn, then safely report back to Miles that we found it. I wasn't thinking we'd crash-land in the middle of it." Her droll look turned concerned. "You're bleeding."

I wiped at my cheek, which was still bleeding freely.

"I landed on pens and bottle caps. Of course I'm bleeding. What part of 'grounded from hunting' didn't you understand? This is exactly why I said it's too dangerous. Random acts of chaos always seem to find you, Vena."

Her gaze shifted to something behind me, and her eyes rounded.

"I swear on Grandma Lucia's hunting boots that there better not be anything even remotely scary behind me like a—"

"Codpiece," she said.

"What?"

"I swear he's wearing a codpiece."

It wasn't the codpiece that had me whirling around but her use of *he*.

A man lay on a long, stone slab. Dust and cobwebs covered him, but not so much that I couldn't see some details. The auburn-haired man looked like he was in his mid to late twenties. Fit and healthy, too, based on how he filled out his clothes. Time had frayed the meticulously detailed fabric of his waistcoat and breeches, but his skin remained untouched, if a bit pale.

From what I could see of his face, he was–or had been–extremely good-looking.

"Look lower," Vena said from beside me, making me jump. My gaze involuntarily drifted to the dust-coated lump at his crotch.

"You have issues, Vena. I'm less worried about what he's packing and more worried about why he's here."

"I think it's a diamond-studded codpiece. That has to be worth a fortune."

"Don't even think about it," I said, grabbing her arm. "We are not robbing the dead."

She was like a mastiff on a leash. There was no holding her back from her treasure, and because I was holding on, she dragged me with her.

Her hand stretched forward.

"Don't you dare touch a dead man's swizzle stick," I hissed frantically.

It was too late. She brushed away the cobwebs and latched onto his codpiece. With a tug, the leather strap attaching it broke free.

I breathed a sigh of relief when I saw nothing was exposed.

"Crap. Not a codpiece." She held up the metal-studded pouch. "No diamonds either."

My stomach gave a weird twist as I glanced between the metal-studded pouch and the fairy hoard pile.

"Why didn't the fairies take that?" I asked.

Fairies went after anything shiny. From jewelry to metal toasters, they coveted it all.

Vena wasn't listening to me, though. She was carefully opening the pouch and mumbling about how old it was.

I took an apprehensive step toward the man and, with a shaky hand, wiped the dust from his face, clearly seeing him. He wasn't in any way decayed like a dead person should be. Especially one dressed from another era.

Free of the blanket of dust, his skin reflected an unearthly paleness in the weak light. Yet, his beautiful, full lips retained a hint of color. My gaze drifted to the auburn-brown hair loosely tied in a ponytail that touched his shoulders.

He didn't look dead at all.

My pulse started pounding harder, and my breathing grew shallow. I stared at his chest, waiting for it to move. If it did, I couldn't tell. I leaned in so my ear was close to his nose. Nothing. Still shaking, I dusted off his chest and set my ear to his jacket right over his heart.

A single thump under my ear made me squeak and scramble away. I latched onto Vena's arm and shook her until her gaze ripped free from the jeweled ring she held.

"I don't think he's dead," I whispered frantically.

Vena frowned and looked from me to the man, taking in the now unencumbered view of his face.

"Shit," she breathed. "You bled on him?"

"What? No."

She brushed her hand against my cheek, the side I'd used to listen for his breath, and her fingers came away bloody. My rounded eyes met hers. The fear I saw there amplified my own. Vena wasn't afraid of many things, which was part of the problem with her hunting. She was too ballsy.

She shoved the ring into my hand and rushed to the guy, swearing under her breath as she took the hem of her shirt and attempted to wipe a drop of blood from his bottom lip. His *lip?* How dumb could I be? His clothes, un-mummified appearance, and lack of breathing with a heartbeat led to only one conclusion.

I'd practically spoon-fed a hibernating vampire.

"Start looking for a way out, Everly. The fairies were getting in here somehow. We need to go. *Now*."

Her barked orders and budding panic broke through my own terror.

Heart crashing against my chest, I raced around the dimly lit cave of horrors, looking for a way out. Cobwebs clung to all the shadowing corners. I picked up a copper weathervane and used it to clear them away.

"Did you find a way out?" Vena called.

I heard the tinkling of metal and looked over to find her shoving shiny things into her backpack.

"What in the hell are you doing?" I yelled. "Help me!"

She closed her pack and hitched it on as she scrambled off the hoard, slipping on the uneven pile.

"I'm taking what I can get. I doubt Miles will get a good bounty for this location," she said as she began searching for an exit. "Most hunters don't want anything to do with a vampire."

I glanced uneasily at the man who was unmoving on the rock slab. I didn't want to think about what would happen if he woke to find us in his cave.

What was he doing here anyway? Like the majority of the public, I knew next to nothing about vampires other than that they existed and lived in secret. I'd always pictured the attractive ones in secluded posh houses, though, and the weathered old ones in mountain caves.

What was Mr. Hot-n-Dusty doing here? And why was I thinking about how handsome he was? Handsome still had fangs.

"Found it," Vena called, ripping me from my thoughts.

She stood near the narrow end of the cave, peering into a crevice.

I hurried to her side and squinted into the space, seeing a faint light farther in. The space was maybe two feet high and a little more than half as wide.

"I'll never fit through that," I said.

"If Fangs can, you can, too."

I glanced back at the man's broad-shouldered form and supposed Vena was right. And, really, did I have any other choice? Sending her out to lower a rope wouldn't do us any good. I didn't have the upper body strength or agility to climb up, which was part of the reason she kept bribing me into rock-wall climbing. It was completely different with a harness though.

Swallowing hard, I looked at the opening again. If I didn't want to stay down here with him alone, I had no choice but to try.

"You go first," Vena said.

"Why me?" I'd face-plant into every cobweb in there.

"Just go," she said, glancing back at the vampire.

I shrugged out of my pack and slid on my side into the opening. The awkward angle made it a tight squeeze and hard to move. But I was able to worm my way along. Vena was right behind me, pushing me to go faster.

As I'd anticipated, every cobweb lodged in my hair and along my face. She owed me big time after this.

The light grew brighter. As I was about to reach the opening, a miniature blue devil flew in. My scream echoed in the small space. The fairy's beady little eyes went wide, and it zipped back out the way it'd come.

"Go, Ev," Vena said, pushing at me

Pulse racing, I scrambled the last few feet and fell out of the opening. Vena emerged more agilely from the side of the moss-covered hill.

She tossed my pack at me and looked up at the sun.

"Let's meet up with Miles. He's going to want to know what we found."

"No. No more Miles. No more fairies. No more hunting." I stood and glared at her.

"What about cheesecake? I have one waiting for us at home."

I picked up my pack, shouldered it, and gestured to the trees.

"Lead the way. No more detours, though, or I'm calling your mom."

A smile played on her lips at my weak threat. "Your hair looks like cobweb cotton candy."

I reached up to feel my hair, and my hand came away with a sticky web. A whimper escaped me.

She pulled a large black spider from my hair and winced apologetically when she saw my horrified expression. I hated spiders almost as much as I hated fairies.

"A shower then cheesecake. How about a caramel mocha latte to go with it?" She scooted me from the cave opening and down the nightmare mountain. "You'll feel so much better after a nice hot shower."

No shower could make me feel better about bleeding on a vampire, but at least, I could get rid of the dirt and cobwebs. I shuddered.

CHAPTER THREE

I WIPED MY HAND ACROSS THE MIRROR, CLEARING AWAY THE STEAM to look at my cheek. The scratch, no more than an inch long, wasn't deep. But it did look red and angry. Squinting my dark grey eyes, I psyched myself up for what I knew I needed to do.

Instead of reaching for the peroxide, though, I gave myself another few moments of reprieve and brushed my hair. It always looked dark when it was wet, but as soon as I blew it out, it would return to its sunny, un-webbed glory.

"I regret letting you go first," Vena called through the door.

She was probably sitting in the hall, unwilling to get anything else in the house dirty since she knew she'd have to clean it.

"I'm disinfecting my cut," I said.

My hiss when I dabbed the soaked cotton ball to my face elicited a quiet apology from Vena. With the scratch still foaming, I tossed the cotton ball into the garbage and opened the door.

"Not what I want to hear from you. I want to hear, 'You're

right, Ev. Hunting is dangerous. I promise I'll never do it again.'"

She stood gracefully.

"You'd really want me to give up my dream? The thing that brings me joy?"

I made a pained face.

"No. I want you to be safe, Vena. I want to be eighty in a senior-living community and look over at my best friend, knowing she'll help steal an extra pudding from the nurse's cart."

"We'll steal the whole cart, and they won't have a clue." She tugged me into a hug, uncaring that I only wore a towel. "Besides, I didn't even get hurt this time. You took one for the team. See? You're my lucky charm. If you start hunting with me, I'll never have a scratch on me again."

"I'd never survive."

She released me with a grin. "You would if you started training."

"Go shower and scrub extra hard. Hopefully, you can wash off the insanity."

While she used the bathroom, I pulled on lounge clothes and went to the kitchen to show a piece of cheesecake that I wasn't the type to take prisoners. Vena had been smart about her bribery. It wasn't some mediocre store-bought confectionery. This creamy slice of heaven had my eyes rolling back in my head on the first bite.

I'd almost forgiven her by the third bite until I heard a key in the front door.

Narrowing my gaze, I moved into the dining room and waited for our visitor, the only other person with a key, to let himself into our house.

Miles' grin faded at the sight of my scowl, and his gaze flicked over my face, lingering on my cheek.

"What happened?" he asked.

"Your sister took me along on the hunt."

"Yeah, but what happened? It was literally supposed to be a walk in the park."

"You knew?" I couldn't keep the fury from my voice.

Vena emerged from the hallway and elbowed him before he could answer.

"Miles, I love you like a brother, but shut up," she said.

"I *am* your brother."

"You won't be for long if you keep yapping. You're upsetting Ev. Hoes before bros."

"Ev was *already* upset," I said grumpily. "You led me to a fairy hoard. Your show of solidarity isn't going to earn my forgiveness over that betrayal."

"You found the hoard?" Miles asked with pure excitement in his tone.

"Yep, and the vampire hibernating in it," I snapped.

His face went pale, and he whirled on Vena.

"We're fine," she said. "The keyword is hibernating. He didn't even know we were there."

Miles' gaze flicked to my cheek. "The vampire was in the fairy hoard cave where you hurt yourself?"

"Don't question me like I did something wrong," I said angrily and forked the cheesecake. "I wasn't even supposed to be there."

"This is serious. Vena, you know what this means."

"What does it mean?" I asked around a mouthful of self-soothing.

"You don't want to know," Vena said at the same time Miles started talking.

"If the vampire wakes up in the next few months, he'll be able to track you by the scent of your blood."

"Which is unlikely," Vena said. "If he was going to wake up, he would have already. The vamp was dressed like George Washington."

"She thought he was wearing a codpiece," I said. "It was a coin purse."

Vena swore and looked at me. "Tell me you still have the ring."

I frowned, thinking back. I remembered her shoving the ring at me and then…

"I think it's in my pants."

"That's what he said," she called, racing from the room.

"Wait, wait, wait." Miles held up a hand, looking sick. "Are you telling me you took something from a vampire?"

"Found it!" Vena yelled. "It was in your pocket. See? You're the perfect sidekick."

"Never again," I said, shaking my head when she reentered the kitchen.

"Vena," Miles said, "you have to put it back."

"What? Why? You didn't even look at it." She held it up and stuck it in his face. "I think it's a ruby. Do you know how much one the size of your thumbnail would go for?"

"As soon as I disclose its origin, no one will buy it."

Her face fell a little. "Why?"

"The vampire will track down the person who took it and kill them—and anyone else who touched it—to get it back."

I stopped chewing and stared at both of them.

"Only if he wakes up," she said quickly.

"It's not a chance we can take. Put it back, Vena."

To my relief, she exhaled heavily and nodded. "Fine. We'll go back tomorrow."

"We? Ah, hell naw! I'm never going back there again. And don't even think of trying to bribe me with another piece of cheesecake. It won't work." The whole cheesecake might, though, and that worried me.

"I wouldn't dream of it," Vena said sweetly. "Did you see the topping that came with that slice you're eating? Triple berry something. I forget what she called it, but it sounded fancy and was made with alcohol."

"I need a new best friend. One who doesn't know me as well," I said, setting down my half-eaten cheesecake.

She took the plate. "But think of all the fancy desserts you'd be missing out on."

"Keep the desserts. I'm not bringing the ring back. You and Miles can go."

Turning my back on the tempting bribery and my traitorous friend, I headed to the living room to relax before my shift.

A whispered argument between the siblings drifted to my ears, but I didn't care to listen. I was done with ancient rings, cobwebbed vampires, and glittery non-codpieces. Right now, my life was all about kicking up my sore feet and watching some mindless TV.

A few minutes later, Miles left with a hasty goodbye and closed the door.

"Ready for some *Other House* drama?" I called to Vena.

"I'm going to hang out in my room for a bit."

The sound of her door snicking close was ominous.

Something was going on. Rather than ask what, I took a breath and settled into the couch. She was either keeping me in the dark for my benefit or wasn't ready to talk about whatever was upsetting her. As long as she wasn't plotting another trek with me as a sidekick, I was content to leave her alone.

After turning off the car, I used the rearview mirror to check my face. The small cut was visible under the transparent medical strip I'd applied to keep it closed and sanitary. Tips would either be really great tonight out of pity or awful out of disgust.

Adrian and Pam were lingering by the lockers when I came in. Neither said anything to me when I stuffed my purse into my locker and clocked in. They didn't need to. I could feel their speculative glances until I turned my back on them and headed upstairs.

Anchor's brown eyes flicked between my scratch and my eyes.

"Trouble I need to take care of?" he asked, not stepping aside. With his wide stance and even wider shoulders, there was no way around him.

"Only if you have a machete and herbicide," I said with a grin that pulled at the bandage. He didn't smile in return.

"The rest of us need to get to work, Anchor," Adrian said behind me. "Flirt with Everly later."

"We'll talk later," Anchor said, stepping aside. "I'm going to want a name."

I patted his arm as I passed.

"Mother Nature. That's the only name I have. She's a cruel lady who likes tripping people with her roots."

Hurrying up the stairs, I inwardly cringed at what I knew was coming and joined the others in the staff room. They all glanced at me, but no one said anything.

Shepard strode in a minute later.

He looked at me, frowned, then glanced down at the tablet he held.

"Adrian, you have upper stage right," he said. "Thomas,

lower stage left. Pam, lower stage right. Sierra, VIP section. Don't screw it up. Everly, upper stage left, but see me in my office before the shift."

He turned and headed out.

"Guess Everly isn't the favorite anymore," Sierra whispered loud enough for everyone to hear.

I shook my head then followed Shepard to his office where he was already seated.

When I knocked on the open door, he didn't glance up but stared at the tablet still in his hands. "What happened?"

"I went hiking with Vena today. I tripped and fell."

His steel-hard gaze lifted and locked with mine. "I hear about women who trip and fall, but I rarely see it happen. You sticking with that story?"

"It's not a story, Shepard. No one hit me. No intervention is needed unless I talk about going hiking again. If I do, stop me. There's nothing good in nature."

He casually dropped the tablet on the desk. "Why's Vena taking you hiking? I didn't think you were outdoorsy."

"You're right there. I'm not. But Vena and I are trying to broaden each other's horizons."

He leaned back in his chair and considered me for a long moment.

"Am I in trouble for a facial scratch? It's covered. If a clear bandage is too gross, I can—"

"You're not in trouble, Everly," he said, standing. He came around the desk and gently clasped my arms. "I'm worried. You're a pretty woman in a world filled with shitty people. Everyone who works here is family. I take care of my family. Do you understand?"

The intensity of his stare and the sincerity of his words made my pulse beat a little faster.

"And that's why I like working for you, Shepard," I managed to say steadily.

He released me and stepped back. "I put you on stage left so Anchor can keep an eye on you. If there's any trouble tonight, he'll step in."

"There won't be any trouble. Promise." I held my smile in place until he nodded and returned to his desk.

Taking that as a dismissal, I hurried from his office and down the stairs. Army waited for me to get in place before opening the doors and letting the night crowd enter. I felt the weight of Anchor's gaze while I took the first table's order.

I got the typical "What happened to your face?" question from a few of the regulars and those bold enough to ask. But for the most part, my shift rolled by like every other Saturday night.

My feet started to ache a little earlier than usual. However, when Shepard called me over and said that Sierra needed help in the VIP lounge, I didn't hesitate to say I could handle it. The money called to me. I wasn't greedy, but I had bills and dreams to fund. My final two semesters wouldn't pay for themselves, and I wanted my degree.

Sierra gave me a pissy look when she saw me, which I ignored. I took over the table at the top of the stairs so I could watch over my tables down below.

From my vantage point, I spotted tonight's troublemaker in Thomas' section. The woman's hand darted out to caress his ass when he moved to deliver drinks to the next table. He didn't react, which she took as an invitation to keep going.

I hurried down the stairs.

"Trouble?" Anchor asked.

"The blonde in Thomas' section needs to be educated on the strict no-touching policy."

"Need Doc?" Anchor asked.

"Not for this one," I said.

Thomas met my gaze as I made my way through his section. He didn't try to stop me, though.

"Excuse me, miss," I said, ignoring the other women at the table. "Blur has a strict no touching the serving staff policy. I'm sure you understand why it needs to be followed for all genders. If a man sees a woman doing it, he will take it as an open invitation to do the same. We're here to pay bills, not get groped."

An embarrassed flush consumed the blonde's previously humor-filled expression.

"Of course. I'm sorry."

"Thanks for understanding." I smiled at the whole table to show there were no hard feelings then returned to my section.

Anchor winked at me, a small smirk on his face for half a heartbeat before it returned to its handsome yet intimidating stoic mask.

The next few hours passed in a pleasant blur, as they usually did. The DJ announced the final call, which caused the typical rush of drink orders. Thanks to the VIP table, I had an extra fifty in my pocket by the time the doors closed behind the last patron.

My feet wanted me to collapse in a chair, but rather than giving in, I cleared my tables downstairs then went up to clean my VIP table. Sierra's tables were already cleared. She sat at one, counting her tips.

"A lousy thirty more for all the ass-kissing I had to do up here," she said, flicking her blonde hair over her shoulder. "What did you get from that table?"

"Nothing crazy. It turned over three times. About fifteen from each."

"Figures," she said under her breath.

I wasn't sure why she was still employed here. Shepard wasn't the type to put up with crappy workers. And while Sierra did her job, she was one of those passive-aggressive types who oozed negativity whenever she opened her mouth. He could have easily found someone equally as good at serving drinks, who could manage a friendly smile without eye-daggers.

She stood and handed over ten percent of her total to Detroit, the VIP bartender. "I swear I have given more money to bartenders over the month I've worked here than anywhere else."

"That means you're making more money," I said. "It's a good thing. And the bartenders bust their butts to get us our drink orders plus theirs. Be thankful."

She glared at me with her hazel eyes. As soon as she went downstairs, I sat at the bar and gave Detroit a weary smile. He smiled back, and there was none of the weariness. There was a reason Shepard kept Detroit up in the VIP lounge. He had a carefree, rugged look with a body of steel, the stamina of a centaur, and a flair for mixing drinks.

"Don't mind Sierra," he said. "She's still new. She'll come around or leave quickly. You've only been here about six months, so you've only seen some of the employees who have come through here. Chalk it up to free entertainment."

"I'd rather have less toxic entertainment. Can I bother you for a glass of water?"

"Sure thing. Did you cash out your card tips already?" he asked, filling a glass for me.

"Yeah, why?"

"Just curious."

I counted out my tips and handed over my ten percent.

"Does ten percent add up to much when you split it with the other bartenders?"

He shrugged. "Along with the tips we get from the people who prefer to drink at the bar, it's decent."

"Are you telling me I should be a bartender?"

"Are you telling me you're tall enough to see over the bar?"

"Ouch. Of course I can see over the bar. And as I demonstrated, I can reach over it to pass your tip money, too."

"From your chair."

"I'm taking my impressively average sixty-four-inch height home now. Enjoy the rest of your night from your freakishly skyscraping height."

His chuckle followed me down the stairs.

Anchor called goodnight to me as I headed toward the back. Shepard was in the kitchen, helping with the cleanup. He looked up when I came in.

"Heading out?" he asked.

"Yes. Unless you need something else."

He shook his head. "I'll walk you out."

I paused. "Why? Am I in trouble?" I couldn't remember doing anything that would land me on Shepard's shit list, but he had an extensive menu of pet peeves. Heaven help the person who came across as a know-it-all or habitually interrupted conversations. Or worse, the unfortunate employee who loved wearing heavily scented perfume or cologne. Shepard's death glare if he ever caught someone on their phone during a shift was completely spine-melting. I didn't want to be on the receiving end of any of his looks.

Shepard's gaze flicked to my cheek briefly. "You're not in trouble. I'm just not taking chances on your safety."

I fought not to roll my eyes.

"There is nothing to worry about, Shepard. No abusive boyfriend is waiting by my car."

"Then humor me."

I wasn't going to argue with my boss about something trivial. I simply didn't want the "boss' pet" label to stick any more than it already had. But since Sierra was already gone, I didn't have to worry about her spreading rumors.

Plus, with the whole vampire and fairy hoard thing still in the back of my mind, having an escort to my car after dark wouldn't hurt.

I really, *really* didn't want this morning's treasure hunt to come back and bite me.

CHAPTER FOUR

THE RINGTONE I ASSIGNED TO VENA JARRED ME AWAKE, AND I grappled for my phone on the nightstand. Tapping the screen to answer, I cut the obnoxious "Bribes are imminent! Bribes are imminent" short and squinted at the time. Eight a.m. Why did she hate me?

With a small groan, I set the phone to my ear.

"Why are you calling me when your room is ten feet away?" I asked, trying to process anything beyond the fact that I needed an injection of caffeine immediately.

"I'm not at home," Vena said, her breath coming out in a staccato rhythm. I knew that tempo from all the times she dragged me out of bed as part of her "Everly needs cardio" campaign.

Vena was running.

I sat up, no longer needing that jolt of caffeine.

"What do you mean? Where are you? Did you go back to the cave? Did you put the ring back?"

I knew I should have knocked on her bedroom door when

I'd returned from my shift the night before. I'd wanted to talk to her about the ring but hadn't wanted to wake her.

"Ev, go to Miles' apartment now."

"Why? What's going on? Are fairies chasing you?" Even as I questioned her, I hurried out of bed.

"I need you to be calm about this—"

"Calm? You are running and telling me to go to Miles' place."

"Ev, I can only talk and run for so long. Miles is either ignoring my calls or sleeping. Take his spare key from the hook and tell him to call me immediately."

"Is this a break-traffic-laws kind of hurry or as-fast-as-you-can hurry?"

"As fast as you can, Ev."

When she ended the call without a sarcastic reply, I knew the situation was serious.

Twisting my hair up, I rushed to dress and ran out the door. I brushed my teeth as I drove and tried not to give into a complete freakout, assuring myself it wasn't a life-and-death emergency. If it were, she would have told me to break traffic laws. It didn't help calm me down much, though. She'd been running for a reason.

If Vena's idiotic hunts didn't kill me, the stress of them would.

I parallel parked at the curb in front of Miles' six-unit apartment building and headed up the walkway to his faded green door.

With my thoughts on Vena, I took out his key without paying any attention to my surroundings. Before I could stick it into the door, a blue-winged devil zoomed out of the bush under Miles' window.

It charged at me, aiming for the key.

Yelping, I closed my eyes and batted at the air. My hand connected with a tiny body. Its high-pitched squeal had me freezing in dread.

Shit.

I peeked down at the fairy wobbling and dazed on the grass then glanced around for witnesses. Thankfully, no one was around.

Jamming the key into the lock, I slipped inside before the fairy could take flight again.

"Miles," I called, turning on a light. "You need to wake up and call Vena. Stat!"

Research papers were strewn on about every available surface. The two-person dining table. His battered sofa. The three-legged coffee table propped up with a cinder block.

Shaking my head, I crossed the space between the kitchen and living room and knocked on the closed bedroom door.

"Hey, you need to get up. I think your sister made everything worse."

When there was still no answer, I cracked open his door.

"Miles? Wake the hell up."

No answer.

With a muttered curse, I peeked inside to find the room empty. The rumpled bed indicated it had been recently slept in. Despite the chaotic mess of research papers in the rest of the house, Miles was a tidy type who made his bed and folded his clothes.

The papers were still spread everywhere, though, which probably meant he'd pulled an all-nighter again. Not unusual with his passion for research.

Most likely, he'd left for coffee and something to eat.

I returned to the main living space and peeked out the curtained window to confirm my suspicion that he'd left. However, the fairy was now flying around like a drunk with one wing jutted at an odd angle, momentarily distracting me. I felt no guilt.

After a quick scan of the vehicles lined in front of the complex, I didn't spot Miles' yellow piece of crap car.

Turning toward the kitchen, I sent Vena a text.

Me: Miles isn't here. Car's gone. Looks like he pulled an all-nighter and is getting breakfast. I'll wait here for him.

I got her auto-reply stating that she was driving and would look at the message when she was done.

Feeling a little calmer now that I knew she was no longer running, I glanced at Miles' sad kitchen. The likelihood of finding something to eat was slim, but my stomach was growling, and I had nothing better to do.

I opened Miles' refrigerator, not expecting much. The sight of a very delicious-looking wedge of chocolate cake surprised me. The alternating layers of cake, mousse, and cream were repeated three mouth-watering times. Other than looking like Miles had dropped the box it had come in on its side, it was unmistakably an expensive splurge.

Miles didn't do expensive desserts. That was my deal.

Maybe it was a peace offering for his accomplice role in the whole Everly-fell-down-the-fairy-hole debacle. Miles was a good sport like that. But, even if the cake wasn't for me, it was still mine. He owed me.

Listening to its beckoning, I appeased my eager taste buds and pulled out the cake, grabbed a fork, and sat at his scuffed kitchen table.

A partial drawing peeked out from under a pile of papers. It looked like one of those really old drawings where all the people had crazy bags under their eyes.

Curious, I pulled the paper out while balancing the plate in my other hand.

The page was covered with information about vampires. Miles had crossed half of it out and wrote "lol" next to a few lines. Like the one about sacrificing a goat on a full moon in the vampire's lair to protect a person's home, and the one about vampires turning the sun red right before a killing spree. However, the one about splashing a vampire with an infusion of garlic and virgin's blood to sedate them he'd marked with a question mark.

Did Miles even know any virgins? I sure as hell was glad I wasn't one, based on the number of ideas I saw that involved the use of a virgin in some way.

After leafing through the pile, I frowned at the repetitive vampire theme. Had Miles been that worried about Vena taking the ring? The previous day's whispered conversation teased the back of my mind.

As Vena had said, what were the odds of the vampire waking up after a few centuries of hibernating? One in a million, right?

Maybe before you bled on him, I thought to myself.

To drown my worry, I skewered a bite of cake and stuffed the bite in my mouth. The flavor made me moan. Definitely an apology cake. Miles was winning brownie points back.

Chewing slowly and savoring the goodness, I continued to look over Miles' research, taking care not to rearrange the papers too much.

The bits of information that the public already knew were marked "common knowledge."

Such as…vampires were made, not born. Turning a human into a vampire was risky business, and the majority didn't survive the transition for whatever reason. Public hate and persecution kept them in hiding and their numbers low. The human populace didn't like identifying as livestock.

No brainer on that one.

Idly taking another bite of cake, I wondered if vampires fed on other creatures, too. The news never reported non-human vampire killings, though. Hell, they rarely reported human ones anymore. Vena's parents, who were researchers like Miles, said there'd been a big drop in missing person cases after some of the lesser creatures had made themselves known to the world. The working theory was that vampires were to blame for most of them, and they knew they would be hunted if they kept it up.

However, given the age of the clothes the vampire in the cave had worn, he would have been hibernating through all of that. The werewolves coming out (and all the supernaturals that followed)... The laws that had been made to accommodate them… The public distrust of his kind... He would be in for a rude awakening if he chose to rise again.

I took another bite of cake and continued to skim the information Miles had gathered. While I had no interest in becoming intertwined with the supernaturals, educating myself was plain smart. The more I understood, the more I could avoid the dangers associated with some of them.

Under the papers about vampires, I found random old articles about the first creature sightings. Things probably related to whatever Miles had been researching before our vampire run-in. A fairy in Norway, which I personally felt they should have squashed immediately. A dervish in the Everglades. A troll in Russia. The oldest article was dated almost a century ago.

Absently, I skewered another bite of cake.

Weight tugged my fork when I lifted it and started to tip my plate. Fumbling to steady it, I looked down to see my fork had snagged on something inside the cake. Something that looked like a frosting-covered baggy.

Cringing, I pulled it out and went to the sink to rinse it off.

The water ran down it, revealing a withered and slightly furred shaft of skin inside the plastic.

Gagging, I dropped it on the counter.

"I ate dick cake!" I wheezed.

Another gag gripped my throat and stomach, and I grappled with the faucet.

Gargling didn't help, so I distracted myself by naming every cast member from *The Other House,* starting with season one. My stomach gradually settled.

"I'm going to kill Miles when I see him. Why couldn't he be normal and use a toilet tank to stash stuff and not a perfectly innocent cake? And why a shriveled dick?" I asked the room.

I felt another gag creeping in and took a calming breath.

By the time someone pounded on the front door, I had my stomach under control.

"It's me," Vena called.

I hurried to let her in.

"I ate dick cake, Vena," I said, tears gathering in my eyes. "Why would Miles do that to me?"

She stepped in and locked the door behind her. "He's here? Miles!"

"He's not here. The cake was in the fridge."

Vena's gaze swept the front rooms.

"Forget about the cake, Ev. Where the hell is he?"

"I don't know." Her worried expression cut through my cake trauma. "What's going on, Vena?"

She blew out a frustrated breath and tried calling him again.

"We need Miles."

"Yeah, you already established that."

A muffled phone rang from the apartment's only bedroom.

Vena ran for the sound, and I followed, confused. She pulled his phone from under his pillow and swore. Then she fished his protection charm from the blankets. The chain was broken.

With a sinking feeling of dread, I stared at both the phone and the charm. There was no way Miles would have voluntarily left his house without those. One, maybe, but not both.

"It couldn't be him," Vena mumbled, fingering the broken chain. "Miles was at our house when it was still light out and left before dark. And he never touched the ring."

"What are you talking about? What's going on, Vena?"

She turned to me, her blue eyes darker with the intensity of her gaze.

"The vampire was gone when I got there, Ev. No sign of him. I told you to get here because we need Miles to tell us what to do next. Returning the ring and hoping the vampire doesn't wake before the scent of your blood fades is no longer an option."

I sat heavily on the bed.

"Don't freak out," she said. "We're safe. It's not even noon, and the sun is shining. But we need to find Miles."

"You think the vampire took him?"

Vena looked at the chain in her hand then dropped it beside me to focus on his phone.

"No, this has to be something else. It doesn't make sense for the vampire to come here and not to our house. It was your blood, your scent, that he would follow."

"So what do you think happened? Where is Miles?"

"I'm not sure. The charm should have protected Miles from whatever wanted to hurt him."

"From supernaturals. But what if a human attacked Miles?"

She glanced at me. "The front door wasn't damaged, right?"

"No, it seemed fine."

"Check the windows," she said, lifting her phone to her ear.

As I inspected the window frames, I listened to her report to the police that Miles had possibly been kidnapped.

"They're sending someone over," she said, pocketing her phone and unlocking Miles'.

"What are you doing?"

"I'm going to look through his phone."

"For what?"

"Any hint about who might want to kidnap Miles."

"The window in here looks okay," I said. "I'll check the rest. You should look in the living room at what he's researching. He's got papers everywhere. Stuff about how to kill vampires and random things about creature sightings."

Vena nodded and turned to leave the room without looking up from Miles' phone.

I followed her out and tried not to let fear overwhelm me. We had been twelve when her grandparents disappeared during a hunting expedition–of the treasure variety–almost ten years ago. I could still remember how the days had turned into weeks and the agony of Vena's heartbreak over not knowing what had happened.

I didn't want her to go through that again. *I* didn't want to go through that again.

Each window I inspected turned out like the rest of the apartment, battered by age but undisturbed.

"None of the windows are broken or look like they were forced open," I said.

Vena paused scrolling through the phone and glanced at me. "This doesn't make any sense," she repeated. "The charm's chain was broken, and his phone was left behind. That sounds human, but then there should be signs of a break-in." She sighed as she deflated into a chair at the table. "This morning, I'd only been worried about the vampire."

My stomach twisted at the reminder. Or from the dick cake. I frowned and rubbed my middle.

"It looked like Miles was worried about the vampire, too," I said, nodding at the table littered with vampire information. "But I didn't see anything that would help our situation. Did you find anything in Miles' phone? A threatening message? A booty call text that made him run out the door so fast he forgot his phone and broke his necklace?"

She gave a small laugh like I'd hoped.

"I wish it was a booty call." She began leafing through the papers, dismissively setting some aside. "There aren't any recent messages or anything particularly informative in his browsing history."

Vena stopped flipping through the papers. "This research is useless. Virgin blood on a full moon? Where is he finding this shit?"

"Probably the Shadow Trade market."

Here in D.C., the local Shadow Trade market ran out of an old brick warehouse. While I'd never been to it myself, I'd listened to Miles talk about it enough to imagine it looked like an indoor flea market. However, the goods found in those vendor stalls weren't human-made.

A person could find ancient fae relics for an astronomical price or simple charms to ward off a common cold. The Shadow Trade market was where Miles had purchased our protection charms. It was also where he sold information to treasure hunters like Vena.

Still sorting through his research, I picked up a ridiculous propaganda pamphlet with a coffee ring on it. Why would Miles even bother keeping this? He was smart enough to know trolls didn't bring the creatures to Earth. They are barely smart enough to open a jar of pickles.

"What are we looking for?" I asked, setting it down again.

"Anything unusual." She stood suddenly and went to the cupboards, looking inside them. "If he was knowingly working on something big, he might have hidden information about it."

She stopped and looked at the baggy by the sink.

"What the fuck is that?" she asked.

"The dick cake. Well, the dick from the cake." I made a face and rubbed my stomach again. "He set me up."

"What the hell is dick cake?"

"A perfectly innocent-looking slice of delectable cake he used to hide that thing. I ate three bites before I found it, Vena. *Three*."

She picked up the nasty skin roll from the counter as I willed the few bites of tainted cake to stay down.

Thankfully, a knock on the door stopped any further inspection and distracted me from my resurrected nauseousness. She shoved the disgusting baggy into her pocket as I went to look through the peephole.

"It's the police," I said, opening the door.

The two officers introduced themselves and listened to Vena explain about the broken charm, the abandoned phone, and the empty apartment. The officer who wasn't taking notes kept glancing at the research articles on the table.

"Did he mention any plans to leave?" the officer taking notes asked.

I saw doubt creep into Vena's expression. "Yes, but he wouldn't have left without his phone and charm. Never."

"What did you say your brother did for a living?" the second officer asked.

"I didn't say," Vena said. "Does it matter?"

The second officer gave a patient sigh. "By the looks of things, your brother is investigating supernaturals. Either he's a vampire hunter, a treasure hunter, or a researcher. If he's a vampire hunter, he knows what he's doing and will be back. Hopefully. If he's a treasure hunter, give him a few weeks. He'll turn up. If he's a researcher, he'll be back for his phone and notes before the day's done."

"He's a researcher," she said, her frustration showing. "And if he's not back tonight?"

"Then it's a standard missing person's report. We have his information and will put it into our system after twenty-four hours."

"Wow. So helpful," she deadpanned.

"We're just following protocol," the officer said, not unkindly.

"Thank you," I said, opening the door for them before Vena could say anything else.

"Our jobs would be a lot easier if people would stay away from shit they have no business being in," I heard one officer say to the other as they walked down the sidewalk.

I turned to close the door and looked at Vena. Anger and worry radiated from her. Closing the distance between us, I hugged her hard.

"Don't worry. Miles has us. We'll figure this out."

She hugged me back and nodded against my shoulder before straightening.

"If he's researching something, we need to follow the breadcrumbs to him," she said, digging her hand into her pocket.

I retreated a few steps as she pulled that nasty relic out of the bag.

She shook the shriveled schlong out onto the counter. A few fragments broke off, dusting the laminate surface.

"It's not a dick. It's a sheep's scrotum."

I gagged and turned away. "That doesn't make it better."

"The fae used to use scrotums for things that they wanted to withstand time's decay. My grandparents told me about them. This looks to be centuries old."

"You're touching it, aren't you?" I took deep breaths.

"The fae don't usually let these get out into the world. I think this is it, Ev. You said it was in the cake? Hidden?"

"Yeah." I finally looked over at her and witnessed her sniffing it. "I'm going to be sick."

"Don't be a baby. It's still too dry to unroll it without cracking it, but it feels like he oiled it. He probably stashed it in the cake to hide it while it softened. Whatever is written inside could point to whoever might want it."

"So Miles was kidnapped because he had a thing for oiling shriveled scrotum?"

Vena cracked a smile. "You were right about it being Shadow Trade related, then. But how did they get his necklace off if they were non-human? Or if they were human, how did they break in?"

"Maybe they knocked, and he answered the door."

She shook her head. "No. He would have looked through the peephole first. If it were someone he didn't know, he wouldn't have answered. And even if he did, he would have put his research away first."

"Unless it was someone he knew from the trade."

She picked up his phone and unlocked it. "Maybe it's one of his contacts. We can probably whittle down the list quickly." She scrolled through his phone. "It's mostly family and research contacts. I don't see any names that jump out at me. But I bet spineless Spawn knows something."

Any small amount of optimism I was shooting for crumbled at Spawn's name. The goblin was currently Miles' best customer at the Shadow Trade market…the last place I wanted Vena to go.

"We need to call your parents and tell them--"

She was already shaking her head. "No way. I'm not having them come back from their research trip early. They'll end up panicking like they did with my grandparents' disappearance. We're going to be smart about this and quietly find out who borrowed my brother to persuade him to share his information. If he's not safely back by the time they get home, I'll tell them everything."

She glanced at the scrotum then pulled the vampire's ring from her pocket. "That gives us seven days to solve our two problems, and I know our first step."

The nervousness that had my stomach tighter than the nutless sheep's sphincter had a lot to do with Miles' disappearance and the fact that, tonight, a pissed-off vampire was going to come for me. But it was also because I knew Vena. Without Miles' calm reasoning and guidance, Vena was going to go rogue.

When she held up her first finger, I cringed.

"First, we have to lay a trap for the vampire tonight. Second, we have to find who wants the nut scroll. There's only one place we can go for the information and weapons we need."

"We are *not* going to—"

"The Shadow Trade market. We're going," Vena said with a nod.

Shit.

CHAPTER FIVE

"NOTHING GOOD COMES FROM THE SHADOW WORLD," I SAID. "How many times have I said this?"

"A million at least," Vena said dryly as she tucked the scrotum into its bag.

I groaned and rubbed both hands down my face. My fingers brushed over the bandage still on my cheek.

"And why don't you ever listen? There's a vampire out there who, according to Miles, will track me down and kill me because I recently bled on him, *and* he's missing his ring. The person who could help us–Miles again–is missing. We're over our heads, Vena."

She strode across the room and wrapped me in a hug.

"I won't let anything happen to you, Ev. I promise."

"That's a dumb promise. Too much has already happened. Promise me instead that, no matter what happens to me, you'll show up at Blur tomorrow, fill out whatever paperwork Shepard needs, and start working a job that won't lead to your disappearance, too."

"I promise. But the vampire and Miles are our priority. Agreed?"

"Of course I agree. What kind of trap do we need to set for the vampire? And what do we do with him once he's trapped? Is there a service we can call? A relocation program, maybe?" I asked hopefully.

Vena pulled back and gave me a flat stare. "He's not a flock of geese shitting all over a park. He's a vampire. Relocating him won't fix our problem. We need to kill him."

I made a face.

"I don't want to be a murderer."

She released me with an arm pat. "Don't worry. Miles found the answer we need, and it's not direct murder."

She went to the table and plucked a piece of paper from the pile she'd been shuffling. It looked like a handwritten list. Before I could read it, she folded the paper and tucked it into her pocket.

"I'll take care of the trap. Now, I know you don't like the idea of going to the market, but given the circumstances, I think it would be better if we stick together."

The thought of investigating further made me nervous, so I distracted myself with lecturing Vena.

"A telemarketer. A pet food taster. Hell, even a portable toilet custodian. All of those jobs would have been better than a Shadow Trade treasure hunter."

"Everything is going to be fine, Ev. You'll see. We'll get Spawn to tell us what information Miles was trying to sell, and once that scrotum softens and relaxes enough to handle, we'll know even more. Miles will be home in no time, and that vampire will be dust once the sun sets."

"Where was this optimism during our job fair in high school?" I grumbled as I followed her out the door.

The fairy from earlier dove for the brush when we emerged as if it had been hovering outside the entrance. I shuddered, glad it hadn't flown toward me again, and hurried after Vena.

We ditched my car at a grocery store between Miles' place and the market so we could drive together since parking near the market tended to be a problem. With Vena's black crossover nearing the end of its lease, she didn't typically drive it more than necessary. However, parking my aging fuel-efficient compact for an extended time in this area was safer than parking hers.

In all honesty, I would have preferred we not go at all. While I was well aware of the darker dealings that went on at the market, to the general public, the market was a place to shop for trendy novelty items. People paid good money for elixirs to enhance their skin's glow, increase stamina, ward off bad luck, and whatnot. That the effects were fleeting at best ensured return business.

"Miles had crossed out most of the ideas written on those research papers regarding getting rid of a vampire," I said. "He'd noted a few with question marks, but I didn't see anything he'd seemed sure of."

"Yeah, he spent a lot of time digging from the way it'd looked. We'll owe him one when we find him."

"You're assuming whatever paper you grabbed will work," I said, pressing my point.

"Ev, if it were that hard to dust a vampire, the world would be crawling with them. The fact that it's not means this bloodsucker won't be a problem."

"It's because most people don't survive the transition," I said.

"They live forever, Ev. That any of them survive means their numbers would be growing...unless they could be killed. Stakes to the heart isn't a myth. It works. But this spell will be a less messy option than a stake."

I snorted. "You say that like you're some kind of hardened killer. You see a snake and run, Vena."

"It's called a 'nope rope' for a reason."

"Okay, yeah, let's bring reason into this. Suppose we screw up Miles' instructions. Or suppose we don't screw up, and they still don't work. We run the risk of making an already pissed-off vampire even angrier."

"So what do you want to do? Leave him an apology note on our kitchen table? 'Please, sir. This was all just a horrible misunderstanding. The ring jumped out of your codpiece and into my pocket. It was all an accident.' Never mind the come-hither blood you left on his lips."

"Hey! No attacking. I wouldn't have been there in the first place if you hadn't dragged me there under false pretenses."

Vena released a long breath. "You're right. I'm sorry. I'm being snipey, and you don't deserve it. I really am sorry for all of this."

"I know you are. And I wasn't suggesting we leave a note and his ring on the table, but is that such a terrible idea? I mean, he looked like he came from an era where men prided themselves on their honor. Maybe we could appeal to his knightly code of ethics."

"A vampire's knightly code of ethics?" Vena shook her head and parked in a free lot two blocks away from the market.

I didn't voice my usual complaints about walking even though my legs were still sore from the hike.

"I want to hope for the best, too, Ev, but isn't it safer to plan for the worst?"

Miles' phone buzzed in the center console. Vena snatched it up, conveniently pausing our conversation.

"What is it?" I asked.

"A text filled with numbers."

She turned the phone toward me. The screen showed, **"3891622277021444+-."** The numbers didn't seem to follow any pattern or reason.

"Who sent it?" I asked.

"It's an unknown number." Vena blew out a frustrated sigh and pocketed the phone. "Come on. We have a lot to do before it's dark."

"We have a lot to do before I have to work," I corrected. "And since we're not splitting up, you're coming to Blur with me later. No arguments." I wanted her where I could keep tabs on her.

"Actually, hanging out in a public place tonight is probably the safest option. We definitely don't want to be home after dark."

We got out of the car and started walking.

"We should get a hotel for tonight, then," I said.

"Nah. We can go to my parents' place since they aren't home. It'll be safer."

A couple strolling in front of us and taking up the sidewalk stopped our conversation. Which was fine since I could see the market ahead. The large building's bay doors were open to allow the flow of foot traffic to come and go.

As soon as we entered, my nose was assaulted by a myriad of scents, both good and bad. I made a face and glanced at Vena, who seemed completely unbothered by it.

Portable vendor stalls crowded the open space between the permanent shops that lined the sides of the building. Even more stalls lined the second floor, a mezzanine of sorts created by the shops below. Natural light flooded the space from the skylights above, adding to the glow from the long industrial pendant lights. Overall, the place wasn't as dark and shady as I'd thought it would be.

"Come on. This way," Vena said, taking the lead. She weaved her way through the crowd, heading deeper into the building.

The farther we moved from the door, the seedier the clientele and the merchandise grew. Instead of charms and pendants neatly laid out on tables, caged creatures howled. Several crates were draped with dirty sheets stained with blood.

"I'm two seconds away from running," I said, clutching Vena's arm. "And you know how I hate to do that."

"We're almost to the cafeteria," Vena said. "Spawn normally hangs out back there."

As Vena dragged us toward the bowels of the market, the aisle broke off into narrower branches made of stacked crates, casting us into shadows. She took the one to the right, pulling me further into the dimly lit maze.

The shady sellers at the booths leered at us. We would be sold to trolls for soup bones, for sure.

"You're cutting off circulation." Vena pried my hands off her arm.

"Did you see that bloody rag? We shouldn't be here. I'm never coming here again. There is nothing here worth dying for."

"Not even information on Miles?"

I glared at her. "Not fair."

"We'll be fine as long as you don't show your fear. If Spawn picks up on it, I'll have to fork out a fortune to get information."

"You don't have a fortune."

"Exactly. The only thing of value we have is the ring. And I'd rather not trade for it."

"We won't trade for it because we're hoping for the best by

giving it back while preparing for the worst," I whispered harshly.

"Won't have to give the ring back if the owner is dead."

Vena turned at a statue of a goblin impaling a human with a spear and strode through a wall of dirty, mismatched sheets. Leathery-skinned goblins sat at a rickety table, eating something fleshy. Blood oozed between sharp teeth.

I gagged.

"There he is." Vena pointed to the one on the other side of the table. The pointy-eared goblin she indicated looked up at us. A brief flicker of surprise showed on his face before he scowled.

"Can't you see I'm eating?" he complained.

"Fine," Vena said with a shrug. "Anyone else here looking for information on a recently found hoard of treasure?"

Spawn slammed his fist on the table when one of his dining companions started to stand.

"She's mine," he snarled.

Abandoning his meat pile, he stood and glowered at us. His head barely reached the top of the table as he walked around it. While some fools might mistake his lack of height as non-threatening, I knew better. Mean things came in small sizes. Case in point: fairies.

Vena and I followed Spawn out of the unsanitary eating area and down another aisle between vendors to a booth locked with floor-to-ceiling steel bars. Spawn waved his hand in front of the lock, and the bars retreated into the ceiling above.

"What do you have for me?" he asked, moving behind the short counter that looked as if it had been used as a butcher's block. The grooves were deep, some flecked with red and brown that I hoped was paint and not dried blood. But that was less gruesome than the shrunken body parts that hung from hooks behind him.

With her warning about showing fear still echoing in my head, I tried not to show my revulsion either.

Vena didn't bat an eye at his goods as she laid her hand on the counter, leaning forward. "What I have depends on what you can tell me about Miles' latest project."

Spawn crossed his arms and glared at her.

"He collects information, and I buy it. How am I supposed to know what he was working on? If you're not here to sell information about the fairy hoard or buy something from me, get lost."

Vena silently snarled and slapped her hand against the counter.

"Don't bullshit me, Spawn. He told me you were the one to give him the lead on the cache. And as you've mentioned, you don't sell information. So, I want to know why you gave him the lead. What was he working on?"

Spawn's eyes shifted briefly to the right, and I followed his glance. There was nothing there but a stack of crates partially blocking the aisle.

"That information will cost you more than you can pay. Especially if the last treasure hunt was a bust."

"It wasn't," Vena said, crossing her arms. "I found a ring with a ruby in it."

"Might be worth something. Might not," he said with an indifferent shrug.

"Same could be said about the information you do or don't have. What was Miles researching?"

"He's searching for things that went missing a long time ago. Things neither of you wanted to lose."

Vena impatiently gestured for him to continue. "That could be many things. We're in a hurry."

The goblin bared his teeth, revealing a caught meat chunk. "Then leave."

"Not until I get information." She lifted the hand that she'd slapped on the table, revealing the ring underneath it.

Spawn's gaze didn't even flick to the ring. He pulled a knife out of nowhere and stuck it into the tabletop inches from Vena's hand. She jerked, shock painting her features for a heartbeat before she balled her fist.

I stepped in front of her.

"Miles disappeared," I said. "We're trying to figure out why. What was he working on? Maybe the ring might be worth bending the rules about selling information."

Spawn looked down at the ring and frowned.

"You found this in the fairy hoard?"

"Yes, along with a vampire."

His gaze shot to mine.

"You stole from the vampire?" he asked incredulously. "Take the ring and leave. Now!"

"It's just a piece of jewelry," Vena said, stepping around me to grab the ring.

The moment she cleared the front of the counter, Spawn slammed the bars down over his store. "It's not *just* anything," he forcibly whispered as he scanned the area. "Vampires never relinquish what is theirs."

"If you want us to leave, tell us about Miles. What was he working on?"

Spawn narrowed his beady eyes at her. "He was researching things far more dangerous than the ring. And if you're smart, you'll stop asking questions before you disappear like the rest of your family."

"Problem, Spawn?" a deep voice asked behind us.

Vena and I looked over our shoulders at the same time. An oversized troll was lumbering by.

"No problem here, friend," Vena said with a smile.

The troll grunted and continued on. However, when we faced Spawn's shop, the little goblin was gone.

"Damn it," Vena swore.

"Miles has other contacts," I said softly. "We'll keep trying."

Vena stuffed the ring into her pocket. She visibly forced the tension from her shoulders and took a deep breath.

"You're right," she said. "We'll keep trying. One stop down and a few more to go. While we're checking around, keep an eye out for a reasonably priced sun charm."

Sun charms were typically used to help winter depression with their mild UV glow and were fairly common. It didn't take us long to find one at a price we were willing to pay.

During the purchase, Vena asked the shopkeeper if he'd ever worked with Miles. The dwarf didn't show a hint of recognition at the name. Vena thanked her, and we headed to a vendor who definitely knew Miles. However, the half-human half-goat faun hadn't spoken to Miles in over a week.

His gaze shifted to me, sweeping me from head to foot.

"I'd love the name of the seller you use for your curve augmentation," he said. "Mmm-mmm. I could eat you up."

My eyes went wide, and Vena hooked her arm through mine.

"Sorry, she's taken," she said over her shoulder as she led us away.

It took us another twenty minutes to check with Miles' other contacts and find the other ingredients necessary for whatever solution he'd found. During that time, I was hit on by a man stroking his miniature chupacabra a little too vigorously and was asked for a lock of my hair from a woman who wore so many charms and amulets I was surprised her neck didn't break.

"Please tell me we're done," I whispered harshly. "I need a shower and some chocolate therapy before work."

Vena's brow furrowed, which I knew had nothing to do with my comment and everything to do with having no leads on Miles. She stopped at a booth with head scarves guaranteed to regrow hair and pulled out her phone.

"Can you tell me what this is?" she asked the kind-looking woman, showing her the cryptic text Miles had received.

"A phone number?" the woman said, as clueless as we were.

"Nah," a customer said beside us. "Too long for a phone number. The plus and minus look more like longitude and latitude to me. It's the kind of stuff hunters use to look for treasure."

Vena turned to look at the bald man.

"You work with hunters?"

He shrugged. "I've been known to sell information a time or two." He reached into his pocket and handed her a card. "Been known to buy it from time to time, too."

She took his card and slipped it into her back pocket. "You might have just saved a life. Thank you."

"That'd be a first," he said before resuming his hunt for the perfect headscarf.

Vena grabbed my arm and pulled me toward the exit. The moment we stepped outside, I inhaled the fresh air and tipped my head back to the sun.

"I am never going back there again."

"It's not so bad. They're only trying to make a buck like everyone else. Besides, getting hit on isn't the worst thing that could happen. Did you see the centaur's face when I told him his sun charm was overpriced? I thought we were going to get donkey kicked into next Tuesday."

"You're lucky we didn't. Do you think that number really is coordinates?" I asked.

"I hope so. I don't know why I didn't see it before he pointed it out. Miles usually writes coordinates down on a piece of paper for me, so it's not one long string of numbers."

"Can we go home now?" I asked hopefully.

"Yep. We'll grab your car then head home so I can brew up a trap and do some research. Once I'm done, we'll head to Blur for your shift. After that, we'll go to my parents' place to wait out the night. Come morning, half our troubles will be dust."

Filled with doubt, I chewed on my lip.

"I know you think killing him is the answer, but what if the spell or whatever Miles wrote on that note doesn't work? What then?" I asked, returning to the questions she'd tried not to answer earlier.

"Then we regroup and try again."

Try again on an angry vampire? I couldn't see a second attempt ending better than the first one.

While she drove me to my car, I debated the wisdom of attempting to kill a vampire at all. He wasn't living in the same world anymore. He couldn't go around killing people and get away with it. Neither could we, even if our victim would turn to dust.

When we returned home, I had enough time before work to pull out what I needed to make bonbons. While Vena worked on her plan, I worked on mine.

Chocolate made everything better. Nothing could soothe rage like the rich decadence of a good dessert. If I added today's modern culinary genius to it, I was sure a batch of bonbons would distract our recently woke vampire from any revenge-focused rampage.

Vena took over the dining area while I took over the kitchen. Too distracted with her research, she didn't notice me measuring ingredients. The bonbons had to be perfect. No one could stay mad for temporarily borrowing a ring after tasting heaven.

I went to pour the condensed milk into the bowl. A loud bang followed by Vena's curse startled the can from my grasp. I fumbled to grab it and cut my finger on the lid.

Blood dripped into the bowl.

CHAPTER SIX

I STARED DOWN AT THE RUINED MIXTURE AND WANTED TO SWEAR.

"What happened?" I asked Vena instead, wanting to know what was so important that she startled me.

"The coordinates on Miles' phone are in D.C. Close."

I wrapped paper towel around my finger and set the can on the counter.

"I thought you were figuring out the sun charm spell-thingy."

"Multi-tasking. I say we check out the coordinates on the way to Blur tonight."

"No way. You heard the creepy goblin. Miles was working on something dangerous. It's not safe."

"Think about it, Ev. We searched his phone and apartment and didn't find anything besides the scrotum to explain what he'd been working on. Then, hours after he disappears, he gets this cryptic text. This could be our clue to finding him."

I knew I couldn't say no. If it was a clue to find Miles, we owed it to him to look.

"Fine," I said. "We'll drive by it. But nothing else. No stopping. No questioning people. Once we figure out what is there, then we can plan our next steps." Which would not involve any more risks. Having to deal with the threat of a recently woken vampire was enough.

I turned to consider the pink milk. I didn't have another can to replace it. But . . . the bonbons were for a vampire anyway. Maybe the extra ingredient would be the perfect addition to this please-don't-be-mad-at-us gift.

And it wasn't as if he hadn't already had a taste of my blood. Unwrapping my finger, I allowed a few extra drops to stain the milk then cleaned and bandaged my cut.

I had the bonbons cooling in the freezer before Vena finished what she was doing.

"I'm going to go pack then shower," I said. "Don't eat those bonbons."

"You made bonbons?"

"Yes, but they aren't for you. They're bribe food, and I counted each one. No eating them. I'm serious."

She made a face as I walked past her.

In my room, I packed enough for several nights away, on the off chance things didn't go as Vena planned, then got ready for work. By the time I finished, Vena was in her room packing as well.

The ring pouch sat on the table, partially covering a note from Vena. There was no sign of any trap or sun charm. Relieved that she'd changed her mind, I read her note.

Didn't know vampires were real. My bad.

. . .

I snorted and grabbed the notebook to write a new one.

We humbly apologize for accidentally transporting your ring away from you. When we discovered the mistake and went to return it, you were already gone. I hope that finding it in impeccable condition and these treats will make amends.

We are truly sorry.

When I finished, I retrieved the bonbons. Vena emerged from her room as I set them next to the new note.

"You made him dessert?" she asked.

"It can't hurt."

"You know what? You're right. It actually might help this look more authentic."

"What do you mean?" I asked, eyeing the ring pouch. "What did you do?"

She plucked the ring, which I'd thought was in the pouch, from her pocket.

"Just a little switch."

I glanced at the pouch again. "What's in there?"

"The sun charm. Miles figured out a way to turn it into a bomb of sorts. The vamp will never know what hit him."

"But I made bonbons as a peace offering."

"Ev, he's a vampire. He's dangerous. Get over it."

She then went to the kitchen and looked around before opening the flour container. She dropped the ring inside and shook it.

"Why did you just pollute my flour?" I hurried to pull it from her hands, but she held tight.

"He'll never find the ring in here. He'll see his pouch and go straight for it. I'll buy you new flour once he's dust. Okay?"

I reluctantly released the container and nodded.

With a contented smile, she placed the container on the counter and headed to her room. "I'll be ready to go soon. Are you packed?"

"Uh, yeah."

I glanced between the ring pouch and the flour. While I knew Vena was probably right and that the vampire was dangerous, he was only coming here because we took his ring in the first place.

Feeling guilty, I crumbled Vena's original note and went to throw it away.

Miles' list that Vena had taken was sitting on top of the trash. It included the ingredients to use with the sun charm. I wasn't familiar with most of them as I skimmed the list. But the last couple of lines caught my attention.

Chemical reactions should begin once the vampire is in range. Vampire should turn to ash. Possible inferno may happen. Proceed with caution.

Inferno? Proceed with caution?

Vena was going to burn the house down along with the vampire? Was she insane? We couldn't afford that kind of damage. What would the neighbors think?

With my mind made up, I dug through the flour to find the ring. After cleaning it thoroughly, I removed the small stone charm from the pouch and slipped the ring inside.

The stone didn't seem like it could kill anything, let alone a vampire, but I wrapped it in a paper towel and tucked it into my pocket. If the vampire hated my blood bonbons, then we'd still have the sun charm as a backup.

Feeling a little better about the situation, I went to grab my bag. It was time to flee.

Vena was only a few steps behind me as I headed for the door.

"I'll drive," I said.

I preferred driving because then I controlled our destination and how long we stayed.

We weren't on the road for long before she said we were close to the texted coordinates.

"Slow down," Vena said, her gaze swinging from her phone to her window.

I pulled over to the side so the evening commuter traffic could flow around us as I idled along the sidewalk lined with nice bars and restaurants.

"Are you sure this is the right place?" I asked as I spotted it. "It's a strip club."

Vena glanced at her phone again. "Yep. This is it."

We both looked over at the three-story brick building with unlit arched window openings.

"Why would someone send these coordinates to Miles?" Vena asked.

"That unknown number was probably one of his friends wanting to grab a lap dance."

"Not Miles. He's too focused on his research."

I knew she was right, but the need to live in my world of denial a little longer had me saying, "He's also twenty-five. Even if he doesn't want to go, his friends probably do."

"Then why send the coordinates? Why not tell him to meet at the club?"

Vena's logical reasoning was sinking my delusion boat. It *was* odd to send numbers instead of the club name.

"Miles could be in there. We need to go inside." Vena opened the door and was out of the car before I could stop her.

"Shit." I swung into the lot and parked. Hurrying after her, I said, "You have sixty seconds. Then we have to leave. I mean it, Vena."

"Yeah. Sixty seconds."

That didn't sound promising.

Vena opened the old wooden door, and music assaulted my ears with the club's version of dance music as she stepped into the dark club.

I followed, hoping this club was of the flashing boob variety and not the pick-up-dollars-with-genitals variety. Thankfully, a large man wearing a tight black t-shirt stood right inside the door and stopped us from going further.

Perfect. We could ask him a few questions then leave. No need to see more.

He eyed us up and down. "You got IDs?"

Vena took out her driver's license.

"Not that ID," he said before she could hand it to him.

"Then what ID?"

"If you don't know, you don't have it."

"How can I get one?" she asked.

"You don't." He stepped forward. "Get out."

"What kind of place needs a special ID?" she asked.

"The kind that is private," he said.

Vena stood her ground even though the bouncer took a menacing step closer.

"Who owns this place?" Vena asked.

"None of your business. Get out before I toss you out."

When Vena fisted her hand, I pulled her toward the door.

"We'll leave," I said quickly. "We don't want any trouble."

The minute we were outside, Vena jerked her arm from my hold.

"No," I said firmly. "You don't get to be angry with me. What were you thinking?"

"I was thinking about Miles," she said in a harsh whisper as we headed to the car.

"And I'm thinking about both of you. The coordinates could be nothing. Or it could be related. We don't know at this point. You going in there like an enraged troll won't help us learn anything. And who's going to help me find Miles when you're in the hospital with a broken face? Or better yet, who will save us if we go missing too?"

I opened my door and slid in behind the wheel.

"You need to be smarter about this, Vena," I said as soon as she sat and closed her door.

"Miles has been missing for at least ten hours." The torment in her voice was almost my undoing.

"He'll be fine," I said as I pulled into traffic. "He's smart and knows what he's doing. He doesn't take unnecessary risks. He'll probably show up tomorrow or the day after with a story about being charmed into spilling everything he knows about a treasure hoard.

"We need to keep it together, Vena. We need to think and focus on what we can control. You're the one always telling me that, and you're right. Now you need to do it. Just in case Miles doesn't show up, let's stay focused on our other leads, which is that shriveled ballsack you're probably still carrying around."

Vena exhaled heavily and dropped her head back against the headrest.

"You sound like Miles."

"I'll take that as a compliment. He always was your voice of reason. Now, what's the plan? What do we need to do next?"

"I checked the ballsack when we were home, and it still needs more time to soften. Tomorrow morning, I should be able to unroll it without damaging it. While you're working, I'll keep going through Miles' phone and see what I can dig up regarding the strip club, just to be safe."

"Good. That's a solid plan." I pulled into Blur's employee parking lot and waited for Vena to grab her laptop bag out of the back.

"Are they going to have a problem with me taking up bar space all night? I don't want to ruin my chance to work at this fine establishment."

I rolled my eyes at her partial sarcasm.

"It'll be fine," I said.

We parted ways so Army could let her in through the main entrance before Blur's doors officially opened. No one was at the employee lockers when I clocked in, but Gunther was washing his way through a mountain of dishes in the sink.

"Hey, Gunther. Is that left over from last night?"

"Nah. Stress cleaning."

I frowned and paused on my way to the door that led to the bar. Was he upset about getting into trouble with Shepard for drinking?

"Stress cleaning? You okay?"

He shook his head. "A body was found a block from here. Throat slit. Shepard isn't happy."

Stunned by the news, I continued to the bar.

Buzz was behind it, hand-deep in a glass, polishing like his life depended on it. Did all the guys stress clean?

Vena was settling at the bar and glanced meaningfully at her laptop bag, which she'd partially hidden with her legs.

"Hey, Buzz. Would it be a big deal if Vena claimed a stool for the whole night?"

He looked from Vena to the cut on my cheek, which I'd rebandaged.

"Why? What's wrong?" he asked, setting the glass down. "You didn't actually fall, did you?"

Vena grinned. "If you ever saw her walk outside, you wouldn't be asking that question. She's only graceful here because the floors are flat." Vena paused and looked at the steps that I regularly went up and down. "How do you manage the stairs without falling?"

"Shut up," I said without rancor before looking at Buzz. "Let me know if she's a pain in your ass tonight."

"That's what he said," Vena said under her breath.

"If she is," I continued, ignoring her, "I'll stick her with Anchor."

Vena glanced over at Anchor with a smirk. "I'm happy to fall on that stick."

Anchor looked over at us. His heavy gaze took in Vena.

Crap. Had he heard her?

When she winked at him, he quickly looked away. Even from this distance, I could see the blush on his tan skin, which made the muscled man ten times more adorable.

"Alrighty then. I should go and find out my assigned area." I wrapped a short black apron around my waist as I hurried away.

When everyone was assembled in the staff room, Shepard appeared moments later.

Sierra eyed my cheek with a smirk. "Looks like another day without the VIP section."

"Quiet." Shepard looked at his tablet. "Adrian, take lower stage left. Thomas, lower stage right. Pam, upper stage left. Sierra, upper stage right. Everly, you're on VIP." He started for the door as he added, "Everly, come by my office before the shift."

"Wait. Can you give the VIP section to someone else?" I asked.

He paused at the door and raised a brow. "Why?"

My reason had everything to do with Vena being a floor below me, but I didn't want Shepard to question it. "I've had it more than the rest. They deserve a shot at it, too."

"No. Meet me in my office in five."

The others hurried out after Shepard.

Sierra glowered on her way past, purposefully shouldering me.

"What's your problem?" I called after her, but she was already through the door.

Shaking my head, I followed everyone to the main floor and veered toward Vena as Shepard disappeared into the kitchen. Buzz nodded to me as I approached, and I marveled at how many glasses he'd polished in such a short time.

"Is our ward behaving?" I asked.

"She demanded three cherries in her Shirley Temple because she hasn't had a cherry in years."

Vena smirked at me while I shook my head at her. "Shepard put me in the VIP section. Do your homework and behave."

"I'll be fine. Go get those tips."

I glanced at Buzz, who winked at me and promised he'd watch over what remained of Vena's cherries. Usually, I had to worry about other people's safety when Vena was around, but tonight, I was grateful for Buzz's watchful gaze. Until she and I knew the vampire was pacified, everything was uncertain.

Shepard emerged from the kitchen with Sierra following in his wake. Her face was flushed and her expression a mix of resentment and embarrassment. Without a doubt, Shepard had reprimanded her for her snarky comment. I felt no pity for her. What had she thought would happen when she acted like a bitch in front of the boss? She was lucky he didn't know about her shoulder check.

Ignoring her, I followed Shepard up to his office, saying hello to Anchor as we passed. He pulled his watchful gaze from Vena long enough to greet me.

Shepard was already in his chair when I entered his office.

"I'm worried about your safety," he said.

I felt a jolt of panic because I was worried about my safety and thought he knew something, but then his gaze flicked to my cheek again.

"Either you're calling me a liar, or you're giving my outdoors skills more credit than they are due," I said lightly.

He sighed and leaned back in his chair.

"How long have you been working for me, Everly?"

"A little over six months."

"A short time and yet longer than any other server. You do the work. You're good with customers. You have a positive attitude. And you work well with the other staff. I don't want to lose you."

"If you're worried I'll quit because Sierra's in a mood, I won't. I live with Vena. Snark and sass don't faze me."

"I've dealt with Sierra. She won't be a problem. But when you leave tonight, no walking to your car alone. You get Anchor, Buzz, or, preferably, me to walk you out."

"Is this about the dead person?" I asked in sudden understanding.

"Not only the dead person but yes," he said, confusing me.

"It's not safe at night, and I don't want you to take unnecessary risks."

"I won't," I promised. "And Vena's hanging out here all night, so she can walk out the back with me if you're okay with it."

He stood, coming around the desk. His stoic expression didn't give away a single thought.

"Why is Vena staying all night? What's going on?" As he spoke, he gently clasped my chin, tipping my face up.

It was the first time he'd touched me like this, and my pulse stuttered a beat as our gazes locked and held for a long, awkward moment. His expression softened as he released my chin and brushed his thumb right below my cut.

"You can trust me to take care of you, Everly," he said, his voice a low rumble.

I swallowed hard and glanced away, unable to maintain eye contact when he was so close.

"I trust you, Shepard. Thank you. Everyone here is like family."

"Good. Remember that."

I nodded. "I will."

Backtracking, I left the office and paused in the hall to take a calming breath.

Shepard was sexy as hell but my boss. I liked him because, to me, he wasn't unreasonable with what he asked of his staff. He had high standards, which sometimes led to staff turnover. But his standards were what ensured a comfortable work environment.

That included his hands-to-yourself work policy.

All the bar staff, who'd been here much longer, were extremely attractive and flirty. But they always kept their hands to themselves.

Until now.

Until Shepard.

I thought about it for a moment and shook my head. No matter how it had seemed, he hadn't meant it as anything more than a caring gesture. I knew that. Yet, it still surprised me how much he cared.

I cared, too. Blur had become my second home. Except for Sierra, I saw them all as my second family. Which made being here tonight even worse.

If what Miles had said was true, there was every chance the vampire would show up here tonight instead of at the house. Was I putting everyone at risk by being here? I hoped not. It wasn't like a vampire could go on a mass killing spree and get away with it in today's age. Not that that thought gave me much comfort.

I smiled at Detroit, who was working the VIP bar and focused on preparing my station. After I had enough napkins and other supplies to keep me going until the end of the night, I straightened the chairs around my tables.

Perfect.

I felt the fae before I saw my first VIPs of the night ascend the stairs. Typically, I'd rather hang with the dwarves. I trusted myself with the dwarves. Fae, not so much.

With alabaster skin, clear arctic eyes, and silvery hair that transcended any beauty salon, the fae were beautiful. And they knew it.

Being near them was like looking at a chocolate cake I couldn't eat and telling myself I could just lick the frosting. Dangerous. Alluring. Tempting in all the wrong ways.

I knew it was their natural effect on humans.

The old tales about the fae hadn't been far from the truth when they first appeared in our world. Their presence beguiled to the point that some humans would do anything a fae asked. Thankfully, the fae weren't malicious. They simply wanted to enjoy the finer things in life, and for the most part, humans were the finer things. They craved our adoration and collected human lovers like Vena collected hunting knives.

Being at clubs like Blur usually meant they were looking for a new flavor of the month amongst the clientele. The VIP section gave them a bird's eye view of the selection.

I gave them my best smile and moved to take their order.

"Hello, beauty. Tell me, what drink graces your delicious lips from this place?" He didn't even have to move his gaze from my face for me to feel it along my body.

"Blur's most popular signature drink is Effervescence," I said.

They both nodded their acceptance.

Stepping over to the bar, I placed the order with Detroit. Not that I needed to. He was already mixing the drinks by the time I got to him.

"If they try anything, let me know," he said quietly.

I was pretty sure I didn't have to let him know. Even though Detroit was one of the flirtiest of the bartenders, he'd watch out for staff.

More VIPs entered my section as Detroit finished the drinks. On my way to deliver the cocktails to the fae, I swung by the new three-top and let them know I'd be with them soon.

When one of the fae saw my approach, he slightly raised his hand to stop his companion's conversation.

I set the drinks down and stepped back. "Can I get you gentlemen anything to eat? Our appi-teasers are phenomenal."

The fae who had been talking looked at me. "Consider our appetites very teased, beauty. Perhaps we will feast later."

There was something about the way he said "feast" that

heated my blood. He smirked as if he knew my reaction and then turned back to his friend.

Fae might not be malicious, but they were absolutely dangerous. Thankfully, I knew better than to fall for a pretty face.

CHAPTER SEVEN

I SAT NEXT TO VENA WITH A SIGH AND COUNTED OUT MY TIPS. She'd moved upstairs to the VIP lounge as soon as the last customer had left.

"Damn, girl. How did you get twenties for tips?"

Detroit chuckled. "She's a brat to the customers."

I gave him an appropriately affronted look then glanced at Vena. "I'm nice, don't flirt, and deliver the drinks quickly. There's not a lot to it."

"Then why was Miss Bitchy-pants crying that she made less than two hundred when you're walking with close to three?" Vena asked.

"Clue's in the name," Detroit said.

More than ready to leave and find out if Vena had discovered anything, I passed Detroit his share of the tips.

"Come on, Vena. You woke me up too early, and I need sleep." The shortened sleep from the night before, plus the day's stress on top of an entire shift, had taken its toll. I wasn't looking forward to the drive to her parents' house.

She stood, her stuff already packed.

Detroit stopped me with a reminder. "Shepard wants to walk you out."

"Oh, does he now?" Vena purred.

"Please don't make this weird," I said before turning my pleading gaze to Detroit. "Shepard said any of you could walk us out. You busy?"

He eyed me, clearly wondering if he would be risking the wrath of Shepard. Tossing the tip money on the bar with a sigh, he walked us downstairs. The main floor was already devoid of staff, and Gunther was almost done with his dishes when we passed through the kitchen.

I clocked out and followed Detroit outside.

After being inside for eight hours, the cool night air didn't feel like a fresh relief like it should have. Instead, it felt ominously oppressive, and a shiver stole through me as I looked around the gated parking lot.

"How close was the murder to Blur?" I asked, keeping up with Detroit.

"Close enough that Shepard's going to want to walk you to the car for the next year," Detroit said softly, his eyes scanning the area as he moved.

That Detroit was on edge made me even more nervous.

"I'll watch you drive off," he said as I unlocked the doors. "Text Shepard when you're home for the night. He'll worry."

I nodded and settled behind the wheel. Vena managed to stay quiet until we left the parking lot. As soon as we were out of sight, she turned in her seat to look at me.

"You have Shepard's number?" she asked with a grin ghosting her lips.

"Of course I do. He's the boss. Now, tell me what you found."

"I found out that Buzz has a romantic streak. He likes

flirting but is waiting for Mrs. Right. He's also a big softy who can't stand the sound of a rumbling tummy. Those lamb skewers were so good."

"Vena, focus," I said as I navigated toward the freeway out of town.

"I am. I peppered him with personal questions until he scurried to the other end of the bar so I could research the strip club without my soon-to-be coworker drawing awkward conclusions.

"Unfortunately, all my research efforts regarding the club were dead ends. I found pictures of the nicely decorated interior, empty of people, but not much more. However, I've seen the club's 'NC' logo somewhere before. I can't remember where, though. With that whole special ID thing, I'm betting it's linked with supernaturals somehow. Once we get to my parents' place, I can go through some of Mom's books to look for it.

"I also searched Miles' email, phone history, and contacts and found a few things. Mostly clients he had worked with in the past. A couple of inquiries for private research. None of it raised red flags."

"So, nothing?"

"Not quite nothing. There's a picture I need to double-check. I found it on Miles' phone while scrolling through his recent pictures. I didn't go too far back, focusing on stuff from when he started compiling information on the fairy hoard."

"You mean the dangerous information that Spawn warned us to stay away from if we didn't want more family to go missing?"

"Exactly," she said, purposely ignoring my sarcasm. "Miles had screenshot a photo of a book cover. The book looked so old the lettering faded from the cover. I looked at the date of that file and combed back through his text messages. Sure enough. He received it from an unnamed contact. No message. Only the picture and a hefty price tag for information on the book."

"How hefty? Like kidnap someone for it hefty?"

Vena shrugged. "It all depends on how hard up a person is for cash. Five grand is nothing to sneeze at, but I wouldn't want to take on my brother for that amount. I think Miles was going to try to find it."

"You're going to try to do the same thing," I guessed.

If Miles needed a book, the first place he would have gone is his parents' house to look. But he wasn't the type to leave his research lying around–the situation at his apartment notwithstanding–so I highly doubted we'd find anything there.

"If the book doesn't have a name, how are you going to find it?" I asked.

"You know my parents have an extensive library and a research database we can access. There's also the research forum. I'm sure we'll turn up something."

I briefly wondered if Vena was grasping for leads where there were none, but I didn't say anything. She was worried about Miles and not the type to sit around doing nothing.

Passing the city boundaries, I drove to the Hunters' sprawling estate. Without streetlights, only the moon and my headlights lit the way beyond the trees to a house overlooking the meandering river.

Vena's family home reminded me of a proper English manor, complete with quarters for butlers and servants. Those little rooms and nooks had been turned into areas of study and research. Hiding places galore for Vena and me when we used to play hide-and-seek.

The shadows played in the trees that surrounded the house, making my hands clench the steering wheel. This isolated spot was beautiful in the day but creepy as hell at night, especially with a vampire on the loose.

Fingering the protection charm tucked into my shirt, I parked in front of the garage. We both raced to the front door with our bags but for different reasons. I wanted safety and sleep. Vena probably wanted to start searching. She crammed the key into the lock and flung the door open.

"Let's check the pantry," she said, already moving that way in the dark house.

So, I was wrong. Her speed had been all about her stomach, which I found odd.

"I thought you ate at Blur," I said as I followed.

While she foraged, I set my bag on the floor inside the room.

"No chips," she said. She stepped over to the garbage and frowned when she peered into the empty can. "Damn. I thought maybe Miles ate them."

Was she hungry or trying to track Miles through his eating habits?

"I don't want to be the downer here, but we don't have a lot to go on, Vena. We need to think about what to do if the book, the sheep scrotum, and the strip club turn out to be nothing. Is there anyone we can go to for help? I know you don't want to worry your parents, but they have contacts that we don't. It's wrong to keep them in the dark."

Vena stopped her search to face me.

"In the past, Miles told me not to freak out if he goes missing for a few days. That it probably has something to do with his research and not to bother our parents, but he wouldn't leave his phone and charm behind. I'm freaking out, Everly. I'm trying not to, but I am."

"Hey, I get it. After what happened to your grandparents, freaking out is normal," I said, trying to be the calm one. "If you don't want us to involve your parents yet, then we won't. We'll give Miles another day or two to show up on his own. We'll also focus on the leads you have and our vampire issue. Miles seemed more worked up about the vampire than whatever big thing he was working on."

"You're right," she said, giving me a grateful smile. "Since we've done what we can about the vampire situation for tonight, let's focus on our Miles leads."

She slapped a hunk of cheese from the fridge onto a plate, pulled out a box of crackers, and handed it all to me, along with a knife. "Take this to Mom's study. I'll run our bags upstairs."

I listened to her footsteps fade away into the house as I sliced the cheese and went to settle into her mom's leather thinking chair. What were the odds Vena would let me sleep if I closed my eyes right now? I was tempted to find out. Feet hurting from a busy shift, I kicked off my shoes and settled in.

"I was right!" I heard Vena yell from above.

I didn't bother yelling back. If it was important, she'd find me.

Closing my eyes, I waited.

"Ev," she said when she entered.

I dutifully opened my eyes and watched her bee-line to her mom's computer. She turned it on while waving an empty bag of chips at me.

"Miles *was* here. This was in his room. He always eats the good stuff first when he comes here."

"It could be from the last time he visited," I said even though I doubted it. Their mom ran a tight ship. Garbage cans were emptied, and cupboards were stocked with non-perishables every time they went on a research expedition.

"You know as well as I do this chip bag means that Miles

was here recently. But was it before or after he received the picture of the book?"

She stuffed the bag into the garbage by the desk and faced her mom's computer. "Now the question is...did he find anything here?"

"What do you want me to do?" I asked, fighting the urge to close my eyes again.

"See if you can find any books that might look like the one in the picture. I doubt it's here, but we should look to be sure."

I peeled myself out of the chair and started with the shelves in the study. Every room in the manor had rows of books except the bathrooms and the kitchen. It could take the rest of the night to weed through them all.

"Vena, what if I look through the shelves in here tonight and leave the rest for the morning? We both need sleep."

Vena made a halfhearted noise, which I took as an agreement, but I wasn't too sure either. Since my feet ached, I scooted the chair close to the shelf and sat down to search the lowest row first.

Before I finished scanning the shelf, my phone buzzed in my pocket. When I pulled it out, the paper-towel-wrapped sun charm came with it. The small bundle landed quietly on the floor. I scrambled to pick it up, accidentally unraveling the paper towel. I palmed the stone and looked at Vena like a kid getting caught licking the frosting off the cake.

She didn't look away from the computer even for a second.

Exhaling in relief, I tucked the sun charm into my cleavage so there weren't any more mishaps and looked at the message on my phone.

Shepard: You were supposed to check in. Are you safe at home?

Crap. I forgot to text Shepard.

Me: Yes. I'm safe. Sorry, I forgot. Long day.

Pocketing my phone, I rubbed my eyes to get them to focus and resumed my search. I'd only meant to lean back in the chair for a moment to rest my eyes. Instead, they stayed closed.

I wasn't sure how much time had passed when Vena shook my arm.

"Huh? What?" Groggily, I blinked up at her serious face.

"I found the book."

I sat forward and scrubbed my face with my hands, trying to spark my brain up to Vena-speed.

"Where is it?" I asked.

"I'm not sure. But I found it listed in the database."

"How can it be listed when it doesn't have a title?"

She pointed at the screen where I saw a picture of the book, similar to the photo on Miles' phone. The database listed the book as "unknown."

"Do you know what this means?" Vena asked.

My sluggish mind couldn't process how an unknown book listing could help us. We still didn't have the book.

"Help me out, Vena. I'm half asleep."

"Look at the name on the bottom."

I leaned in and glanced at the history of who had the book. The last reported person was Barnaby Hunter.

"Your grandfather?"

She nodded, looking grim. "Spawn told us not to dig, or we'd disappear like the rest of my family. I thought he meant Miles, but now I think he meant my grandparents. I think Miles was looking into–"

She stopped and glanced at my chest.

"Ev, what's going on with your cleavage?"

I looked down to find a subtle glow from underneath my shirt. The sun charm was illuminated, but it shouldn't have activated. The instructions had said it would only react if a vampire was nearby.

My eyes went wide. "Shit."

"What did you do?" Vena demanded.

"I switched the ring with the charm. I'm sorry! But the side effects listed a possible inferno."

"So you thought the safest place to keep something that can ignite is in your cleavage?" She grabbed my arm and dragged me toward the door.

A window shattered somewhere in the house.

Vena and I froze and looked at each other with wide, fearful eyes. I could almost see her mind racing. The only thing of mine that was racing was my heart. It was doing its best to send me to an early, panicked grave.

"What do we do?" I whispered.

We were both wearing our protection charms, which in theory, would keep us safe from any form of supernatural with malicious intent. I wasn't sure I wanted to stake my life on it, though. Neither did Vena, apparently. She hurried to the bottom drawer of her mom's desk and pulled out a wicked-looking knife.

"Out the window," she mouthed.

I spun around, ready to torpedo myself through the glass, when the sudden heat from the sun charm had me clawing at my shirt. It felt like I'd dropped a freshly made nugget of caramel corn down my bra.

"Shit. That's hot!" I yanked out the radiating stone, chucked it toward the chair, and dashed to the window.

A burst of blinding white light exploded behind me, reflecting off the glass. I staggered as Vena crashed into me, swearing up a storm.

The smell of burning leather clogged my nose as she

clutched me, and for a horrifying moment, I thought we'd started her parents' house on fire.

However, the smell dissipated faster than the spots dancing in front of my eyes.

"Ladies." The smooth baritone wasn't a voice I recognized. "I am quite put out by the inconveniences you've caused me."

Knees growing weaker by the second, I turned and repeatedly blinked at the person standing near the chair.

As the spots began to clear, my stomach dropped at the sight of the man from the cave. Although he still wore his ancient clothes, he was free of dust and webs.

If I'd thought fae dangerously tempting, the man standing in Vena's mom's office proved I knew nothing. The lamp on the desk ignited the red hue in the shoulder-length russet hair he'd tied back at the base of his neck. His strong jawline and perfect skin were illuminated in the light. Warm, light-brown, almost amber eyes stared directly at us.

I swallowed hard at how his gaze dismissively flicked over Vena before settling on me. He looked curious and slightly amused as he studied me with his mesmerizing eyes.

"Now what, pray, can you offer as recompense?" he asked.

"How does a serving of silver in the jugular sound?" Vena asked, widening her stance in front of me and lifting the knife she held.

"Decidedly uncomfortable," he said blandly. "Though I would expect no less than a coarsely worded offer from women of ill repute, I had hoped for a modicum of reason."

"Ill repute?" Vena echoed, sounding more confused than offended. "What the hell is that supposed to mean?"

"I believe he thinks we're loose women because we're wearing pants. Look at how he's dressed, Vena. He's old. He doesn't know."

He smiled slightly, the barest tilt of the corner of his mouth, and brushed his thumb over his bottom lip. My stomach fluttered in response. I was so distracted by his perfect mouth that I barely noticed the glint of ruby decorating his finger.

"An astute observation." He inhaled deeply, and his gaze swept over my face as his teeth lengthened noticeably. It didn't detract from his beautifully shaped lips. "It would seem you are the reasonable one of the pair, so let me speak plainly.

"It will take far more to make amends for your wrongdoing than the tantalizing samples you've provided. Although, I do appreciate the effort you put into the confectionery."

"Samples?" Vena questioned without taking her eyes off him. "What's he talking about, Everly?"

"I cut myself while making the apology bonbons," I said without clarifying that it had been an accident. "We truly are sorry about the misunderstanding. I'm sure you saw how the ceiling was caved in when you woke. We fell into it while hiking. Our intention was never to rob you."

His gaze swept over my face again.

"Apology not accepted. We both know my ring did not slip into your hands of its own accord. No matter the changes the world has undergone, honor is not dead. And thievery holds no honor."

He turned to the side, giving us a view of his chiseled jawline as he looked at the books on the desk then at the computer.

"However, I am not heartless. I will allow you to repay me."

"You're not getting more of our blood," Vena said.

His gaze flicked at her with annoyance before clearing and settling on me. "While feedings will help me acquire the knowledge I need, it will not be enough to ease my transition into this new world. I require a liaison."

"Not happening!" Vena snapped.

"Vena," I harshly whispered as I pulled at her arm. "Stop provoking and listen."

As far as I could tell, the vampire was merely asking for help. As long as it wasn't of the chomping-into-arteries type of help, I'd take being a liaison over being an unwilling donor any day. Besides, we had stolen his ring and woke him. Considering Miles' and Spawn's reactions to the news, I thought the vampire would have already killed us, not asked for aid.

The vampire nodded at me as if thanking me for continuing to be reasonable.

"Help me acclimate to this new world, and I will consider your honor debt repaid in full," the vampire said before Vena could say anything else.

"You'll forgive us if we don't trust you since vampires are not known to be *creatures* of their word," Vena said.

A slight narrowing of his eyes was the only indication he didn't appreciate her emphasis on how she viewed him.

In a blur of motion, he switched spots with Vena. Her mouth dropped open when she realized she stood by the desk and he now stood in front of me.

He angled himself to keep watch on her. "I know quite well the reputation of my kind, but this offer does not concern you."

Vena looked from her empty hand to him. He arched a brow at her and glanced at the knife now embedded in the wood trim above the door. I hadn't even seen him throw it.

"This offer is for Everly only, and she has my word. I will not harm her in exchange for her assistance."

He glanced at me, and I swallowed hard, feeling way over my head. Dwarves? No problem. Fae? They were a little tricky, but I could still deal well with them. A vampire, though?

"For how long?" I asked, sounding reasonably calm.

"Until I no longer require your assistance."

"Not happening!" Vena snapped. "That could be forever."

"A mortal cannot give me forever," the vampire said. "Would you rather amuse me with more of your parlor tricks?" He gestured at the leather chair, which had a scorch mark on the seat with a small pile of dust in the center.

"Also a misunderstanding," I said weakly.

He turned his intense gaze on me.

"It is warming to hear that you weren't trying to kill me." He leaned closer, his gaze sweeping over the medical tape on my cheek and down to my throat.

When it dipped to my gapping neckline and to my bright red cleavage that stung like a sunburn and carpet burn had a baby, I quickly secured the buttons I'd pulled apart to remove the charm.

"Counter offer," I said.

He raised a brow but gestured for me to continue. I glanced at the ring on his pointer finger again.

"Both Vena and I will help you acclimate, but there's a time limit of ten days, and discretion is required. I also want your promise that you will not harm us even after the acclimation period has ended."

"Ten days is oddly specific," he said, considering me.

"Vampires aren't openly accepted in today's world. Most people still think they're a myth. If you're obvious, you will endanger yourself, and us as well. Ten days are all we can risk. If you haven't caught on how to blend in by then, we'll all be dead."

He chuckled lowly.

"I'm already dead, or didn't you know?"

I thought back to the single beat of his heart that I'd heard in the cave and wondered if that was true. There was so little I knew about vampires.

"Do we have a deal?" I asked.

His amber gaze considered me for a long moment.

"We do."

He reached up to brush his thumb over the fluttering pulse on my neck.

"And I very much look forward to the next ten days, Everly."

CHAPTER EIGHT

WITH THE VAMPIRE SO DANGEROUSLY NEAR, I RETREATED A STEP, but my foot collided with the wall.

"I caution you against running," he said with a smirk. "One thing you should know about vampires is that we love a good chase." He straightened away from me as he scanned the room. "So many new inventions. I want to learn everything."

"Not tonight," Vena said quickly. "Everly needs to sleep first."

I knew Vena's sudden concern about my lack of sleep wasn't real. She wanted him gone...likely so she could yell at me for agreeing with this proposal and to come up with some new way to try to kill him.

He ignored Vena and looked at me. "I require a few questions answered before I take my leave."

"Okay," I said.

"When I entered the cave where you found me, humans only knew of humans. When did humans become aware of the others?"

Vena moved from her position at the desk and went to her

mom's scorched thinking chair. He turned with her, ensuring he could see both of us as if *we* were the threats, which I found interesting.

"About a hundred years ago," I said.

"How did that happen?" he asked.

"No one knows."

"The supernaturals just appeared." Vena wiped the ruined seat with the hem of her shirt. "My mother is going to be pissed when she sees this."

"She will become inebriated?" he asked, looking slightly offended.

"No. Getting pissed or being pissed isn't only about drinking. At least, not here in the States," I said. "It means she'll be angry."

"As she should be," he said. "That's a fifteenth-century chair. In its day, it would have been paid for in gold. It's the only thing in this dwelling that I recognize. Well, that and the books."

Vena stopped dabbing to look at him, and I could already hear her inner mind at work, wondering if he would know the contents of the faded book. But she kept silent, now watching him like he was the prey and not her.

I had to admit, the vampire wasn't the terror I'd expected he would be. I'd thought he would have gone for our necks at the first opportunity. He'd proven he could move fast, and he'd been close enough to my neck. But he hadn't done anything. Only his elongated teeth betrayed his need for blood.

I actually felt a little bad for him. He'd clearly been sleeping for a very long time. Waking up after the entire world changed must feel confusing, and maybe even a little frightening. Not that he looked frightened. Wary, yes. Afraid? Absolutely not.

He prowled through the study, making his way back to me. "Who are the leaders of the fae, dwarves, and wolves?"

"Why do you care?" Vena asked before I could say anything.

He gave a slight snarl of warning that had her crossing her arms.

"We wouldn't know," I said quickly to keep the peace. "Supernatural groups mostly keep to themselves. I know I agreed to help you, but is there a chance we can call it a night for now? I've been up since eight yesterday morning and need sleep."

He didn't look as if he was ready to call it quits, and I didn't blame him. He had to have so many questions about the world, but I truly was beyond exhausted.

"Very well. I will take my leave for now and return tomorrow."

"I work in the evenings but can answer questions after," I said so he would know that I was previously committed.

"I would prefer not to wait so long. Perhaps we can speak as you break your fast?"

I didn't like the way his gaze dipped to my neck when he was talking about breaking a fast.

He moved closer again with a satisfied smirk on his face when I backed into the wall again.

"I didn't mean you. Unless you offer, of course."

"Not offering," I said weakly.

"A pity. I shall return in the morning. Rest well, Everly."

He stepped away.

"Wait. What's your name?" I asked.

He hesitated a moment before answering. "Brodier Ashley Cross. You can call me Cross. And I trust both of you will keep the knowledge of my existence, including my name, to yourselves."

Faster than my eyes could process, he was gone.

"How's he going to be back in the daytime?" I asked Vena. "I thought vampires couldn't survive in sunlight."

"They can't. Hopefully, he'll walk out into the sun and turn himself to dust so we don't have to worry about the vampire you've fed *twice*."

I bristled at her tone.

"But did we die? No. So maybe that second helping saved our lives. Be more grateful and less cranky." I sighed and rubbed my face. "If he didn't kill us now, what are the chances he'll kill us when we close our eyes?"

Vena looked down for a moment, thinking. "He has his ring back and could have fed on us already if he wanted to, so probably small. But we should sleep in shifts to be on the safe side."

Our sleep time was already too short.

"Nope. We're going upstairs, barricading ourselves in your closet, and both of us are getting at least six hours of sleep before we head back to the city. No looking like death when you fill out your paperwork for Shepard."

"Fine. But be honest. You're worried about looking good for Shepard."

I was too tired to verbally wipe the smirk off Vena's mouth. Instead, I trudged upstairs with her following closely.

Fifteen minutes later, Vena and I lay on a makeshift bed in her closet, her phone illuminating the modest space.

"Turn it off," I said sleepily.

"I will. I can't stop wondering what this book is. Grandpa was the last one to have it, and he and Grandma disappeared. Miles starts looking for it, and he disappears, too. Related or coincidence? I can't decide."

That woke me up a bit.

"Do you really think that's why he's missing? Are we going to disappear next because we're looking for it?"

"Don't worry. I used Miles' log-in to search the online archives. If anyone is watching, they won't know it was me."

"No, they'll only know it was someone close to Miles. He's got tons of friends, right?" I said sarcastically. Miles had acquaintances and a few tight friends, but the circle was small.

Vena cringed and turned off the phone.

"Go to sleep," she said. "Things might look better tomorrow."

I doubted it.

I woke up alone in the closet to the faint sounds of thumping somewhere else in the house.

Heart pounding, I crept from my hiding place and grabbed Vena's emergency baseball bat before silently making my way down the hall to Miles' room–the source of the noise. Morning light poured in through his windows, showing the lower half of my crazy best friend's body wiggling out from under his bed.

"What the hell are you doing?" I asked, setting the end of the bat on the floor and leaning on it.

Vena popped the rest of the way out and looked up at me.

"Nice to see you're out of the closet," Vena said with a smirk. "Miss me?"

"How long have you been up?" I asked.

"About an hour."

I looked left and right dramatically. "An hour and not a crumb of breakfast in sight?"

Vena snorted and stood. "It's not my turn to bribe you. You owe me this time."

"For what?"

Looking far too cheerful, Vena pulled her phone from her back pocket and showed me the picture of the book.

"While I was rubbing more lube into the scrotum this morning, I noticed something. Do you see it?" she asked, excitement lacing her words.

"First, gross. Second, yeah, I see the book. Third, did you get any sleep? You're descending into nutty squirrel mode again."

"I'm not nutty from lack of sleep, and I don't mean the book. Look next to the book."

There was a corner of a wooden desk, a little worn. Nothing about it looked particularly interesting.

"What exactly am I looking at?" I asked.

"That's Grandpa Barnaby's desk. The book was in this house, Ev. What if it's still here? What if that's why Miles came here?"

"That's a lot of what-ifs that don't explain why I owe you. Why are you looking under Miles' bed if the picture was of your grandpa's desk? Isn't it in your dad's research room now?"

"You owe me cuz I let you sleep longer. And yes, but I already looked there. I came here because this was where the bag of chips was. I was kinda hoping that Miles already found the book and hid it."

"Okay. First, we eat; then I'll help you tear this place apart. But we leave by eleven, no matter what, so we're at Blur by noon. We told Shepard we'd be in early today." Technically, we told him we'd be in this morning, But noon was only one minute past "morning," right?

As if Shepard knew I was thinking of showing up late, my phone buzzed.

"It's Shepard."

Vena arched a brow at me. "Exactly how good is his hearing?"

I ignored her and answered.

"Sorry to call you so early, but I know you and Vena were planning on coming in this morning. Would it be a problem to postpone until your shift?"

"Are you having second thoughts?" I asked, and Vena crossed her fingers.

"Not at all. I have a uniform here waiting for her if she's ready to start tonight."

"I don't mind coming in later," I said. "And Vena's evening is open, so that works."

"Good. Come fifteen minutes before your shift. I'll have someone waiting for you in the parking lot to escort you inside."

I tended to arrive a lot earlier than that for my shifts, and he knew it.

With the recent murder excluded, Blur's neighborhood wasn't a bad place considering it was downtown D.C. And we were arriving when it was light out.

"What's going on, Shepard?" I asked.

"There's been another death nearby. Happened sometime before dawn. I want to give the enforcers some time to make sure the area is safe."

"The police are still there?"

"Don't come before four. Okay? Promise me that."

"I promise."

All playfulness missing, Vena watched me closely as I hung up.

"Another person died," I said. "That's two deaths in the last two nights."

"Right about when our recently resurrected Mr. Cross left his cave."

"Do you think he's responsible?" I asked.

"Responsible for what?" Cross asked as he appeared suddenly at the bottom of the stairs. He stood in a pool of blue light from the stained-glass hallway window.

Startled, I dropped my phone and watched it bounce down the stairs and skid to a halt at his feet. He picked it up and inspected it.

"What is it?" he asked.

"A phone."

"Phone?" He looked thoughtful for a moment. He then nodded and held it out to me. "I see."

I grabbed Vena's arm and dragged her down the stairs with me so I could take my phone from Cross.

"Good morning, Everly," he said, steadily watching me.

"Did you sleep in our basement?" Vena asked.

The annoyance that flashed in his eyes didn't bode well for us if he was the killer.

"Good morning, Cross," I said, drawing his attention away from murdering Vena. "We were about to make pancakes. Please join us."

Vena's jaw dropped at me. Ignoring her, I tried for a friendly smile at Cross and forced myself to lead the way to the kitchen as if having a vampire walk behind me was no big deal.

"Your mood is far preferable to your companion's," Cross said from right behind me. "She reminds me of a fishwife."

"She's upset for a reason. We heard people are dying near a place we know, which is why she asked where you were last night."

"Pardon?" His hardened tone warned me that we were walking a fine line.

Apparently, Vena was tone-deaf, though.

"My guess is that you woke up hungry and had a feeding frenzy." Vena went straight to the kitchen cupboards like she wasn't purposely antagonizing him.

I watched him as she continued.

"I don't blame you. You had to be starving in that cave. Just thinking about it makes me hungry."

Cross didn't look hungry, per se, but he did look annoyed.

"In today's world, you can't kill humans or supernaturals for food," I said, cautiously.

"I believe in a catch-and-release system." His steely smirk was aimed at Vena, but it softened when he turned his attention to me. "I could show you if you like. It doesn't hurt. Some have even described the experience as euphoric."

"So, you didn't kill anyone?" Vena asked.

He shook his head, his gaze never leaving me. "I will admit to killing the first rabbit I came across. As the fishwife stated, I was starving."

Cross seemed to sense the doubtful look Vena shot his way.

"It's a pity you cannot gain knowledge from me as I can from you," he said, glancing at her. "One taste of my blood, and you would know I've done nothing but watch and learn these past days."

"Wait, what?" I asked. "You can read the mind of the person you drink?"

He gave me a slightly disappointed look.

"I learn from the blood I consume. The small samples you provided gave me a glimpse of today's world. Your world. Or rather, your life in it. A full feeding would give me a very intimate knowledge of you. Your hopes. Your dreams. Your secrets."

"Are you *kidding me*?" Vena shot me an accusing look. "You

might as well have strip teased in front of a peeping Tom's window."

"Hey. You're the one who dragged me up the hill to the fairy hoard," I said, briefly forgetting our audience. "I wouldn't have been there or bleeding if you hadn't tricked me."

"Ladies. No need to quarrel," Cross said smoothly. "You'll simply need to trust that I didn't kill anyone."

Vena snorted. "We're a long way from trust. Hurry up and get your daily question quota met. We have a lot to do today."

"Like what?" he asked as he made himself comfortable at the kitchen table.

"None of your business," Vena snapped.

"Three sets of eyes are better than two, and he can ask questions while we work," I said.

"No." She took a box of pancake mix from the cupboard and a bag of blueberries from the freezer. My tastebuds started a preemptive revolt. Box mixes were for those uninterested in culinary works of art or those low on time. Unfortunately, we were the latter.

Cross stood and walked over to the pancake mix. Picking it up, he shook the box and sniffed it. Based on his expression, he agreed with my silent opinion as well.

Vena snatched it back from him and emptied it into a mixing bowl.

As I watched the interaction, I saw Cross' actions for what they were. Curious. Cautious. Frustrated. But not threatening. Not even when Vena was being extra provoking.

As I'd already acknowledged, I knew nothing about vampires. Did I think he was safe? No. But I didn't think he was a murderous, killer vampire like everyone stated.

"Vena, after what you said last night, I think we need to find Miles sooner rather than later. We should let Cross help us."

"No," she said at the same time he said, "I am not here to help you find lost people. You promised to help me."

Cross resumed his seat at the table. "I have a few questions."

"Fine," I said, slightly annoyed with both of them. Nudging Vena aside, I took over making the pancakes and started a blueberry compote to go on top.

When Cross didn't ask anything, I looked over to find his gaze running the length of me. It wasn't to check me out. He was studying.

"Do all women wear tight breeches that reveal their shapely legs and shirts unencumbered by bodices?" he finally asked.

"We even show ankles," Vena said with heavy sarcasm. "And knees."

He looked thoughtful. "I approve the change. But I don't approve of women working. Where are your men to provide for you?"

I glanced over at Vena, who was holding a knife like a shank as she eyed him. I reached over and took it from her.

"He's from another time, remember?"

As I whipped the water into the mix, I said, "A lot has changed for women since you were last awake. We can provide for ourselves. We can make our own money, purchase our own property, and even vote."

"There's only one thing we need a man for, and not even then," Vena said. "There are toys that take care of that. Most of the time, it's even better than the real thing."

I gave her a what-the-hell look and glanced at him to see his confusion.

"She means sex," I said with a sigh as I placed the bowl down and dug out a pan. I knew Vena didn't like Cross because of what he was, but she didn't need to make it sound like she hated all men. Not when we both knew how much of a lie that was.

"Surely you still need a man for procreation," he said, looking insulted.

Vena smirked. "Sure, for a quick donation. Otherwise, men are overrated."

I rolled my eyes at her.

"You are content to be spinsters?" he asked.

Vena went for the knife again, but I blocked her with the frying pan. "Why don't you go look for the book while I finish here?"

"And leave you alone with fangs?"

He growled softly.

"Then make coffee, and stop making things difficult."

While she grudgingly turned and dug through the cupboard to find the coffee, I placed the pan on the stove and turned on the burner.

"Next question, and please make it one that doesn't insult Vena. Women have fought hard for the independence we have. I can't deal with an angry Vena before breakfast."

"Do you have a manservant that could dress me appropriately?"

I glanced at his cave clothes and agreed he would need a wardrobe change to blend in. Even though his clothing looked like it had once been expensive and fashionable, age had ruined them.

With a grin that worried me, Vena turned from making the coffee. "We don't have a manservant to pamper your lordliness, but I have the perfect outfit for you."

"You do?" I asked.

"Oh, yes. Allow me to fetch it, my lord chauvinist." She bowed like a deranged jester and spirited away, yelling, "Don't

MELISSA NICOLE

you dare pull your fangs out on Everly, or I'll kill you with pleasure."

He raised a brow at her departure.

That was it.

A brow.

Definitely not a cold-blooded killer.

I poured the batter even though the pan wasn't as hot as I would have preferred. But to prolong breakfast and this encounter sounded like its own version of hell.

"I have a question for you," I said.

"That is not in our agreement."

"But helping you is, and I need to understand how to best help you."

"Very well."

"Why were you in the cave?"

"I should have thought it obvious."

"It's not obvious to me."

"Your blood smells of confectionery," he said, changing the subject. "It is sweet like those bonbons you left for me."

"If you don't want to answer the question, say so."

"I do not wish to answer."

"Okay. If you won't tell me why you were in the cave, will you at least tell me why you aren't drinking blood to gain knowledge? Why pester me for it when you can easily sip and learn?"

"Are you offering?"

"No." I flipped the first pancake and faced him again. "I'm asking why a creature with the ability to learn a lifetime of knowledge within minutes would choose to ask tedious questions?"

"I find the term "creature" offensive."

"Noted."

110

"I first walked the Earth as a human, not a vampire. I am a man, born and raised like any other."

"Got it. So do you have an eating disorder? Is that why you were in the cave? Maybe you can't bring yourself to drink blood? I don't blame you. It makes me nauseous to look at it."

He was on me an instant later, his eyes pitch black and the skin around them pale and darkly veined. The edge of the counter dug into my back as he loomed over me.

I felt regret and panic pooling in my middle. Why had I thought he wasn't a murderous killer? He sure looked like it now.

"I hunger for blood every waking moment. It calls to me. Begs to be consumed. I am fully willing to answer that call. The only disorder my appetite knows is the revulsion of humanity at my choice in sustenance."

I swallowed hard at the menace in his tone.

"Do your eyes always do that?" I managed to ask.

His fangs flashed in his anger, and he reached for my neck. A sizzle and a burnt smell resulted. He jerked back.

I stared at him as he slowly shook his hand, and his eyes returned to their previous light brown.

"Why can I not touch you?" he asked.

A shaky breath escaped me before I tentatively said, "I wear a charm that is supposed to protect me from anyone who means me harm."

"My apologies. I don't behave well when I'm hungry."

"Neither does Vena," I managed, unsure where I stood with him. "Is your hand okay?"

The tightness in his expression softened as he studied me.

"It's fine." He returned to the table, and I warily finished flipping the pancakes.

"I was in the cave because I grew tired of the world," he said after a long silence.

When I glanced over my shoulder at him, he did look tired. And a little sad.

"I'm sorry I woke you. It wasn't intentional."

"I know it wasn't. But I'm glad you did. So much has changed and at a rate that I didn't anticipate. To answer your other question, I try only to drink what is freely given, which is why I need you."

"Whoa," Vena said as she rushed back into the room holding a suit bag. "Did I just hear what I thought I heard? You are not feeding on Everly."

"That is not what you heard," Cross said calmly. "I need Everly to help me acclimate to this world so I can find willing feeders."

Vena thrust the dress bag at Cross. "I think you should change into this outfit, and then we'll talk about blood banks, a fairly new concept, historically speaking. You might find that you don't need Everly at all."

He accepted it with a frown. "Men wear dresses now while women wear pants?"

Vena snorted and showed him how to open the bag. "It's a suit. I figured you looked like a suit kind of guy."

"I am. Thank you."

He took it and left the kitchen.

"What's with the change of heart?" I asked, fully suspicious. "When he asked for clothes, I thought for sure you'd tell him to sit on a stake."

"I thought about it. Then I thought of giving him Miles's favorite jogging suit. You know the one."

I did. It hugged Miles' ass perfectly.

"It would serve Miles right to have vamp balls rubbing in

his favorite shorts for all the worry he's putting me through. But I couldn't do it. I'm his sister, and I love him. And I also don't like Cross' highhanded attitude toward women."

I plated the pancakes and slid them to Vena.

"Cross' thoughts are archaic because he's archaic," I said.

"Exactly," Vena said with a mischievous grin before drowning her pancakes in syrup.

"What did you do?" I demanded before flipping my own pancakes.

"Patience, my young one. You will see."

She made me nervous. I didn't do nervous well.

As soon as my food was done, I turned off the stove and topped them with the blueberry compote and whipped cream.

I was bringing the first bite to my mouth when Cross entered the room. I choked on air.

"Vena, I thank you for the attire. It is a bit ill-fitted, but it will suit me until I acquire a tailor."

The old, tan corduroy suit had to be from the seventies and hugged him like a second skin. Everywhere. The man had an impressively muscled, lean build.

The suit accentuated his broad shoulders and narrow waist. And he was packing. His long john, which was noticeably impressive, wasn't the only impressive bulge. He also had another one in his pocket.

He smoothed his hands over his sleeves, pulling my attention from his double bulges.

"Other than the fit, it is quite comfortable."

I struggled to be impressed by the ruffled shirt and the collar that jutted out three inches longer than what was currently fashionable.

Vena sniggered, and I closed my eyes.

CHAPTER NINE

AFTER DRESSING CROSS IN HER GRANDFATHER'S LEISURE SUIT, Vena's good mood lasted through breakfast but vanished the moment we entered her father's study.

"Don't touch anything," Vena said to Cross as if she were talking to a naughty toddler.

She crossed the study, which previously belonged to her grandfather, and stopped before the desk. While she ran her fingers over the mark that had been in the picture, Cross veered over to one of the antique bookcases in the room.

"I had one like this," he said. "This one has withstood the test of time remarkably well."

I couldn't help but watch as he studied everything around him. It was as if new and old blended for him, and all of it enthralled him.

When he had fanged out before, I felt fear. But now, horrid suit excluded, he seemed like a completely different person with his wonder.

"What are you seeking in here?" he asked.

"None of your business." Vena eyed the clock. "Haven't you been here long enough?"

"Not nearly. I've several more needs and will require assistance."

"We don't want to hear about your needs." Vena pulled open a desk drawer and weeded through the contents. "There are hookers, er, wenches in the city who'd be happy to help you with your needs."

"I meant blood."

"They might be willing to give you that, too, if you pay them enough."

Cross shot her an annoyed glance before focusing on me. "The fishwife spoke of blood banks."

I pulled out my phone as Vena continued her search.

"Places for humans to donate blood. It's usually for helping save another human's life, but maybe you can find what you need there. It looks like there are several blood banks in the city to choose from. I'm sure you're not the only, um, person interested in blood. But I have to be honest; I haven't heard of a vampire drive-through, and they have regular daytime hours. Nothing at night. Oh, and I'm betting you'd need money."

"I assume you know what money is," Vena added.

I understood Vena tended to get testy when she was stressed and sleep-deprived, but she was taking her frustrations out on the wrong person.

"I wasn't born in the cave. I simply slept there," Cross said dryly. "Currency was coin before I came here, but it's paper now, correct?"

I nodded. "Paper and plastic."

"Plastic? I have yet to procure any paper currency and have not heard of plastic."

"Procure?" Vena's head shot up from behind the desk. "Are you planning on robbing a bank?"

"I'm not a thief."

"So you're going to what? Get a job?" She smirked. "I don't see you as the job sort, but perhaps Ev can get you in at Blur."

I glared at Vena for flippantly revealing where we worked.

"Actually," I said, "She makes a valid point about obtaining money. You're not exactly employable without playing a bit of catch-up and getting identification. So, how *do* you plan on getting money?"

"Tell me, where would your lombard reside?"

I glanced at Vena, who shrugged before she dipped back under the desk.

"What is a lombard?" I asked.

"Perhaps you would call them a pawnbroker."

"There are plenty of pawn shops in D.C.," I said. "What are you selling?"

"Gold."

Vena popped up like a groundhog. "Gold? How much?"

"Enough," he said vaguely as his hand drifted to the bulge in his pocket. It looked like he had a fist in there.

"Enough for the dark ages won't be enough now," Vena said.

"Then enough to procure blood, perhaps," he said.

"Depending on the quality of the gold, you should be able to sell it for enough to get what you need," I said before Vena could say more.

"Then there is no issue. Shall we go now?"

"You can go," Vena said. "We're staying. But I'd be happy to walk you out."

Cross flashed her another annoyed look before exhaling and focusing on me.

"Everly, as the only reasonable female in this room—"

"Oh no he didn't!" Vena said.

"—will you kindly tell me what it is that you're looking for so I can address my increasing hunger in a safe and acceptable way?"

Well, when he put it like that...

I held out my hand to Vena. She scowled at Cross but pulled Miles' phone out of her pocket and unlocked it. The book we were searching for was on the screen.

"We need to find this book," I said as she showed it to him. "We think it might be here because that little corner is that desk."

"Hmm," Cross said, already looking at the desk. "I assume you've checked the hidden compartment."

"Not a fan of your condescension, Cross," Vena said.

"And neither am I every time you open your mouth."

"Okay. No more attitude from either of you," I said before either could say more. "Cross, would you mind showing us the hidden compartment?"

"And maybe explain how you know there is one?" Vena added.

"I'm familiar with this brand of desk. Like many other pieces in your home, it's older." He walked over to the desk, removed a drawer, and pulled a latch inside. The decorative front piece in the center popped open.

"How is it that two women with no men can afford a house filled with luxuries of which they are unfamiliar?" he asked.

"It's Vena's family home," I said as she opened the drawer.

"And where is her family?" he asked.

"Gone for now," I said.

"Holy shit," Vena breathed. "It's here." She pulled out the book from the picture and laid it on the desk.

"Delightful," Cross said in a dry tone. "Now, may we leave?"

Instead of answering him, I went to Vena's side as she opened the book to the first page.

Herein rests the original accountings of the first encounters. Lest the reader believe this fiction and fallacy, be assured it is not. The truth is a danger to all who read. Proceed cautiously lest the shadows devour you as well.

"Dramatic much?" Vena said under her breath before turning the page.

"Ladies, I understand that the fairer sex is recently enamored of the written word, but I'm afraid my needs can no longer safely wait. I can hear your racing pulses, and they are tempting me within a breadth of reason. Unless you have a large family pet you wish never to see again, we must leave."

Vena and I both slowly turned to look at Cross. His eyes were black again, and he was gripping the back of a chair.

"I'm not getting in the car with him," Vena said under her breath.

I agreed with her but didn't voice it.

Instead, I said, "Eating pets isn't a good idea. But there are deer in the area. You can find them all along the river. We can go to the pawn shop after you feed."

"Yeah," Vena said. "Deer are delicious. Go out and hunt like a manly man."

His eyes darkened with vivid black veins as he pushed away from the chair and left the room.

We cautiously followed him to the front door, where he

opened it and walked out into the sunlight. He didn't burst into flames or even smolder a little as he lifted his head and sniffed the air.

He disappeared a moment later.

"What the hell?" Vena said.

I glanced from the sunny front yard to Vena. "How is he able to be in the sun? Wasn't that supposed to kill him?"

"I've never heard of a vampire walking around during the day before."

Closing the front door, we returned to the office. She went over to the shelf and weeded through the books until she found one that was leather-bound and closed with a clasp.

She opened it and flipped through to the back.

"I'm so glad I took the sun charm. It wouldn't have done a thing," I said. "No, not true. It would have *really* pissed him off. You have to stop taking risks like that, Vena."

She snorted. "Like making him blood bonbons wasn't a risk?" She shook her head and closed the book. "Nothing." She slid the book back onto the shelf. "If there is a way for a vampire to walk in the sunlight, he's probably the only one who knows how."

Vena smirked. I thought for sure she'd be upset by the lack of information.

"Why are you smiling?"

"People would pay good money for his secret."

"That's mercenary, even for you, Vena."

"He's a vampire, Ev. We may not know much about them, but there are documented cases of killing sprees. Why do you think yesterday's murder and this morning's murder aren't on any news feeds? It would scare the 'sheeple.'"

"We both know that Cross hasn't gone on any killing sprees. He's hunting deer instead of feeding on us."

"Don't tell me you think he's as docile as a dwarf."

"No. But, he hasn't ripped out our throats. All he's done is ask a few harmless questions."

"And all I want to do is ask a few harmless questions of my own."

I gave her a look. "Harmless to you but not to him."

She shrugged. "I still want to know."

"So do I, but I'm not dumb enough to ask. Risks, Vena. Less of them. Please."

However, as soon as Cross returned with a spot of blood on the corner of his lips, Vena asked, "How come you didn't light on fire?"

I leaned over to grab a tissue from the box on the desk and handed it to him.

"You have a little something on your mouth," I said.

"It is like paper and cloth," he said, feeling the tissue. "Extraordinary."

"You throw them away instead of washing them." I pointed to the garbage next to the desk.

After he wiped his mouth clean, he placed the tissue in the garbage.

"Well?" Vena asked. "According to what I've been told, vampires can't survive in the sun. Why can you?"

"The reason is none of your concern," he said. "Can we be off? The sooner I can exchange for blood, the better."

I studied his light brown gaze, completely devoid of any hint of blackness, and nodded. "I'll get my keys."

He followed me out to the entry where I'd deposited my keys the night before. I picked them out from the antique ceremonial bowl and slipped on my shoes.

When I straightened, I glanced at Cross' outfit and felt a stab of pity for him. He had no idea Vena dressed him to look like a vintage pimp daddy. Thank goodness she didn't have a feathered fedora to go with it because I was pretty sure Cross would have worn it. His face was so attractive it was almost a crime to let him walk around the city dressed like that.

I opened the door and called for Vena.

"Hang on!" A moment later, she appeared with the book in her hand. "I'm reading this on the way."

Cross was intrigued by the car and ran his hand over everything as soon as he settled in the front passenger seat. I showed him how to buckle for safety, which made him smirk when my hands grazed against his chest.

As I drove, I explained the gearshift, gas, and brake.

"You will teach me this skill, too," he said. "It looks relatively simple."

"It's not difficult, but it does take some practice. Why bother with driving a car, though, when you can move so fast?"

He arched a brow at me. "I wish to blend."

"Ah. Right."

"This is a bunch of nonsense," Vena said abruptly from the back seat.

"What is?"

"It's all stories. Which are written badly, I might add. There's one about a guy who established his farm on some new land in Russia. When he went out to check on his cattle the following week, they were all sliced open, and their hearts were eaten. That one's from the late 1500s. The next one is from the 1700s. Two girls were stolen from their beds right after their 'first bleeding.' Why the hell would my grandpa be reading this?"

"It sounds like an accounting of a werewolf attack and a fae abduction," Cross said. "Why are the numbered signs along the road?"

"They tell me what road I'm on and how fast I should be

going," I said quickly so we could get back to the concerning information he'd shared. "Werewolves are nice. They don't eat hearts."

Cross laughed. Head thrown back, sexy neck exposed, full-on laughed.

"Uh..." Vena's eyes met mine in the rearview mirror. "That's not comforting."

"Which part are you laughing at, Cross?" I asked. "The niceness or the hearts."

"Both. Werewolves are not nice. They will kill anyone who jeopardizes what they protect."

"Well, there's this reality show we watch–called *The Other House*–that follows people living in the same house. It always has a werewolf in it, and there haven't been any deaths," I said.

"Are you ready to cry wolf?" Vena said, repeating the show's jingle.

Cross turned toward me, a weird look flickering over his face.

"You truly cannot be this naive, can you?"

"She can," Vena said. "And also, don't ever talk to her like that again. It's rude, and you're tarnishing your gentlemanly reputation."

I frowned out the windshield. "You know what? Both of you can stuff it, or I'll pull this car over, and you can walk."

Vena chuckled and went back to reading her book.

Cross asked another question about a sign, but I didn't answer. I was too irritated with both of them. I wasn't naive. I simply took things at face value. There was a difference.

"Everly, I apologize," Cross said after a moment of silence. "Perhaps there are a few good werewolves in existence. It has been a long while since I've walked this earth."

"Like there are a few good vampires?" Vena asked innocently from the back seat.

Cross' expression turned thoughtful. "Point well made. I would not consider my brethren nice by any means. Nor the fae, particularly."

"What about the dwarves?" I asked, needing to know.

"The treasure seekers do have their usefulness."

I made a face and didn't talk to either of them again until we reached the city. Vena paused her reading to pull up the directions to the nearest pawn shop and impressed Cross with the concept of the internet.

Finding a parking spot a few blocks away from King's Pawn Shoppe, I paid the meter, and we walked to the store.

Vena was the first one inside, like always. While I preferred to browse bakery cases, the cabinets in pawn shops were like a treasure hunt for her. She veered off to look at the display cases. I stuck with Cross, knowing he would have questions.

His gaze swept through the hodgepodge pickings locked behind cracked glass. There was everything from human antiques to creature goods. He sniffed a hookah pipe that was sitting on the display counter.

"Interesting," he said as he continued toward the shop's only other occupant.

"Sell, pawn, or buy?" the man behind the counter asked. He was as shabby as his store. The grease stains on his shirt were too numerous to count.

Cross leaned close to me and whispered, "Is there a more reputable establishment?"

"Let's start here and see what he has to say about your gold."

The man eyed Cross. "If you got a thing for vintage, I got

some great belts and hats. I might even have a pair of platform boots in the back."

I shot Vena a look over my shoulder. Her wardrobe choice was going to get us into trouble once Cross figured out what she'd done.

"I'm in need of currency," Cross said.

"What are you offering?" the man asked.

"A trade. How many papers will you give me for a gold coin?"

"Papers?"

"You know. Cash," I said.

"I guess it depends on the coin. Right now, the gold rate is about fifty per gram. After my cut, you're looking at thirty. If you're looking to trade it for the value of the coin, I'd have to know the dates and such."

"He'll be able to give you a more accurate estimate if you show him a coin," I said to Cross.

Cross dug into his tight pants, wincing a little when the fabric pulled across his pleasure python. He withdrew a single gold coin the size of a dime and placed it on the counter. Both the broker and I leaned in to look at it.

The symmetry of the disc was a bit off as well as the placement of the stamp. While I knew Cross was old, this coin proved exactly *how* old.

The man glanced at it and then at Cross. "Is this legit?"

Cross looked at me. "Legit?"

I nodded to the man. "Yes. It's real."

He picked it up and inspected it with a magnifying glass. "Damn. Well. Um. I can give you two hundred for it." A bead of sweat sprouted at his brow.

I didn't know the value of the coin, but from his reaction, I knew he was attempting to cheat us.

"Try again," I said.

More sweat popped up. "Four hundred. Best offer."

I plucked the coin from his hand. "Thanks for your time."

Taking Cross by the arm, I turned us toward the door.

"Wait!" the guy said. "I don't have the capital to buy it, but I know a collector who has an interest in coins like this. Let me send him a picture of the coin. Whatever he says, I'll only ask for a percentage as the broker."

"How much of a percentage?" I asked.

"Twenty."

I scoffed.

"That's my going rate. I need to make a living."

"I know jack about coins, but I know to question the way you're trying to stop us from leaving. If that coin's worth a million, two hundred grand for making a phone call is pretty hefty for a daily wage. We're not interested in paying a brokerage fee. I think we'd be better off finding an online auction site."

I turned again.

"You're killing me," the guy said. "Okay, okay! Two percent."

I glanced at Cross. "It's your call. He might have a contact; he might not. He might also try to rip you off."

Cross gave the man a look that would have chilled me to the bone.

"I recommend against trying to rip anything from me. Take your picture," he said, returning to set the gold coin on the counter.

The man took out his phone and snapped several pictures from different angles.

"I'm not sure how fast I'll hear from him," the man said. "He travels a lot. But I can guarantee he will be interested. What's a number I can reach you at?" He slid a pad of paper and pen to Cross.

"Number?" Cross asked.

"I'm more likely to answer, so here's my phone number." I took the pen and jotted it down for the broker. "If it takes longer than two days, don't bother calling. We'll have found a different buyer by then."

He didn't try to stop us again when we turned away. I grabbed Vena, and we headed to the car. On the way, I checked the time before searching for the nearest blood bank.

"What's the backup plan if getting blood from a bank doesn't work?" I asked Cross.

"I am fully capable of procuring my own blood supply."

"Then why are we going to a blood bank?" Vena asked as I pulled away from the curb.

"I'm intrigued," Cross said with a disdainful look at her.

Twenty minutes later, we were walking toward the donation center.

"Not it," I said, grinning at Vena.

She rolled her eyes at me. "Fine. I'll be the pincushion while you do the nice asking thing."

The moment we opened the door, though, Cross' eyes went dark. He turned around and walked back out without a word.

CHAPTER TEN

"I GUESS THAT MEANS I DON'T NEED TO DONATE TODAY," VENA said brightly as we turned and hurried after Cross.

"Or you'll be donating in a different way," I said when Cross glared at her over his shoulder.

He paused several yards down the sidewalk and waited for us to catch up.

"We will need to revisit this blood bank option another day. After I've properly fed. The deer was not enough."

"Not it," Vena said under her breath.

I shot her a warning look and unlocked the car door.

"Cross, this needs to be where we part ways for today," I said when he moved to get in. "We have previous commitments, and I did answer a lot of questions."

"Very well. I will speak with you again tomorrow."

He turned and strode down the sidewalk, his suit making soft sounds with every step.

"I really hope he finds something else to wear," I said when Vena got in next to me.

"I really hope someone thinks he's a vampire from the

seventies and stakes him so we don't have to."

She didn't sound nearly as bloodthirsty about it as she had last night.

"Vena, he helped us find the book. You would have never found it without him."

She muttered something as I started the car and pulled out of the lot.

"What did you say?" I asked.

"Fine. He helped a little. But he's still a vampire. You saw him nearly lose control."

"Sure, he's had a few moments, but so have you, Miss Stabby-pants. Instead of focusing on his almost slips, recognize his restraint."

"You're putting too much faith into a creature we know nothing about."

"And you're putting a label on a person who you know nothing about. What if everything we think we know about vampires is wrong? You already said he's not like other vampires. He's walking around in full sunlight. He ate a deer instead of either of us."

"Exactly. We don't know anything about him."

"You're fearing the unknown far too much for being the thrill seeker you are. Where's the Vena who takes life by the horns?"

"She's still here with her best friend who is always telling her to be more cautious. Where's your caution? He didn't kill us today, but what about tomorrow? Or the day after? There's a reason that vampires haven't come out into the open. They're killers, Ev. We've heard the stories about mass murders. Villages wiped out. One of these days, he'll turn on us. I'd rather stake him before that happens."

Vena made valid points, but I had a hard time reconciling

her picture of a murderous monster with Cross. He was just so…proper. Controlled. Most of the time.

"Let's head home and get ready for work," I said. "We'll worry about Cross tomorrow."

Vena buried her nose in the book the rest of the way home, and I took refuge in the silence.

Our neighborhood was already lively, with a few kids playing on the sidewalks by the time we arrived. The old man across the street scowled at us as his granddaughter rode her bike up and down the driveway. I waved as if his perpetually crabby self didn't bother me and grabbed my bag.

As soon as I neared the front door, I saw the tilted handle.

"Looks like your fanged friend was eager for your confectionery." Vena shook her head and walked right in.

I made a face at her and did my best to close the door behind me.

"Still think he's so useful?" she asked.

Something clinked, and I glanced back at her to see her standing near an empty plate and pouch. While I didn't like the broken lock, he had said he'd liked my bonbons, and, oddly, that made me happy.

"He's reimbursing us for the damage when he trades his coin," Vena said, disappearing into the kitchen.

I walked over to the empty plate and spotted a note in old, flowing cursive.

The bonbons were sweeter than the apology.

The apology had been sweet enough, but maybe not for a newly woken and hungry vampire.

Stowing the plate in the kitchen to clean later, I saw Vena at the counter, carefully unrolling the scrotum. She'd already tainted my flour. Now she was defiling my counters as well?

"Can you do that somewhere else?" I asked.

"The light's better in here."

I had been thinking of making a sandwich before work, but not anymore. I glanced at the clock and went to my room for a nap before our shift.

When I reemerged a while later, Vena was in the same spot.

"We have an hour before we have to leave."

"It will take me two seconds to get ready, and there's still a lot I need to do before then. If you want to be helpful, fondle this scrotum open while I read."

"I am not fondling that scrotum."

Vena smirked at me. "If not the sheep's scrotum, maybe there's a Shepard's scrotum you'd like to fondle."

"You're going to make me regret getting you a job at Blur, aren't you?"

"No way. I know you're only doing it because you love me. I'll save my match-making comments for when it's just the two of us. Maybe. At least I'll try really, really hard."

I snorted, not believing a word of it.

"Miles had this scrotum, and he was looking for the book," she said, getting serious. "I think the two might be connected."

"I thought the book was just old stories."

"So far, yes. But there are a lot of pages I haven't read." She gave me a pointed look. "Hint. Hint."

"I am not touching that thing." I dug the book out of her bag instead. "Tell me what I'm looking for."

"I'm not sure. This ballsack and the book are around the same age. So something that ties them together?"

"Not everything your brother does has to have meaning

behind it. Don't forget he also had the coordinates to a strip club on his phone."

"You're right. Maybe some of this is random. But until we know for sure, I'm following up on every lead."

"And we already followed up on the strip club one, right?" I said, needing her to agree with me.

She shrugged. "Getting kicked out isn't much of a follow-up. Unless we get something out of the book or the ram-bam-thank-you-ma'am balls, I'll need to go back and look around."

I groaned at her and opened the book. While she continued to work the scrotum-from-hell gently, I read stories about weird deaths and abductions.

"Half of these read like the original fairy tales," I said after a few minutes. "Dark and disturbing. What happened to happy thoughts?"

"Happiness is new age thinking. Back then, it was survival and suffering. You might want to remember that when dealing with Lord Cross."

"Take your own advice," I said, shooting her a dry look. "I'm noticing a pattern. A lot of these stories have notes about towns. I paged through the book and found a drawing of stones."

"Yeah, I saw that too. Keep reading. Maybe we'll–holy sheep balls! This thing is huge."

There were folds in the four-inch-wide strip Vena had been carefully unrolling. Her nose was inches from it as she poked at the layers.

"No wonder it's taking so long to soften. I think it's been folded in half lengthwise twice. This thing's at least, what? Twenty inches? Can you imagine the sheep this belonged to? How did it walk?"

"Your fascination with sheep scrotum is concerning."

"You have to admit this is impressive."

"I'll admit I was starving a few minutes ago before you started feeling up dead sheep balls."

She frowned. "Well, I opened it somewhat, but the oil didn't touch the inside. It's as dry as a mummy."

"Mummy testicles. Thanks, Vena. I'm never eating again."

She grinned as she oiled the dry skin, getting her fingers into all the folds.

I closed my eyes and willed myself not to barf all over the book.

"You can open your eyes," she said moments later. "I'm going to let it soften again while I get ready. I need black bottoms and black shoes, right?"

"Yes. Shepard will give you the shirt, tie, and apron."

She washed her hands and headed to her bedroom. I set the book down and went to the kitchen to clean up the plate from earlier. Vena's phone sat near the oiled nastiness. As I walked past it, the phone lit up with a message. I was about to holler for Vena, but the few words I had accidentally read made me look closer.

I'll trade information about Miles for the ring.

My stomach sank as I glanced at Vena's door then back at the phone. The number didn't come up as one of Vena's contacts, and only a few people knew about the ring and Miles.

Vena would go crazy when she saw the message, especially since I'd returned the potential bargaining chip. Yet, I couldn't keep it from her.

Picking up her phone, I went to knock on her door.

"Vena, you got a text."

She opened the door. One leg was out of her pants, and the other was still in.

"Who is it?" She held out her hand for her phone.

"Before I give you your phone, I need you to promise you won't overreact."

She stilled. "You're scaring me. Is it about Miles?"

"It is. Someone is asking to trade for information about him."

Her eyes widened as she grappled for the phone. I tugged it away before she could get it.

"But they want the ring."

"We'll get it and meet up with the person for the information."

"Vena, Cross has the ring, and I doubt he'll give it to us after we stole it."

"Stake to the heart. No problem."

"Even if you could kill Cross, we don't know where he is. But he's not the problem here."

"Sounds to me like he is."

"Vena, someone knows about Miles *and* the ring. Who would know that? Cross knows about both, but why would he want to trade for his own ring?

"We were just at the Shadow Market and showed the ring to Spawn. So, he knows about the ring and Miles, but that place was loaded with people. What if someone else overheard us? Or what if that little demon, Spawn, told someone?

"This could be a trap. We need to be cautious, especially since we have the book that's making everyone disappear."

"And sit on information about Miles? He could be in trouble or dying somewhere."

"That's what I'm talking about, Vena. You can't overreact

and make assumptions. We don't know what we don't know. And the more we don't know, the more danger *we* could be in.

"Ask questions. It's a trade for information. The information they're offering could be useless. We already hit dead ends with the strip club, the book, and maybe the sheep skin, too. We need to be level-headed about this and have a plan.

"And we won't see Cross until tomorrow, so we can't actively chase this lead until then. So, ask for proof that they're offering information we're looking for. Ask why the ring is important. Ask who's asking."

"Okay. I get it. There are a million questions to ask."

"Exactly. Rushing in half-cocked and getting ourselves killed won't help Miles. And while you wait for answers, we can work so we can pay rent.

"Tomorrow morning, when we have more information, we'll talk to Cross about the ring and find out why someone would cold text you a trade offer like that. If the person is willing to trade information for the ring, the ring is obviously valuable."

"It's a ruby. Of course it's valuable."

"It's a vampire's ruby. You saw Spawn's reaction to that fact. No one should be willing to risk their necks over a vampire's anything. Why is this person? Cross might be able to enlighten us or at least help us understand what we might be getting ourselves into."

"Ev, you saw him today. He's not our pet. He has no reason to cooperate with us."

"Yes, he does. He needs us. The pawn shop guy is going to contact me about the offer on the coin. Between that, helping him blend, and finding a blood supply, we have leverage, too. Let's use it wisely."

Vena frowned as she plopped onto her bed, one leg still stuck in her pants. "I'll sit on this lead tonight. But that's it."

That was all I needed. Once she started thinking rationally, she'd see waiting was the best option.

I hurried to get us out the door before anything else could happen. Never in the history of ever had I been looking forward to a shift at Blur as much as I was that night.

My anticipation died when we approached the employee parking lot and saw Doc standing at the gate.

"They're really taking these murders seriously," Vena commented as the metal bar slid open for us.

Managing a smile at Doc, I didn't comment.

"Are you going to be back here all night?" I called to him as soon as I was out of the car.

"That's the plan."

"If there's trouble in the bar, who do I call?"

"Shepard. And pity any soul he has to deal with tonight."

Inwardly cringing, I nodded and hurried inside with Vena.

Shepard was waiting for us by the time clock. After he handed Vena the paperwork, he set her up with the time clock, using her fingerprint. He wasn't abrupt, but he wasn't his usual self either. Tension radiated from him.

As soon as she was clocked in, he told me to give her the tour and have her fill out her paperwork in the spare office upstairs once I was finished.

I stared after him as he walked away. Vena elbowed me and waggled her eyebrows. I shook my head at her and quickly showed her the employee lockers.

"I'm glad they actually lock," she said, carefully tucking her oversized handbag into the one beside mine. "With our door busted at home, I didn't want to leave anything valuable behind." The way she patted her purse made me cringe in disgust.

"When you say valuable…"

"Yep. Bedtime stories and ba-ba-black sheep can't be left alone."

"Just keep them in the locker. That sheep has to be five different health code violations."

"Not sure why. It's animal skin and oil. This would be a delicacy in some countries."

"Please. For my sanity and appetite, stop."

"Speaking of appetite." She nodded at Anchor as he popped into the kitchen and grabbed a stack of clean plates. She winked at him before he left.

"Weren't you ready to go on a rampage thirty minutes ago?" I asked.

"I'm distracting myself the best, most enjoyable way I know. Well, it'd be more enjoyable if I could sample some of the beefcakes in this place."

I inwardly groaned, wondering again if it was a good idea to get Vena a job here. But I grudgingly admitted my options were slim compared to the vast and numerous ways Vena could get into trouble.

After giving Vena a quick tour of the kitchen and the food prep area, I grabbed her a server pager that would let her know our orders were ready and explained the order process. When I finished, I veered toward the back kitchen to introduce her to Gunther and Griz.

We walked in on Gunther shaking his head as Sierra tried to give him something that was fisted in her hand.

Not wanting to have anything to do with Sierra, yet curious about the exchange, I stopped near them.

"Vena, this is Sierra and Gunther."

Sierra turned her lethal gaze to Vena. "Another pet for Shepard?"

"What's in your hand?" I asked.

"Mind your own business." She jammed her hand into her apron pocket and, with a huff, stalked away.

"Gunther, what was that about?" I asked.

He shook his head and returned to his station.

"Wait. Where is Griz?"

I didn't get a reply.

"Charming coworkers," Vena said. "I can see why you like working here, Ev."

Ignoring her sarcasm, I said, "Griz is the chef. He might be in the walk-in cooler. You can meet him some other time."

We went out to the main bar so I could explain the sections.

"It's pretty straight-forward," I said. "Upper and lower left. Upper and lower right. VIP up at the top."

"I might need a refresher later."

Rolling my eyes at her, we headed up to the spare office so she could fill out paperwork. She sat at the desk.

"Do you have a pen?" she asked.

"First rule about being a server: Always have tons of pens."

"Or, have a best friend coworker who has tons of pens." She held out her hand with a grin.

Tossing a pen at her, I settled into the guest chair and waited while she filled out the forms.

A low, murmured conversation coming from Shepard's office caught my attention. Had it been in regular speaking tones, I might have ignored it. But between Shepard's off behavior and the murders, I pressed my ear to the wall.

"What are you doing?" Vena asked.

I shushed her with a wave and said, "Impatiently waiting for you to fill out the papers. Army is going to open the doors soon."

"I'd like him to be my drill sergeant."

I returned my attention to the murmurs. I couldn't hear

much, but I picked up the words vampire, nest, killing, and attack. None of those words made me feel better.

"Done," Vena said, piling the papers and handing the pen back.

"Let's get these to Shepard and get your uniform."

"Did you figure out what they're talking about?" she asked.

I did not want to tell Vena that I'd heard Shepard say "vampire." She'd be on him like a fairy on glitter.

"Not really, but we can talk later."

Knocking on Shepard's door, I waited for his "enter" before I opened it. Buzz was inside but quickly exited when we walked in.

I set the papers on Shepard's desk. "We only need her uniform."

He pointed to a neatly folded stack on the side table next to the printer. "That should be the right size. I'm going to put you both on upper next to Anchor tonight."

"Sounds good." I turned to Vena. "I'll meet you by the bathrooms downstairs after you're changed."

She smirked at me but left without comment, closing the door behind her.

"Was there something else on your mind, Everly?" Shepard asked when I stayed behind.

"I heard you through the wall. You said 'vampire.' Is that who the police are saying is responsible for the murders?"

Shepard stood and came around the desk.

A second later, I found myself wrapped up in the best, yet most awkward, hug of my life. My cheek was nestled between two glorious pectorals as my hands hesitated at his sides. What the hell was I supposed to do with my hands? Touch him? Touch my boss while his heart thumped rhythmically under my ear?

"There is nothing for you to worry about," he said, breaking through my unrelated panic. "I promise you're safe here."

"Um. Okay. Safe. I got it." I gave him an awkward pat on the side, and he got the hint and released me.

"Sorry about that. You looked so…"

Did his eyes just dip to my chest? Damn it, this was Vena's fault. She broke my brain with her Shepard talk.

"Worried," he finished.

"Well, I was. I mean, I don't know anything about vampires except that they're rumored to be bloodthirsty killers."

"It's not a rumor. It's true."

"How do you–"

A knock on the door interrupted me, and Shepard gave me an apologetic look.

"Can we talk about this later?" he asked.

"Sure."

I went to the door and was surprised to see Gunther there. He looked between me and Shepard, and I thought he even sniffed me as I walked past.

Once the door was shut, I paused to sniff myself. Nope, I'd remembered my deodorant. Weird.

From the top of the stairs, I saw Vena leaning against the railing below, grinning at Anchor.

"Looks like I should officially introduce myself," she said, holding out her hand. "I'm Vena, your newest *cock*tail-slinging co-worker."

Not liking the way she'd stressed the word "cock," I hurried down the stairs.

"It's a pleasure to meet you officially, Vena," Anchor said a little formally as he took her hand and started to bring it to his lips. My mouth dropped open at his old-world charm, and Vena's lit with giddy excitement.

139

Not good. Not good at all.

At the last second, Anchor pulled back.

"Why do your hands smell like–?" He shook his head and dropped her hand. "Never mind."

Panting, I reached the bottom and swatted her hand down before she could sniff it herself.

"We'll be right back," I said, flushing in embarrassment and steering her toward the restrooms. I waited until we were inside before rounding on her.

"What were you doing? You can't flirt with him anymore. You're working together."

Vena waved away my comment with one hand and sniffed the other.

"Do you think he could smell the sheep scrotum? I mean, I washed."

"Focus, Vena. The staff is off limits."

She snorted.

"Hell no. Anchor officially has my attention now. I need to find out what else he can smell, and I know right where to put my hand."

"Don't you dare. We serve people food and drinks."

She heaved a sigh. "Fine. I'll wait until after closing. Then we're testing his sense of smell."

If worry over her treasure hunting didn't drive me into an early grave, working with her probably would.

She caught my look and grinned at me as she pulled off her top to exchange it for the uniform one.

"Just remember that you love me."

"Vena, please don't make this awkward for me. I'm already second-guessing everything Shepard does, and it's your fault."

She smirked. "And exactly what did Shepard do that has you second-guessing?"

"He didn't sniff my hand, that's for sure."

"Sniffing elsewhere?"

"Vena!"

She snickered. "Lighten up. This is a cocktail lounge, not Wall Street."

After Vena buttoned her shirt and slipped on her tie, she pointed to it. "Do the knot thing."

I tucked her charm inside her shirt and hurriedly fixed her tie as she glanced at her phone.

"You can't have that on the floor."

"That's why I'm looking at messages now. I replied to the mystery texter for more information."

I adjusted the finished tie and stepped back. "Anything?"

She shook her head and tied on her apron, slipping her phone into the apron's pocket. "Nothing."

"We'll have a plan tomorrow after we talk to Cross."

"I know. But no matter how much I flirt with Anchor, I can't stop the worry."

I gave her a hug that she partly resisted then double-checked my hair while she gave her hands another wash.

The DJ was welcoming the early birds when we headed back out to the lounge. I watched Anchor's attention drift from the patrons entering to us.

While I knew why Shepard assigned Vena and me the station closest to Anchor and I appreciated the added security, Anchor would now need his own safety detail.

Vena winked at him as we walked past, proving I was right.

When I realized her eyes were fixated on Anchor's *anchor*, I poked her in the ribs.

"Focus."

"Aye-aye, Captain."

It was going to be a long night.

CHAPTER ELEVEN

THE FIRST FEW TABLES OF THE NIGHT WERE HEAVY DRINKERS WHO kept Vena and me running. They also tipped really well. Vena grinned as she shoved money into her apron pocket.

Technically, they were my tips since I was the trainer, but if she loved this part of the job, maybe she'd take it seriously.

"We have to pay the bar staff at the end of the night," I reminded her.

"I know." She elbowed me. "Hey, check out Goldilocks."

A group of fae men sat in our section. While they were all beautiful, as fae tended to be, one stood out. He was perfection, and it nearly hurt my brain to keep my gaze on him without looking away.

Vena and I reached their table as they settled in.

"Welcome to Blur. I'm Everly, and I'll be your server. This is Vena. She is training tonight. What can I get you to start?"

"I heard your cocktail, *luxure*, is good," the beautiful one said. His voice was like a siren's call, and Vena took a step toward him before I gently nudged her back. She was already hopped up on Anchor hormones, and this fae was giving off serious come-hither vibes.

"A round of *luxure*?" I glanced at each of them to make sure before Vena and I headed to the bar.

"Holy hell," Vena said under her breath.

"I know. You get used to it. Keep your distance, and you'll be fine. And if that doesn't work, don't worry. Anchor and Army won't let us leave with anyone."

We placed our order at the bar and waited for the drinks. I made Vena carry them back and serve them since she was pocketing the money. She did great, even talking up the food options we offered.

Keeping half an ear on her, I checked with the next table.

About an hour before closing, Vena was running her own set of five tables without a problem. She'd even jumped in to help Thomas with one of his. When I heard her making idle conversation about other clubs with one of her tables, I knew she'd need her own section on the next shift, or she'd get bored.

At the end of the night, we pooled our tip money, and I wasn't disappointed with the total.

"Fifty more than I see on my own," I said.

"Then that'll be my take," Vena said, swiping up the difference. I didn't begrudge it. She'd earned every penny plus more.

A good friend would have done a fifty-fifty split with her. Then again, a good friend wouldn't have dragged me up a mountain to fall into a fairy cave. I didn't feel a smidge of guilt when I counted out the bartender's share and pocketed the rest.

"Finish wiping down the tables on that end, and I'll get this end," I said, already moving away from her to give Tank and Boulder, two bartenders Shepard regularly worked into the schedule, their cut.

On my way back, Anchor waved me over.

"Maybe you can have a word with Vena," he said with a low voice and a glance at Shepard's office window above.

"About what?"

"Talking about the other clubs in the area isn't good for business." He tugged at his earlobe and frowned. "Does she work at another one?"

"Another club?"

"Yeah." He cleared his throat. "Juicy, the strip club?"

My eyes went wide then narrowed. Anchor quickly held up his hands.

"I don't mean anything by it. I wasn't even sure she knew what it was. But she kept asking customers if they'd been there. And with the way she smelled before…" He gave an apologetic shrug then asked, "Does she have a boyfriend?"

"No." I wasn't sure if he was asking because he was interested or because he was trying to figure out why Vena's fingers smelled like scrotum. So I added, "Thanks for keeping an eye on her tonight."

"Tonight and any night. She's easy to watch."

His gaze went to her, and I glanced over as she winked at him then bent over a table to wipe the far side instead of walking around it.

"Trust me," I said, shaking my head at her. "She is not easy to watch. Trouble has a way of finding her."

"I can imagine."

I went to wipe down my tables. When my back was turned, the rat snuck away to the bathroom. I looked up in time to see Anchor's gaze trail after her.

As soon as the bathroom door closed, he glanced at me.

"Since you're almost done, I'll get Shepard to walk you out," he said.

He took the stairs two at a time.

Vena's uh-oh face when she reemerged and saw Anchor missing and Shepard coming down the stairs nearly made up for the trouble she was trying to cause. She did an about-face and marched right back into the bathroom. I laughed my way to the time clock.

"How did she do?" Shepard asked when he caught up with me.

"Good. She was bored by the end of the night. Five tables was too easy for her."

He nodded. "I thought the same thing."

Vena joined us after clocking out and grabbing her things.

"What kind of schedule are you looking for, Vena?" Shepard asked as he walked us out. "Same hours as Everly?"

"If they're available. I'll be back at university full time in the fall, same as Everly, though."

"Not a problem. We'll be able to accommodate that."

"Great. Thanks for giving me a chance," she said.

A slight grin tugged at his lips. "You have Everly to thank. I'll see you both for tomorrow night's shift. Be early."

He opened my car door after I unlocked it and closed it for me after I was in.

"Call me when you're home safe," he said, looking at me through the window.

I waved in acknowledgment and pulled out of the parking lot.

"Call me?" Vena said with a smirk. "Not text me. But 'call me' from the boss?"

"Cut it out. He's understandably worried. People are dying. Did you hear anything back from our mystery texter?"

She hurried to dig out her phone.

"I stopped checking an hour ago because Anchor did that

'I'm watching you' thing." She scanned her phone. "There's a message."

"What does it say?"

"They have proof the information is about Miles and want to meet at our place."

"Hell no," I said.

"My thoughts exactly. But if they know my phone number, and they mentioned meeting at our place, do they already know our address? They could be there waiting for us."

"Should we go to your parents' house to be on the safe side?"

She groaned. "Like that was any safer. Besides, I worked a long shift and want my own bed. Just drive past and see if there are any lurkers."

Since I was also tired and didn't want to drive an hour to her parents' place, we swung by the house. The lights were off. No cars were parked nearby. No bushes rustled from hiding lurkers.

Vena cursed.

"What?" I asked, scanning for an intruder.

"I forgot our door was broken."

I deflated against my seat as I pulled to the curb near the house. "Me, too."

"Cross owes us a door."

"We have no way of contacting him tonight. And I'm not going in there to check if it's safe or not."

Vena grinned as she pressed a name in her contacts.

"Was that Anchor's name?" I asked.

"Anchors away, matey."

"Why do you have his number?"

"Don't act like you don't know me," she said, laughing. She then composed herself to talk to Anchor when he answered.

If I didn't know Vena, I would have said Vena sounded like an innocent girl who needed rescuing as she explained that we'd broken our doorknob before work and didn't feel safe going to sleep with it like that.

I hoped Anchor could see right through Vena's bullshit act as she sweetly asked for his assistance. But since I wasn't going to step one toe out of the car until the house was secure, I kept my mouth shut and let Vena work her devious magic.

"He's on his way," Vena said when she ended the call. "I have a mind to thank him by hoisting his jibs."

"Can you try to go a week of work before hoisting anything?"

She gave a noncommittal shrug.

"Vena, I have to work with him, and our walls are thin. The last thing I need to hear is his bedroom moans."

"Think he would be the loud kind? I'm thinking more guttural."

I swatted at her.

"You wouldn't be so high-strung if you got your own hookup," she said. "Shepard is giving you every signal in the book."

"He's only protective. And he's my boss. Not happening."

"I bet he'd be good, though."

"Not happening," I repeated.

With a sigh, Vena turned her attention to her phone. "What should I tell our mystery trader?"

"That you want to see the proof without a meet-up."

After a moment of hesitation, Vena typed a reply then placed her phone on her lap.

"I asked around about the strip club," she said.

"I know. I had an awkward conversation with Anchor about it."

147

"Really? What did he say?"

"That you shouldn't talk about other clubs while at Blur. Shepard won't be happy if he overhears you, Vena."

Vena waved off my concern. "I didn't find out any information, anyway. No one had a membership to it. What kind of strip club makes you have a membership? Wouldn't they want all the horny men to flock to their door?"

"It does seem like an odd business model."

"Exactly. If membership is that exclusive, what was Miles doing with coordinates to it? Something is definitely up with that place. I have to get inside to find out."

I willed my hands to stay on the steering wheel and not strangle my best friend. "Let's focus on getting the door fixed first. We'll talk to Cross tomorrow."

"Did you hear back from the pawnshop guy about his coin?"

"I haven't looked at my messages." I pulled out my phone and saw a text waiting. "Looks like the collector is interested. The pawn shop guy isn't saying how much he's thinking, only that the collector wants to inspect the coin himself."

"Wasn't he supposedly out of town?"

I shrugged. "I'll text back and see when the collector wants to meet."

I knew I might not get an answer until the morning. However, the pawn guy responded within minutes.

"He wants to meet up tomorrow morning at the pawn shop. Seven o'clock, before it opens." I glanced at Vena. "That's not suspicious at all."

She nodded, scanning the shadowed street around us.

"It means that coin's worth a lot more than they'll want to admit. Too bad there's no way to contact Lord Fangs-a-lot to confirm the meetup. Don't answer the text right away. Let's see how long it takes him to send you another text."

It took five minutes. Vena whistled a low sound.

"I wonder how many of those coins Cross has," she said. "I might need to start being nicer to him."

I kept my doubt she'd be able to manage that to myself and responded to the message that I wouldn't be able to confirm the time until my friend got back to me.

A truck pulled up behind us a few minutes later. Anchor got out and waved at us. Vena was out of the car before I even opened my door.

"I knew you'd come through for us," she said, smiling up at him. "What do you have there?"

He held up a plastic package with a new door knob.

"I wasn't sure how yours was broken, so I figured I'd bring a replacement to be safe."

"Wow. That's a big knob. I bet it'll feel good in my hands when I give it a twist."

My mouth dropped open, and Anchor, the poor guy, surprised me by looking down at the knob as he blushed. Vena's grin widened. She loved the bashful ones. According to her, hot and bashful was unicorn level.

"Anchor, thank you so much for helping us out," I said. "Please ignore everything coming out of Vena's mouth. Her filter is broken."

He tugged at his earlobe and glanced at the house. "I'll look at the door."

"Please." I gestured for him to go first and, when his back was turned, elbowed Vena hard.

"Ow," she whispered.

"Too much," I whispered back.

"But look at him."

I glanced at Anchor as he crouched in front of the door.

"All that sexy is begging for my attention," she whispered.

"*Nice* attention. Not bend over and hold your ankles so I can molest you without lube attention."

Vena's face went completely blank; then she burst out laughing so hard a dog started barking three doors down.

"I can't believe you just said that," she wheezed. "That was freaking hilarious."

"No, it's not," I said quietly, trying to shush her. "You made him uncomfortable. Tone it down a little."

Anchor stood abruptly, pocketed his phone, and strode toward us. "Get back in the car and lock the doors."

"What?" I asked at the same time Vena said, "Why?"

"Someone's been inside your house. I've already called Shepard. He's on his way with a couple of others."

"What?" I said again, sounding as horrified as I felt. "The counters are dirty. And there's laundry. And–"

Vena took my face between her hands. "Breathe, babe. It's going to be okay. Shepard will not look at yesterday's panties." She side-eyed Anchor. "Mine are already in the wash. Sorry."

He made a choking sound.

"If someone broke in, wouldn't it be better to call the police?" she asked him.

Again, if I didn't know Vena, I would have said it was a logical thing to ask. Something I should have asked. Something that shouldn't have made Anchor stutter out a lame excuse about the police being busy with other stuff.

"Like the murders that are going on around Blur?" I asked.

"I, uh, would feel a lot better if you got in the car now," he said, neither confirming nor denying my guess.

I grabbed Vena's arm to haul her to the car, locking us inside.

"Why would he think someone had been inside?" Vena asked. "It's not like he had time to check the place out."

"I don't know. But we're staying here until we're given the

okay."

Vena groaned. "This is going to be a long night. Maybe I'll work on the scrotum."

"No!" I whispered harshly, watching Anchor's back through the window. "You are not bringing that nasty thing out in my car. It's bad enough that Anchor smelled it on your hands. You are not making my car stink like a funky jock strap."

"It's just skin and oil." She glanced at Anchor, too, and looked like she was two seconds from drooling. "Wonder what he'd look like all oiled up."

I breathed for patience. When Vena's libido kicked into overdrive, I could normally switch her focus to treasure hunting with one little comment. But with Miles still missing, that was a dangerous topic.

Thankfully, it didn't take long before an SUV pulled in behind Anchor's truck. Shepard was the first one out, followed by Doc and Buzz.

Shepard glanced at us before he and the others went to Anchor.

They spoke a few words at the door before Shepard and Anchor headed inside and Doc and Buzz went around back.

Vena smirked at me, knowing I was about two seconds away from freaking out over dirty laundry and dishes.

"Shut up."

"I didn't say a word."

"You didn't have to. This is serious, Vena. Our house has been violated. And with everything else going on, I don't know that I feel safe anymore."

"You're right. A lot *has* happened. But the guys are making sure the house is okay. We'll have a new lock, and we can even bunk together if you want. Safety in numbers and all that."

"Maybe."

After a few minutes, Shepard came to the car. Vena and I got out to talk to him.

"There was someone inside," he said.

"How do you know?" Vena asked. "Did they leave something behind?"

Shepard paused as if choosing his words. "There was evidence of a vampire."

I glanced uneasily at Vena.

It had to have been Cross. But what evidence did he leave behind? And then I thought of the note he had written. No, I'd thrown that away, and I'd cleaned up the bonbon plate. There hadn't been a thing left out to say a vampire had been there.

Vena seemed to have the same thoughts.

"A vampire?" she said, sounding skeptical. "How can you tell a vampire was in the house? Was there a blood trail or something?"

Understanding she was still on her werewolf kick and trying to figure out if they all had keen senses of smell, I discreetly reached over and pinched her side as Doc and Buzz came from around the house.

"No other signs," Doc said.

Did they think the vampire would try to break in again when the front door was already busted?

"So the vampire's gone, then, right?" I asked.

"Right. But I don't want the two of you staying here alone. Anchor will stay with you tonight."

When Vena brightened, I shook my head. "No. That's okay. We'll be fine. He's already installing the new lock."

"By the looks of it, the previous lock had been easily broken. Either he stays, or I stay."

Vena raised a brow at me.

I felt a flush stain my cheeks as I struggled not to glance at

Doc and Buzz as they went to the SUV.

"Anchor can take my bed, and I'll sleep with Vena."

"He'll be on the couch by the door," Shepard said as if his word was law.

I doubted Anchor would fit comfortably on our couch, but I wasn't going to argue. It was late, and I was tired.

"As long as he's okay with it," I said.

"He is. Go inside."

"Thank you." I headed into the house and past Anchor. "Sorry you're stuck with us."

"I volunteered."

That made Vena smile at him. He glanced at her and then back at the knob. I made a note to wear my headphones to bed. I didn't want to know what happened beyond my bedroom walls.

In addition to worrying about Anchor staying the night, I worried about when Cross would appear tomorrow. As much as I wanted to pretend otherwise, Vena was right about Shepard and his crew. There was something more going on with them. And I really didn't want Cross and the Blur guys to meet until I knew what.

By the time I washed up and got ready for bed, Shepard and the others were gone. Anchor sat rigidly on the couch while Vena perched on the armrest next to him. Her open stare was sending all the inviting vibes.

Anchor cleared his throat. "So how did you and Everly meet?"

"In kindergarten. Some other girl took the brownie from Everly's lunch that her grandma made her. I wasn't a fan of bullies. Then or now. I got the brownie back, earned myself a lecture on fighting, and found myself a best friend."

"That's a long time to be friends. You're both so different."

"Not really. We balance each other. She is a positive, calming influence, and I help her have fun and stand up for herself." Vena leaned toward Anchor. "I could help you stand up too if you want."

"I'm out of the bathroom if anyone needs it," I said loudly, making Anchor jump even though he wasn't the one doing anything wrong.

Vena stood and winked at me before looking at Anchor.

"Anchor, let me know if you need any help working the shower. I'd be happy to show you." With that, she sauntered to her room.

Her bedroom door closed softly behind her, and Anchor let out a big, long breath.

I was about to apologize for her when Anchor looked at me.

"Do you think there's any chance she'd want something more than too-fast-to-last?"

I chuckled. "Maybe. You'd have to wear her down with awkward silences when she hits on you and sweet compliments when she's least expecting it. Blushing is her catnip. Oh, and plan to sleep with one eye open, or you might wake up pregnant."

He groaned and let his head fall back to the couch.

"I wasn't planning on sleeping anyway."

"Night, Anchor."

I left him in the living room and kept my door open a crack in case he needed anything, like a bodyguard, in the middle of the night.

The sun was barely making itself known to the world when the persistent buzzing of my phone woke me just past six. Groggily,

I looked at the caller, saw it was the guy from the pawn shop, and tossed my phone back onto the nightstand with a groan.

A light tap sounded on my door.

"Hey, Everly?" Anchor called softly.

"Yeah?"

"I'm going to take off now. Shepard said to call him if you need anything and to come a little earlier for your shift if it's possible. He wants to talk."

I let out a second groan, and Anchor chuckled.

"I'll tell him to text you in a few hours to remind you."

I mumbled something about overbearing bosses as the front door closed.

Knowing I couldn't ignore the call I'd missed, I rolled out of bed. I needed caffeine and a wake-up shower. After that, I would figure out what to tell the pawnbroker.

Used to Vena being up before me, I fumbled my way through starting the coffee then shuffled to the shower. I was reaching for the conditioner when I heard the door latch snick closed.

"Vena, I'm barely functioning. No drama until after coffee."

"This place reeks of wolves," came the low voice outside the shower curtain.

I squeaked and ripped the curtain aside enough to be sure I heard right.

Dressed in the same atrocious leisure suit as the day before, Cross stood in my bathroom, a sexy smirk tugging at his lips. His light brown gaze swept over my wet face and down to where I clutched the curtain to my chest.

"What the hell, Cross!"

I chucked the bottle at him without thinking.

He easily caught it and smirked.

CHAPTER TWELVE

I COULDN'T BELIEVE I'D JUST THROWN A BOTTLE OF CONDITIONER AT a vampire. Did I think that throwing it would do anything other than piss him off? No. I did not. Yet, as my brain registered my own potential-death stupidity, it also registered Cross' growing humor.

As I'd realized the day before, he wasn't what I'd thought a vampire would be. Good looking. Sense of humor. Gorgeous eyes…when they weren't black with hunger.

Right. Dangerous, Everly, I silently reminded myself. *Don't be pulled in by pretty eyes.*

"Would you care to explain why it smells like a wolf's den in here?" Cross asked.

"I don't know…maybe I stink from my shift at work. It's an everyone's-welcome kind of place."

He shook his head, his fathomless gaze holding mine as the shower continued to rain down on my back.

"Wolves have been here, in your home," he said. "One recently and another less than a day ago."

The only people who'd been inside were Shepard and

Anchor, and I defeatedly acknowledged what I'd been trying so hard to ignore. The men at Blur were overly protective of those they considered family, excessively strong, and had ridiculously good hearing and smell. If I were watching *The Other House*, I would have already laid money on them being wolves.

Dammit.

"Can wolves smell vampires like you can smell them?" I asked, thinking of Shepard's similar reaction to Cross' scent last night.

"Yes."

Well, that explained how they got their "evidence."

Any anger at Cross for interrupting my shower dissipated until I remembered our busted front door from yesterday.

"Cross, you didn't break in again, did you?"

"Not this time. The train rattled the window latch in the pantry loose. I came in through there. When I broke in through the front door, I was in a temper."

"What are you now?"

His amber eyes leisurely scanned me from head to curtain as if he could see through the material.

"Curious," he said finally. He turned and opened the bathroom door. "I will wait for you in the living room."

No longer needing a shower to wake up, I finished quickly and wrapped myself in a towel to go change in my room.

I didn't look into the living room when I scurried from the bathroom to my bedroom and snapped the door closed behind me.

Picking out comfortable jeans for a day of hopefully non-life-threatening activity, I changed and tucked my charm into my t-shirt. As protection against malicious intent, it'd already proven its worth when it had repelled Cross. And with Vena determined to chase down leads, who knew what today would bring? More vampires, wolves, and who knew what else, probably.

Once I was decent, my first stop was at Vena's door to pound on it loud enough to wake her. "Anchor's gone. Cross is here."

Ignoring Cross' inspection of our living room, I headed to the kitchen to pour a giant mug of coffee, topping it with enough sugar and creamer to make it palatable.

"Do vampires drink coffee?" I asked.

Cross appeared on the other side of the counter. "Some do. Some don't."

"Let me rephrase. Do you want coffee?"

"No. Thank you."

I nodded and showed him my phone as I sipped my sugary concoction.

"The guy from the pawn shop messaged. No offer for your coin yet, but they'd like to meet at seven to take a closer look. I would have told you right away, but I didn't know how to contact you."

"There is always a way to contact me." His slow smirk made me nervous about asking. I lived by the motto, "Ignorance is bliss." So I didn't question him.

"Vena thinks asking us to come in at seven before the shop opens is a little shady."

"It's a lot shady," Vena mumbled, ignoring Cross as she dragged herself to the coffee pot.

"What does that mean? Is it not a simple transaction?" Cross asked.

"If it were simple, he would have asked us to come in during shop hours." Vena sloppily poured a cup and drank it black.

"More than likely, the buyer knows the coin's value and will try to take advantage of our ignorance and pay less than what it's worth," I said.

Cross didn't seem concerned. "I'd still like to go. But I'll need to feed first."

"There are woodland creatures everywhere," Vena said. "Go grab a squirrel from a tree."

Cross' eyes did that scary black vein thing, and Vena set down her cup.

It felt like a standoff as we all stared at each other. Yet, despite the obvious threat behind Cross' hunger, he didn't make any menacing move toward us.

Vena seemed to think the same thing because she sighed.

"Fine. Let me get dressed," she said. "Ev, contact the pawn shop. Tell them we'll be there."

Keeping my eyes trained on the phone screen and not the intimidating vampire who'd begun pacing, I texted the pawn shop owner. He immediately responded that he'd be there waiting for us.

"Were you able to eat yesterday?" I asked Cross while we waited for Vena.

"Yes. Vena was correct that women of loose morals would sell their blood without hesitation."

"You found a prostitute?" I asked, surprised.

His gaze slid over my clothes, and I could see a hint of doubt in his expression.

"I'm not entirely sure that was her profession. However, she did emerge from a drinking establishment reeking of spirits and proclaiming to her female companions that she wanted to 'get laid,' which I assumed meant she was either ready to take a paid companion or that she wanted to sleep."

I struggled between wanting to laugh and covering my mouth in shock.

"I asked if she was interested in a respite," he continued, "but she kissed me. And in poor taste, I might add." He shook his head.

"After inquiring about the price of her services and her assurance I could have her in any way I wanted her, for free, I fed. Unfortunately, there were more spirits than blood in her veins, which did little to appease my hunger."

I opened my mouth to help him understand what he'd done, but Vena stopped me.

"Hold up!" she called from her bedroom. "There is so much wrong with that explanation that I want to see his face when you explain it, Ev."

I snapped my mouth closed, hating that she knew me so well.

Cross' confused gaze flicked from me to Vena, who joined us in the kitchen while still pulling back her hair.

"M'kay. I'm ready. Let him have it," she said.

I rolled my eyes at her, then looked at Cross.

"The girl was drunk, not a prostitute, Cross. You can't feed on drunk people."

"Obviously. I just told you that it did little for me."

"But did it make you smarter?" Vena asked. "Did you get any useful knowledge from feeding on the girl?"

He shook his head slightly. "Most of what I gleaned from her was a life filled with celebration after celebration. Music and spirits." He focused on me. "This is why I need your assistance. I cannot afford to choose poorly again."

"Okay, so what are you looking for in terms of a meal?" I asked. "Sober, of course."

"Yes. Sober and knowledgeable about the city, its customs, and its people."

"Why not feed on the pawn shop guy?" Vena asked. "You'd at least know what the coin is worth then, right?"

Cross shook his head. "I only feed from the willing."

I filed that interesting bit of information away as Vena crossed her arms.

"Well, there are no volunteers here." She looked at me. "Where are we supposed to find a willing victim?"

"I can find my own source," Cross said irritably. "I simply need assistance understanding the social differences for now."

"Okay," I said. "Let's take this conversation to the car. We don't have a lot of time before the shop opens. We'll figure out something on the way."

We locked up the house and went to the car. Cross sat in front, and Vena took the seat directly behind him. I knew she'd taken a defensive position because she didn't trust Cross. I didn't fault her logic. He'd proven that he struggled with control when he was hungry. But he'd also been showing us the less predatorial side of himself. The almost human side. She seemed comfortable enough with that side that she pulled out the book and began paging through it.

"I think you were on the right track with the bar," I said to Cross as I drove. "But late at night is a bad idea. That's usually when everyone's already drunk."

"Ah. I see. Are bars open at this hour?"

"Not usually. We could try a grocery store."

"Wait for a bar to open," Vena muttered. "'Excuse me, my good sir. Would you be willing to part with a pint?'"

"Not funny, Vena," I said, glancing at Cross. His eyes were growing dark again.

"We'll try the grocery store. It's full of sober people browsing for food, like a market." I wasn't sure how he would feed off someone at the store, but that was a problem we'd deal with when we got there.

I executed a U-turn and pulled into a smaller store near the pawn shop. Vena got out of the car with me. While I knew she was joining us to spectate, I was still glad for her company. I had no idea how a vampire went about asking someone for a willing donation.

"Since we don't want to cramp your style, we'll pretend to shop and stay out of your way," Vena said, hooking her arm through mine.

She veered us to the frozen foods, and we watched Cross wander the store from there. He struck up a conversation with a young stocker a minute later. The stocker nodded then started walking away.

Cross followed, and they both disappeared into the back.

"Didn't think Cross was into men," Vena said softly.

"How did he get someone to agree just like that?" I asked.

"Especially in that suit," Vena added.

We waited a few minutes while I gazed longingly at a tub of ice cream with caramel cups in it.

Vena pulled out her phone and read a message. "It's the person asking about the ring again."

"What did they say?"

"Just asking about a trade. They're a little more insistent this time, but still no details about the information."

Vena flashed the screen at me. And she was right. It sounded like the person was desperate to get the ring.

"Do you really think they have information on Miles? Or is this bait so they can get the ring and leave us with nothing but a pissed-off vampire?"

"I don't know. But we need to follow this lead."

"How? After what he did to get it back, there's no way Cross is going to hand over the ring. You saw what he did to our lock when he was angry."

"We take it from him again, give it to the person to get the info on Miles, and let Cross track the ring again. Simple."

"It's not simple, and you know it."

When Cross reemerged, he walked beside the stocker as he returned to where they'd started then shook the guy's hand.

"Do you see any blood on the guy?" I asked.

"None. But I doubt Cross would go for the neck. He probably went for a place no one can see. I heard the groin is a great place for blood flow."

I cringed at the picture that formed and Vena smirked.

With a smile, Cross came toward us.

"Are you good now?" I asked.

"I am."

"And you got some insight into our world?" Vena asked. "This babysitting stuff is getting old."

"I will still require assistance, especially for the pawn shop."

As soon as we were out of the store, Vena asked, "How did you get him to agree to a little sucky-sucky so quickly?"

I winced at the word choice but waited for Cross' answer. That guy had agreed rather quickly, especially for someone who had no money or anything to barter.

"I can be convincing when necessary," Cross said.

"Just how convincing?" Vena pressed.

"Enough to allow willing people to be flattered by my attention."

Vena frowned as we got back in the car. I thought that was the end of our conversation until she asked, "Seriously, how are you in the daylight? You should be an ash pile right now."

Cross shot me a look like I often gave Vena when someone was being too much, and I felt a connection with him. Not magic or anything out of the ordinary. Simply two people who knew Vena was a dog with a bone about him walking in daylight.

He smiled slightly, and I could see how easily someone might be charmed by him. Was that what had swayed the stock person? Simple charm?

Ignoring his silent plea for intervention because I was curious too, I pulled out of the parking lot and headed to the pawn shop.

"There must be something that keeps you from frying in the sun," Vena continued. "A charm? Vampire sunscreen? Blood of a fairy?"

"Must she persist?" Cross asked dryly.

"She will continue until she gets an answer," Vena said.

As she kept naming outlandish reasons why a vampire could walk in sunlight, I parked down the block from the pawn shop and glanced at the time.

"We'll need to walk fast."

"Not too fast," Vena said. "We don't want to seem eager. Cross, did you learn anything about pawn shops with the blood you sucked down?"

He exhaled like my mom did after grandma answered with one of her "that's what she said" comebacks she loved.

"Hints," he said. "The man knew of their existence, but I doubt he ever frequented one."

"Okay. Then here are the cliff notes. Never say yes to the first offer. And if I have to step in and negotiate, I'm asking for a cut."

"How much of a cut?" he asked.

I saw the treasure-hunting dollar signs light up Vena's eyes. She was on the hunt again.

She gave Cross a thoughtful look, her gaze dipping to his

hands where the ring graced his pointer finger. I knew right where her thoughts were headed, and I wanted to groan when she gave him a slight smile. She was going to make this visit all about gaining the ring.

"Let's see what happens. We can negotiate the details later."

When we tried the pawn shop's door, it didn't open. Vena shaded the glass, peered inside, and knocked hard on the pane.

"I can see the little weasel in there. Come on, sloth-man," she muttered, "pick up the pace. We have shit to do."

No doubt, she was thinking of the text message and getting the ring.

"Are you nervous, Everly?" Cross asked, watching me closely.

I managed a weak smile.

"Not really, but I'm a little worried about him cheating you. Pawn shops aren't my specialty. Bake sales? Yes. This? No."

"But they are mine," Vena said. "Don't worry, Cross, my friend. I have your back."

If he found her sudden helpfulness odd, he didn't show it. He gestured for us to go first when the guy finally unlocked the door.

"Ladies," the man said. "Mr. Cross. Sorry about that. I was getting the call set up."

He led the way to the main counter.

"The call?" Vena asked.

"Yes. Mr. Davies is out of state but knew you were in a rush to sell. Even though he hasn't heard back from his authenticator, he was willing to do a live video call to accommodate you."

"How nice of him," Vena said dryly.

I elbowed her.

"Thank you," Cross said. "Let's proceed."

I glanced at him, noticing that his speech seemed a little different. Less stuffy.

"Yeah," the owner said, turning the laptop on the counter to face us. "Just give me a second here."

He hit a button, and a few seconds later, the screen filled with the image of a middle-aged man dressed in a casual button-up shirt. I wondered if Vena was doing the same thing I was…assessing the background.

From years of waitressing and my time at Blur, I'd gotten pretty good at profiling customers. The troublemakers. The cheapskates. The big tippers.

This guy was dressed like the average blue-collar working man, and the office behind him wasn't anything special. But the band on his finger wasn't beaten up or simple. Same with his glasses and the watch on his wrist. All three of those things gleamed with newness and quality. And that screamed money to me.

"Stan mentioned that you were looking for a little quick cash," he said with a friendly smile. "Hopefully, I can help you out."

"I appreciate you taking the time to speak with us," Cross said smoothly.

"The pictures Stan sent over were interesting. Not interesting enough for my authenticator to get back to me within twelve hours but still interesting."

Vena snorted softly, and I hoped no one but me heard.

"Can I ask where you found it?" Mr. Davies asked.

"It's an heirloom," Cross said.

"One that holds a great deal of value to him," Vena added. "It's been a fight just to get him to consider parting with it."

Mr. Davies nodded like that was no news to him.

"Sentimental pieces are hard to part with. Often, they have

more emotional value to the owner than market value, which is why it's sometimes better to hold onto them. If you have the piece with you, would you allow Stan to show it to me again?"

"Certainly," Cross said, digging his hand into his overly tight pants pocket. He produced the gold coin and placed it on the counter.

Mr. Davies leaned toward his camera as Stan picked it up and held it near the laptop's camera.

"A little closer," Davies said.

I was surprised he didn't pull out a magnifying glass. His nose distorted as he leaned closer. "Looks authentic enough. But I can't say for certain. I tell you what, as a sign of good faith that it is most likely authentic, I can offer you two thousand. I'll wire it to you right now if you want to make the trade."

"Why would you do it if it's possibly not authentic?" Vena asked.

"There is value in the gold no matter what," Davies said. "And even if it is a forged copy, I can add it to my collection as decorative."

While Cross glanced at Vena, I was watching Stan. He was trying really hard to keep his poker face but failing. Hope and greed were shining through.

"We need time to think about it," I said.

"Very well," Davies said. "You have about thirty minutes before I have to leave. Let Stan know your decision by then."

When he disconnected, Cross looked at me. "Was it not a good deal?"

"Not according to Stan," I said, pointing at his slipping mask of indifference.

Vena nudged Cross. "Maybe use some of that persuasiveness of yours."

Stan took a step back. "Hey, now! Violence doesn't work on me. I own a pawn shop in D.C. I know how to fight."

"She wasn't talking about fighting," Cross smoothly said as he leaned forward. "I have no wish to harm you. I would simply like to ask what you think the coin is really worth."

Stan shook his head. "I'm not saying anything. This guy gives me a good commission for the things I find him."

I almost snorted. Stan wanted to take a cut of our price and get a commission from Davies?

"But I'd really like to know," Cross persisted, holding Stan's gaze. "How much is the coin worth?"

"Two point six million." As soon as the words were out, Stan's eyes rounded. "But you didn't hear it from me!"

And if one coin was worth over two million dollars, exactly how much was Cross holding in gold coins? I knew the bulge in his pocket was likely an ancient coin pouch. Our cave vampire was going to be a multi-millionaire soon. And he was walking around in a suit that should have been burned decades ago.

Vena grinned. "Then tell him we won't take less than two point four. I'm sure he'll want it appraised, so get that all set up for us. You have our contact information. We'll be leaving."

Vena's grin stayed in place as we walked out. She reached over and placed her hand on Cross' pocket lump. His affronted glance, as if she had actually touched his honey hump and not his coin purse, had her laughing.

"You, my friend, are going to owe me big time," she said.

I was still curious how Cross had so easily gotten the information from Stan. What made people want to give him what he wanted without a bribe? And what did that mean for me and Vena?

"Vena, please stop touching him," I said.

She dropped her hand away.

"Right. This isn't about the money." She glanced at Cross. "I'm curious what your ring's worth. You know, the one that accidentally found its way into our pockets when we fell into your cave. Wouldn't it be easier to have that appraised instead of a coin? I could help you with that."

"The ring isn't for sale," he said. "It's an adornment meant to be worn. The coin is being used as it is meant. As currency."

CHAPTER THIRTEEN

VENA OPENED HER MOUTH TO PRESS CROSS FOR HIS RING, BUT I gave her a look that had her snapping it shut.

"Cross, I know you're still catching up to all the changes that have happened, but I've realized trading the coin is not going to be as easy as we thought," I said. "You're going to need more help than we can give you."

"How so?" he asked, stopping beside my car.

"Mr. Davies wanted to send you the money electronically."

"Not paper currency?"

"No, not for as large of an amount as we're talking. And an electronic payment means you would need a bank account somewhere. To have a bank account, you need some form of ID."

"And IDs tend to be for the living," Vena said, understanding what I was getting at.

He gave her a dark look. "I am living. My heart beats. I am simply living differently now than how I once was."

"Whatever," she said with a shrug.

"What is an ID, and how do I obtain one?" he asked, still annoyed.

"An ID is a small plastic card with your picture that identifies you as you," I said. "Normally, a person would have to provide a birth certificate and proof of address to get one. I'm not sure your birth certificate would work, though. Did they have birth certificates when you were born?"

"Were you even born here in the States?" Vena asked. "If not, you're technically an illegal resident."

Ignoring our questions, he asked me, "Do you have a bank account?"

"Yes."

"Then I can transfer the money to you for the time being."

Vena was practically bouncing on her toes in excitement.

"That's a perfect idea," she said before I could object.

"Then it's settled. If you will excuse me, I must search out more grocery stores. I will check back with you in an hour or two." With that, he walked away.

I waited until Vena and I were in the car before glaring at her.

"What is wrong with you? Why did you agree that he can store millions of dollars in my bank account? Don't you think someone's going to notice that? I'm going to get flagged in some system, and we're going to get audited by scary people in suits."

"Speaking of suits, I think it's time to give our vampire an upgrade," Vena said.

"You think? And since when did he become *our* vampire?" I asked, driving back to the house.

"The moment I felt what he was packing. It was so…heavy. I cannot wait to get my hands on it." She shook herself. "But first, we need to figure out what to do about this mystery person who wants Cross' ring."

She tapped her fingers over the bag that held the book.

"He isn't going to give you the ring, Vena."

"No," she said, brightening. "He won't. But you saw the way he let Stan hold his two-million-dollar coin. All I need is a picture of the ring. I can arrange a meeting. Showing a current picture should at least be enough to negotiate for the information on Miles."

I was already shaking my head. "You're going to try to trick someone who's probably shady as hell, and we're going to end up dead."

She didn't even pretend to listen to me as she typed out a rapid message on her phone.

"There. Sent. Let's see–" Her phone pinged, and she looked down at it. "They want us to meet tonight at seven. You're never going to guess where."

"Where?"

"At Juicy." She was already digging in her bag for Miles' phone. "It's the same number. How did I not notice it was the same number?"

A sick feeling settled into the pit of my stomach. She wanted to meet the people who texted Miles right before he went missing about the book Vena now had in her purse? Hell no.

"We can't go," I said. "We have to be at Blur early to talk to Shepard."

She started texting without talking to me.

"What are you saying?" I tried to swat the phone away from her before she made the situation worse.

"I said seven wouldn't work. I suggested we meet this afternoon at one. Plenty of time to find out what they have and get to work. And we'll have our friendly neighborhood vampire with us, so we'll be perfectly safe."

"He's not our bodyguard, Vena. I thought you didn't want to involve him in this."

"I didn't. But circumstances have changed."

"Yeah. I know what circumstances have changed. The treasure-hunting gleam in your eye is blatantly apparent."

"We're helping him; he's helping us. It's a working relationship," she said with a shrug.

I didn't like using anyone for any reason, but I stayed silent for now. It was no use trying to persuade Vena while she had money on her mind.

By the time we reached our house, Vena's nose was back in the book.

"This is why towns die," she said, following me inside. "Get this. Twelve girls between the ages of twelve and twenty went missing within the span of a year in this one town. Stolberg. This story was recorded in the eleven hundreds. Do you know why they didn't just get up and leave? It was a mining town. Precious metals. Maybe even some gems by the looks of it. I mean, what are a few girls for riches, right?"

She flipped the pages. "I wonder if that's why there's this random drawing at the back with four stones. Maybe these are stories leading up to finding riches?"

"Doubt it. Read that warning at the front again."

She turned to the first page and read it out loud.

"*Herein rest the original accountings of the first encounters. Lest the reader believe this fiction and fallacy, be assured it is not. The truth is a danger to all who read. Proceed cautiously lest the shadows devour you as well.*"

She huffed a sigh. "If the danger is that other creatures exist, this is an outdated warning. We already know they exist."

She closed the book and drummed her fingers on the cover.

"Miles was looking for this book, went missing, and got a text from the same people asking about the ring. Coincidence? Doubtful," she said, thinking aloud.

"The notes on those stones say one was red. Maybe the stone was used for Cross' ring? Maybe it's an antiquities collector who needs the book to authenticate his ring's origin and value."

"Yeah, because collectors usually meet at strip clubs," I said sarcastically.

She continued tapping.

"Shady ones might. But there's still the scrotum. Miles tends to work on one lead at a time." She was silent for a moment. "I bet it's soft enough that I can open it today."

I didn't understand how her mind jumped from the book to that nasty thing so quickly.

"I'm starving, Vena. Can you please look at it *after* I've eaten?"

"We're on a tight schedule. How about if I open it up on the coffee table?" She pulled the baggy out of her purse and started massaging the skin.

"Protect the table. I don't want oily skin residue everywhere."

"Got it. I'll take care of this while you make us something to eat."

Making a beeline for the refrigerator, I pulled out everything for lemon ricotta pancakes. She reached around me to confiscate my roll of parchment paper and headed to the living room.

While I was not happy about having to buy more paper, I was glad she was working on her "project" somewhere other than my kitchen.

"It's opening!" she called.

My stomach roiled, and I willed it to behave until I could gorge on large quantities of delicious pancakes.

"Don't want to know!"

By the time I got the mixing bowl and pan out, Vena was back and hopping on her toes again.

"It's a map, Ev."

"A map of what?"

"I'm not quite sure. There are some towns noted but with really tiny and horrible penmanship."

"If it was written in ink, the oil probably made it bleed."

She was quiet for a long moment while I measured the ingredients.

"Not pen ink. I think they tattooed the skin before it was dried. Do you have a magnifying glass? Or maybe your glasses from fifth grade?"

"We agreed never to bring up that phase again, Vena," I said with a dark warning glare that I didn't truly mean.

She left the kitchen, and I heard the crinkle of parchment in the living room.

"Wait," she called. "I think I recognize one of these names from the book." A flurry of pages turning sounded from her end of the house. "Yep. Stolberg, where the story of the girl abductions is from. And here's another one. I knew they would be related somehow."

I mixed the ingredients, inhaling the scent of fresh lemon as she continued her mad chatter. Not even her talk of maps and stones could drag me down when I was in my happy food place.

Until she said, "We need to check these locations."

"How?" I asked suspiciously. "You just said you didn't recognize some of the names."

"That's easily fixed with a bit of research."

Research might distract her for a bit, but I knew I'd be dragged into it.

"Somehow, Miles knew the map and the book were tied together," Vena said. "But for what? Why did he care? What's this map showing us?"

I heard her moving around. The crinkle of parchment grew louder. I leaned back to see through to the living room and saw her laying the parchment paper and scrotum on the dining room table.

"Vena!"

"Sorry, but I need better lighting."

I made a face and turned back to my lemony prize.

"I was right," Vena said. "Light's better. I can see more of the names from the book on the map."

I flipped the pancakes. "Why put the towns from the book on a map? Is there some kind of significance to the stories? Are they all mining towns?"

"You and I are thinking the same thing. It's got to be a treasure map, right? But the stories are mainly about horrible things happening to humans. Thanks to Cross, we know they're creature stories, but I haven't found anything to link them to the stones at the back of the book."

"Put the map away for now, and let's eat. We'll think better on a fed stomach."

She snorted. "You think a fed stomach can solve everything."

"I haven't been proven wrong yet." I took plates out and placed heavenly, plump pancakes on them.

Vena came around me to wash her hands. "They do smell good."

"Better than what you've been playing with."

"Nothing wrong with playing with oiled balls. I wonder if Anchor will smell them on me again."

I debated telling her what Cross had confirmed about Anchor and Shepard this morning then decided against it. Vena tended to fixate, and she was already over the top flirting with Anchor. If she knew he was a wolf, she'd never let up. She was as obsessed with *The Other House* as I was.

"Let's not test it," I said. "If you get fired from Blur in the first week, I swear I'm getting you a job on the assembly line at a toothbrush factory. And not the vibrating kind."

She held up her hand in a solemn promise gesture that I didn't believe for a second and took a bite of her pancake.

I'd barely managed a few bites before my phone rang.

"Answer!" Vena said, seeing the screen before me.

Her enthusiasm made sense when I saw the pawn shop's number.

"Hello?"

"Hi, Everly. Mr. Davies accepted your counteroffer. He's willing to purchase the coin tomorrow morning at ten."

"Okay. We'll be there," I said, hoping I wasn't over-committing for Cross.

"See you then."

I looked at Vena after I hung up.

"What did he say?" she asked.

"Mr. Davies accepted your counteroffer."

Her grin was huge. "We're rich."

"No, *Cross* is rich. I'm not touching a dime of his money. Do you not remember how mad he was about the ring?"

"Do you not remember my negotiation skills? I did at least fifty percent of the work. If not for me, he'd have a measly few grand in his beautifully bulged pocket."

"Are you seriously going to ask him for fifty percent?" I asked in disbelief.

"Yep. It's not like he doesn't have more coins."

I took another bite of pancake, trying to console myself that her boldness was going to put us in a grave someday, while she inhaled hers.

"Hurry up. We have a lot to do today," she said, picking up her plate.

"Not really. All we have to do is go to the strip club, which I'm not happy about. And then go to work."

"I think a reconnaissance mission might be in order."

I paused the fork halfway to my mouth. "You know I hate it when you use that word."

She smirked as she walked into the kitchen. "This will be easy. I say that we go to the strip club before our appointment and look around."

"They won't let us in."

"Not unless they think we're applicants."

"I'm not applying to be a stripper, Vena."

"My beautifully bosomed best friend, we're not actually applying. We're just using what your grandma gave you to get us in the door so we can see things we might not otherwise see. We'll have more of an advantage than we do right now. We'd be going into the meeting blind otherwise."

"What happened to waiting for Cross?" I asked. "He said he would see us in a few hours…"

"I thought about it, and you're right. He's not our bodyguard. Plus, it's a little hard to get a hold of him when he doesn't even have a phone. We'll do this meeting with our brains instead of his muscles. Scope out the place first, and if everything seems legit, we show up at one as ourselves."

I stuffed the fluffy pancake into my mouth, not finding a hole in her plan other than the danger of going to a strip club.

She grinned as if she could read my thoughts. "With your pushup bra, we'll get in, no problem."

"Do you promise that this is the last lead we'll follow today?"

"Promise. Go and bring out Lucky."

"Stop naming my bras. Let me finish eating so we can get this over with."

Vena rushed me through my food in record time and dragged me to my room to dig through my closet for the tightest and skimpiest clothes she could find.

"Perfect!" Vena tossed a low-cut top onto the bed and a tight miniskirt. She then fished out neck-breaking high heels.

"Do I get to go through your closet and pick out your outfit?" I asked.

"No need. I already know what I'm wearing."

Her outfit would have more fabric to conceal some sort of weapon, and I was okay with that.

By the time we were dressed and in the car, Vena was searching the internet on her phone while I drove to the strip club.

"I wish Miles would have told me what he was up to," Vena said. "Following his trail would have been so much easier. I can see the potential value in the book and the map if it leads to gems, but what's with the strip club? How does it tie in?"

"That's why we're going, right? To find out?"

"Yep. And thanks to you, we'll have no problem getting in." She smirked at me.

I hoped she was right because I wasn't sure if I'd have enough courage to try again.

Parking in front of the club, I turned to Vena. "Do you promise we're going to be smart about this?"

"I swear, if there is any trouble, we'll leave."

The extremely short skirt I wore showed half my ass to the world when I got out of the car. I took a moment to tug it back into place.

"Fluff the girls," Vena said, watching me over the roof.

"I'm not fluffing anything in the middle of the street."

"Then what were you just doing to your butt?"

"Covering it! I should have worn pants."

"No way. Legs are a stripper's asset. We need to show off that yours are decent. You can wait to fluff the twins until we get to the door."

I glared at her. There would be no twin fluffing. They were barely in the bra the way it was.

"I should have burned this thing after the last time you made me wear it," I said, joining her on the sidewalk. If not for the valiant efforts of my questionably sized button-up shirt, the world would be viewing the healing scorch mark from her dumb sun charm.

"No way. That's our free drinks ticket when we go out." She glanced down at the unbuttoned vee in my shirt and grinned. "You have more cleavage than I have crack. I just want to put my face in there and motorboat."

"Seriously, your parents must have experimented on you as a kid. It's the only explanation for you."

She grinned at me and hooked her arm through mine. "Show time," she whispered, turning us toward the club.

I took a deep breath and strolled to the door with her. This time, it was locked, though.

After knocking, the same bouncer from the previous time opened it. The faint sound of music filtered out.

"Any chance you're looking for new talent?" Vena asked with a wide smile.

His gaze swept over her face, my tits, then her face again.

"Sure. There might be a few openings. Come on in."

I could almost feel Vena's triumph as he stepped back and gestured for us to join him in the dimly lit entry. She strode forward with confidence, pulling me with her. The music grew louder, and I breathed in the lingering scent of fruity-flavored vape pens while I looked around.

Either Vena's definition of nice needed to be questioned or the internet had lied. With dark walls and older, red accent chairs outside the bathroom, the place came across as dated and not nearly as nice as Blur. No wonder everyone Vena asked hadn't heard of it.

The click of a lock sliding into place had me gripping Vena's arm harder.

"This way," the man said, heading down the wide hall.

I shot Vena a panicked look, and she mouthed, "Be cool" before towing me with her. The dude just locked us in, and she wanted me to be okay with that?

She leaned in. "You're cutting off circulation. He's a bouncer at a member's only club."

Right. I took a calming breath. Of course he'd lock the door until he could send someone else to answer it.

I eased my grip as we emerged into the main bar area. The room had four mini stages between the bar and the main stage. Tables with lounge seating were interspersed throughout. Most of the tables were empty, which explained why the mini stages were dark and only two dancers gyrated on the main stage.

Two male dancers.

Naked.

One saw me looking and did a sudden hip thrust, making his semi-hard length slap against his sack.

"That can't feel good," Vena said under her breath.

The other dancer grabbed a pole and slid down its length. I couldn't imagine that feeling any better.

An inquisitive meow shifted my attention to a throne-like chair taking center stage. A black cat was curled up on it. The cat's yellow eyes blinked at us as we moved through the room, following the bouncer.

"Is the cat part of their act?" I asked.

"The owner's companion belongs to the cat," the bouncer said. "You'll meet him later."

Before I could question what he meant by that, he pushed open a door that led to a changing room for the dancers. I saw the normal feathered and sparkly costumes and long tables filled with containers of body glitter situated along the walls. My head swiveled as I took it all in.

It wasn't until the bouncer opened another door that what I saw registered. The costume pieces had no tops. Only bottoms. Bottoms with extra room in the front.

"Here you go, ladies," the man said. "If you wait right here, I'll get the house mother."

"Sure thing," Vena said.

As soon as he was gone, I swatted at Vena. "This is a male strip club!"

"I noticed that when I saw the guys' junk. And when I saw all the pouch thongs on the costume rack. Did you see the one with the beak on it? I think there was a hole between the bills."

"If it's an all-male strip club, why would they want to hire us?"

"Maybe they have men during the day for the stay-at-home moms. Night time might be different."

"Then where are the female costumes?"

"Would you want to chance some guy's sweaty junk in your feathered thong? They probably swap costume racks when the other dancers are here."

I considered that for a moment. "You might be right, but I'm still getting a bad feeling about this place."

"You had a bad feeling before we walked in the door. Calm down. We're not actually going to work here." Vena prowled along the room, looking at the shelves that contained boxes of tubes and syringes. "What is up with this stuff? I wonder if this is some kind of kink club."

That did not help calm me.

"Ah-ha! Check this out." She held up a blank ID card with a uniquely designed "NC" logo in a circle. "This must be their member's only ID he was asking about. Wonder if I should take one."

"Vena, we need to leave."

"We're here to look around, Ev. When the house mother gets here, ask to use the bathroom. It'll give you a chance to check this place out."

"Why me?"

"Because if I volunteered, you'd think I would do something reckless."

She wasn't wrong.

"I'll stay here and ask a few questions. Once you get back, we'll say that we've rethought our career path, thank her for her time, and get out of here."

Her plan sounded reasonable enough until I thought about exploring a currently all-male strip club on my own.

She pulled down a box from higher on the shelf. It was taped shut. Vena inched up her skirt to pull out a small knife.

"Do not open that."

183

"Why not?" she asked, sliding the blade along the tape. "I'll take a peek then put it back. It's not like I want to steal it."

She handed me the knife and lifted the lid.

"Just some cheap boas."

She replaced the box and reached for another one. Nervous that the house mother would catch her snooping, I went to the door to play lookout. However, when I grasped the knob. It didn't turn.

"Vena," I hissed. "We're locked in."

She paused her riffling and glanced at me with a slight frown. "Probably for security."

I knew she was trying to come up with a reasonable explanation to keep me from completely freaking out, but it wasn't working. I'd heard the hesitancy in her voice.

"Or they locked us in to *kill* us. What kind of kink club has syringes and locks applicants into a back room that houses storage? There are no windows. No chairs or a table to sit at for an interview..."

"It's not like we were applying for an office job, Ev."

I was past listening to her reason. "This is how people go missing, Vena."

"Calm down, and give me the knife. I'll jimmy the lock."

"With a knife?"

"Pressure and leverage. And the tubes might not be weird in an all-male strip club. Maybe they use them for, you know, cleansing if more than stripping goes on here."

I paused as the picture of how those tubes might be used filled my head, purposely ignoring the fact that she didn't mention the syringes.

"Are you saying we tried getting hired at a gay male strip club?" I demanded in a whisper.

Vena had the nerve to grin at me. "It does make you wonder why Miles received the coordinates for this place, doesn't it?"

"Just get us out of here. And you can forget about coming back later."

I shoved the dagger at her, handle first, and cut myself in the process. A hiss of pain escaped me.

She pointed to the box of boas. "Grab one to stop the bleeding."

"Sure. Right," I said sarcastically. "Because throughout history, people used boas to soak up blood."

"Well, you're dripping on the floor."

While Vena turned her attention to the lock, I found a pack of unopened paper towels and pressed a wad to my palm.

"I can't get the lock open," Vena said. "We have a few options. We can wait until the house mother shows—"

"No. Next option."

"Or we can try to force the door open."

I looked at the steel door and shook my head. "Next."

"Okay. Then, we create a distraction and jump whoever comes to check on us."

"I'm not doing the jumping."

"Nope, you're the distraction. Give me that bloody paper towel."

She grabbed it and collapsed onto the floor, doing her best dramatic faint.

"Start pounding on the door and sound frantic," she said.

That wouldn't be hard to do.

"Help!" Pound. Pound. Pound. "My friend fainted and hit her head. She's bleeding." More pounding. "We need help."

My hands were starting to get sore, and the cut one was leaving bloody smears on the door.

The door opened suddenly, swinging outward, and I fell

forward. The bouncer grabbed me roughly, and the already straining center button on my shirt pinged free.

Keeping with the act, I didn't even flinch when my left boob toppled from its demi-cup. Nipple out, I grabbed the guy's shirt.

"She's bleeding," I repeated. "She hit her head."

I released him and turned to point at Vena.

Instead of rushing to her aid, he grabbed my arm and shoved me inside. I landed on top of Vena with an 'oof.'

"Make noise like that again, and the next time I open this door, you'll both see the back of my hand."

The door slammed shut, and I lifted myself off of Vena, already starting to hyperventilate.

"Did you hear what he said?" I asked, my voice high-pitched. "We're fucked."

Vena pressed the paper towel into my fist and caught my face between her hands.

"Breathe, Ev. In and out. Keep your cool. We still have our phones, remember? We're not fucked yet."

I nodded and scrambled off her, already digging in my cleavage for my phone.

My fingers found nothing but sweat and regret.

CHAPTER FOURTEEN

As Vena picked up the knife my fall had knocked out of her hand, she pulled her phone from another strap on her thigh. I scanned the floor for mine, and realized it must have fallen out along with my boob due to the bouncer's grabby hands.

I tucked myself back in as much as I could, but Lucky had lost its charm. The strap was broken, and my left side hung heavily in the wilted lace cup. If I needed to run, there would be major problems. And with the center button missing, everyone in the world would know it.

"I can't get reception in here," Vena said, holding her phone in the air as if the cellular gods would find her by her will alone.

We were in over our heads.

"The bouncer must have known who we are," I said, looking for something to use as a weapon as I continued to panic. "It's the only reason he would have let us into a member's only male strip club."

"We'll be okay."

"Okay? You're waving your phone uselessly in the air, and we have nothing to defend ourselves with."

"I still have my knife."

That made me only feel slightly better. There was no way the bouncer would come back alone. He'd have people to help him. And one little knife wouldn't be enough.

I frantically continued my search for something. The needles were a possibility. But they'd break easily.

"Maybe if I get closer to the wall." Vena touched her phone to each wall. "Nope."

A sound outside the door caught my attention. It was muffled at first. Then I heard a loud bang. More shouting.

I backed away from the door as the sounds grew louder.

And louder.

Then nothing.

My heart raced faster in the ominous silence.

"What the hell is out there?" Vena whispered as we retreated farther. She stood poised, ready to throw her knife.

The door groaned then burst off its hinges. I yipped as the door fell to the floor. Vena threw her knife.

The man standing there caught it before the point could reach his forehead and casually tossed it to the side as his black-veined eyes scanned the room.

"Cross?" I said in shock.

"This is not what I meant when I said I would see you in a few hours, Everly," he said, radiating anger.

I didn't even care. Not about his anger and not about how damn happy I was to see a vampire. Cross was a gift-wrapped miracle who also now looked like a supermodel.

The long coppery hair he'd tied behind his head was gone, cut short on the sides and long enough on the top to style. The seventies monstrosity of a suit was gone, too, and in its place, he wore a fitted black suit, red tie, and crisp white shirt. Or what used to be a crisp white shirt. Blood had sprayed between his lapels and was smeared across his mouth.

As we stared at each other, his eyes cleared slightly. But they darkened again when his focus drifted lower.

"Where are you hurt?" he asked, his gaze locked on my chest.

"Not there," Vena said, snapping her fingers at him with one hand while she picked up her knife with the other. "Stop leering at the twins and get us out of here."

He crossed the room and tugged the edges of my shirt together. When he saw the missing button, he swore under his breath, slipped out of his coat, and wrapped it around my shoulders before I could even think to cover myself with my hands. Not that there was a need.

He carefully buttoned me into the bloody coat and adjusted it to ensure I was covered.

"Are you all right?" he asked, nudging my chin up with a finger so he could look at me.

The tender kindness in his gaze was almost my undoing.

Was I okay? Hell no. I understood very well how close Vena and I had come to serious trouble.

"They locked us in a room," I managed. "I won't be all right until we get out of here."

He took my hand and led me from the storage room. The dressing area looked like a tornado had hit it. Sequined thongs were everywhere, and tiny feathers from a torn boa still drifted down in the air.

My phone lay on the floor in the chaos. A bloody feather was stuck on the screen. I pointed at it, and Vena scooped it up.

"Got it," she said softly.

The first body I saw was one of the dancers we'd spotted

earlier. He lay face down in a pool of blood, and my steps faltered.

"Why?" I whispered.

"Don't look," Cross said, urging me forward.

"It's hard not to look," Vena said. "Especially when we're slipping in blood. Not complaining since the assholes did lock us in a room, but I'm not sure it's worth their lives."

"Isn't it?" Cross asked with an angry edge. "I promise they wouldn't have hesitated to take yours."

My hands started to shake as I gave into Cross' urging. We passed several more bodies on the way out. The bouncer lay in a heap right inside the door. I wasn't as upset seeing his eyes vacantly staring at the wall.

However, as soon as we were out of the building, my shaking increased.

"I'm driving," Vena said, noticing my composure dissolving.

I nodded and got into the passenger seat that Cross held open for me. His eyes had mostly returned to their normal soft brown. Vena started the car and waited for him to get into the back before peeling away from the curb.

"Not to be a Debbie Downer, but we just drove away from a murder scene. How attached are you to this car?" Vena asked me.

I hadn't thought of that and started to hyperventilate again. Cross reached around from the back and set his hand on my shoulder.

"There's no need to worry," he said. "No one will report any murders."

"How do you know that?" Vena asked, shooting him a look in the mirror.

"That place was a feeding ground for my kind. I smelled old blood when I entered."

The tubes… The syringes…

I clenched my hands in my lap to try to stop the tremors wracking through me, and Cross' hold on me tightened. "Why would you go there?" he asked softly. "If you wish to donate, I am happy to accept."

"We weren't there as feeders," Vena said. "We were looking for some information pertaining to my brother."

"Is he the person you mentioned who is missing?"

"Yes, and we didn't know it was a feeding ground when we went there."

"You should have waited for me."

"Waited for you?" she asked. "Why?"

"Because you're reckless and foolish and could have died."

Vena's grip tightened on the steering wheel.

"Do you want to know why women changed so much? Because we got tired of the disappointment of waiting for a hero that never showed up. We learned that if we wanted to be saved, we needed to save ourselves. You made it clear when we met that you weren't here to help us…that we're here to help you. So don't act all upset now. You didn't earn that right."

He sighed, gave my shoulder another reassuring squeeze, and released me. I took a few calming breaths and told myself we were safe for the moment and that I wasn't going to go to jail for accessory to multiple murders.

As the panic slowly faded, I started to think more rationally. It'd been stupid for Vena and me to go there alone. If not for Cross–

"How did you know where we were?" I asked.

"I always know where you are," he said. "But I knew you needed me when you bled."

That had to sink in for a moment before I twisted in my seat to look at him.

"How far away were you?" I asked.

"Across town. I was acquiring more appropriate clothing." His eyes turned dark as he stared at Vena. "The clothes you provided were not helping me blend."

She cleared her throat guiltily and opened her mouth. Probably to say something snarky. I cut her off.

"You smelled me bleed from all the way across town?"

"No. I sensed you bleed," Cross clarified.

"You can sense me bleed? Why?"

"Vampires are proprietary. Once we acquire a human, that human is ours."

"Acquire? I'm acquired?" I asked, feeling the panic rising again.

"I've tasted your blood twice, Everly. We are linked on a very intimate level. You are not owned; you are protected."

That helped me feel a little better. As did the soft smile he gave me.

"I won't allow anyone else to feed from those I feed on," he assured me. "Sensing when you bleed is like an alarm."

"Or like a dinner bell," Vena said under her breath.

I shot her a warning look.

"Well, it came in handy," I said, preferring to focus on the positive. "Thank you for coming. And I'm sorry about the clothes. The old ones and the new ones. I'm not sure that much blood will come out."

"Don't bother yourself over it. I'll find more."

"Speaking of clothes, how did you get the suit without money?" Vena asked.

"I can procure anything when people are willing to give."

That "willing to give" thing kept coming up. After the blood alarm comment, I didn't want to dwell on it, though.

"You can take a shower at our place," I said. "We'll figure out new clothes for you unless you have more."

"I only accepted what I'm wearing. I will have to acquire more once I have money."

There was that word again. I wasn't sure I liked it anymore.

"I'm sure Vena will happily lend you some of her brother's clothes, which will blend. At least until you can get your own."

"Or he can wear your fuzzy pink robe while finding something on his own."

Cross leaned forward toward Vena...within biting range. "Have you forgotten what I did to save you?"

Vena glanced at me but then returned her eyes to the road. "Shower first, and we'll deal with clothes later. Your bloody face is already attracting attention." She flipped half a peace sign to the gawking couple in the car next to us.

"Maybe you should lie down," I said.

He tossed an annoyed glance at me.

"Or not."

"I want your promise that this will not happen again," he said.

"Bad clothing choices?" I asked, confused since I'd already said I was sorry.

"Walking into a feeder den," he said, eyes flashing black briefly.

"We can't promise anything," Vena said.

He narrowed his gaze on her. "I'm only asking for Everly's promise."

Vena raised a brow at me.

"It's not like we meant to ignorantly walk into a strip club for feeders and allow them to kidnap us," I said. "Anyway, I don't need to promise anything because Vena isn't going to drag us to unknown or potentially dangerous places ever again, and I'm not the type to wander into one on my own." I looked pointedly at Vena. "Right?"

With a determined scowl that faded to pleading, she glanced between Cross and me.

"We were following up on a lead," she said. "I can't stop looking for Miles. Especially not now that we know that place was for vampires. Why were vampires looking for him, Ev?"

"You will fill me in on your quest thus far, and I'll help you," Cross said, looking marginally calmer.

"Our quest thus far?" Vena snorted. "You really need to match your English with your modern clothes."

"I'm trying," he said. "But it's easy to fall back into old speech habits, particularly when I'm irritated. Do you at least agree to let me help you to spare your friend from further danger?"

Vena shot me a guilty glance and grudgingly agreed. She didn't have to tell Cross everything, but having him scout the dangerous locations would be enough to appease both sides.

Whatever Miles had been involved in was looking more dangerous than either Vena or I had guessed. If not for Cross' offer to help, I would have been speed-dialing Vena's parents by now. Part of me still thought that was the smarter idea, but I wasn't sure how the Hunter family would react to our newly formed association with a vampire.

I still wasn't quite sure how to react myself. Considering the lack of police interest in Miles' disappearance, Cross' help was better than no help. And he'd just proved that. However, while I did appreciate the save back at the strip club, I did not like being "acquired." I barely bled on him or in the bonbons. Neither could count as an actual feeding, could they?

I was bleeding now more than either of those times. I

glanced at my fist and unfurled my fingers from around the wad of paper towel I was still gripping.

Please don't let me need stitches, I thought, removing the paper towel.

Fresh blood pooled in the inch-long gash.

Cross reached over the seat and grabbed my hand. I yelped. Vena swerved. He pulled my bleeding palm to his lips.

I was too shocked to do anything but stare into his amber eyes as I felt his tongue swipe over my skin.

"Hey! Cut it out," Vena said. "You only feed on the willing, remember?"

His tongue moved over my palm again before he pulled back slightly to answer Vena.

"I am stopping the bleeding, not feeding," he murmured, licking me a final time.

A shiver ran through me, and it had nothing to do with revulsion. He drew back enough to press his lips to my palm and closed my fingers over my no-longer-bleeding-but-still-raw wound.

"Take care, or it will start again," he said.

I nodded and held my loosely fisted hand to my chest, pretending like my heart wasn't racing from the intimate contact.

When we finally arrived at the house, Cross was quick to get out of the car and open my door for me. I glanced at my hurt hand as I got out. He was only being nice…right?

As soon as we were inside, I led Cross straight to the shower.

"Have you used one of these yet?" I asked.

"No."

I showed him how to turn on the water to warm it.

"Put your clothes on the floor for now. I'll clean up later. The towels are here for drying off. This is shampoo for your hair, and this is face wash to clean off the blood. Don't get any of the soaps in your eyes. It'll burn. Yell if you need anything else."

"I will. Thank you, Everly."

I closed him into the bathroom and hurried to my bedroom to ditch the bloody suit coat I was wearing. Before I did, I looked at my palm more closely. The cut was blood-free and looked like it was sealed together. When I eased my hand fully open, I felt the stretch and tug on the skin. Cross was right. It could easily break open again if I wasn't careful. But my wound was on its way to healing.

Storing away that little nugget of information, I removed the suit coat. My shirt underneath was a mess, and enough red smeared my skin from the saturated coat I'd been wearing that I started to gag.

"Don't look," I breathed, staring up at the ceiling while I held the coat with one finger.

"Vena!" I called.

She came into my room a second later.

"I got it," she said as soon as she saw me.

She took the coat and waited for my shirt. I debated taking off the bra, too, but why bother? It was wrecked beyond repair, and I wasn't clean enough to put something else on until I washed off.

"Your phone's clean and on the table. Think he'll get mad if I throw this in the washer?" she asked, inspecting the coat. "I bet it's dry clean only."

"What dry cleaner would be okay with a coat that bloody? None. We'd have the police knocking at our door in seconds. Toss it in the washer. I'll explain why we had to wash it here."

"At least he listens to you," she said with a hint of bitterness. "Since I'm washing this, can you grab his other stuff?"

"Why me? You had to rescue me from my bloody clothes."

"Cross doesn't like me. If I go in there, he'll go all black eyes and fangs."

She wasn't wrong.

"Maybe he wouldn't do that if you were a little nicer to him."

She rolled her eyes and motioned for me to hurry. Supporting my left boob with my recently healed hand, I opened the door and reached in for his clothes.

"Everly? Which one was for my face again?"

I tossed the clothes to Vena.

"The one in the small yellow bottle."

"Nothing is coming out of it."

I wrinkled my nose.

"Hand it out through the curtain."

The bottle emerged, and I shuffled closer to grab it. The door shut behind me. My eyes went wide, and I looked at the door instead of taking the bottle.

"Is there a problem?" Cross asked.

When I turned to him, he was leaning around the curtain. His glistening wet face was blood-free and beautiful. So was the bare shoulder, ribs, and hip not hidden by the curtain.

My inner Everly was pleading for a train to rattle the house so the curtain rod would fall. My inner Vena was laughing with giddy delight, thinking about ripping the curtain aside herself. Maybe Vena was right. Maybe my current dry spell was running a little long.

Face heating at my racing thoughts, I held out my hand.

"No. No problem."

I took the bottle, and his gaze went to my barely-covered top half.

"My apologies. I should have allowed you to wash first." A

small, incredibly sexy smile tugged at his lips. "Unless, perhaps, you would care to join me. I could attempt to heal that burn for you."

I swallowed hard.

"Thank you for the offer, but no. Could you step behind the curtain again? I'm going to need both hands for this."

His gaze dipped to the hand holding up my bra, and his eyes gleamed black briefly before he snapped the curtain closed. I quickly fixed the pump so it faced the right direction and handed it back.

"Thank you, Everly," he said. "I will only be a moment more."

I fled the bathroom and almost ran into Vena.

"Stop waving those things around," she said, gesturing to my boobs.

I held the girls while I glared at her. "I'm not waving anything around. I'm just trying not to get blood all over everything."

She sighed as she glanced down at her own chest. "Come on, ladies. Let's not be jealous. Remember, size doesn't matter." Vena lifted her gaze and smirked at me. "Well, not for some things. Did you get a look at our vampire in the flesh?"

I rolled my eyes and was about to head to my room when I heard the water turn off. A few moments later, the door opened.

A water droplet rolled from Cross' toweled, damp hair. It slid down his firm chest muscles, down the swells of his tight abs, and stopped at the towel wrapped around his waist.

It took me a second to tear my gaze away from him.

"The shower is yours," he said. "Is there something I can change into?"

"We're washing your clothes," Vena said when my tongue decided it was only interested in licking the droplets from his body. "Should be done in an hour or so." She nudged me toward the bathroom.

I stepped around him and closed the door.

What was the matter with me? I'd seen naked men before. Cross was nothing new. Well, he was decidedly more attractive than any past men, but still.

As I scrubbed the blood off, I could feel his lips on my palm.

He was a vampire. Nothing could happen. Nothing should happen.

Once I had that firmly in my mind, I turned off the water and dried myself enough to return to my room and change.

I heard a thread of the conversation coming from the dining room as I left the bathroom. Vena and Cross were talking about the sheep scrotum. Apparently, the disgusting skin sack was of good quality and prized by the fae.

After a quick change, I walked out of my room to find both Vena and Cross nose-first in the skin.

"So, what do you think?" she asked as she straightened.

Cross gave the map one last look before he stood up as well. "I think you are both over your heads, and you're lucky I rescued you. Anyone looking for this map is not out for treasure."

"What do you mean?" Vena asked.

"I mean, stop looking into this before it's too late. Information like this will get you killed."

"We've heard that warning already," I said.

"What about my brother?" Vena demanded. "He had this map when he went missing. He had it before someone sent him the coordinates to Juicy. They're linked. I know it."

Cross' jaw clenched. "If I tell you both to leave him to his fate, you will try to skewer me."

Vena glanced at me. "He's smart."

Cross scrubbed his hand over his face, looking a little older than he had moments ago. Clearly, the map was trouble.

"If I look into this, I will have your word that you will not attempt any more capers like you did today." He stared hard at Vena. "You will not endanger your friend for your brother."

She eyed him. "How are you going to look into it? You're still barely functioning in society. No one says caper anymore."

He leveled her with a glare. "I have you to thank for impeding my progress. However, I had enough skill to rescue you, didn't I? Now, do I have your word?"

Vena looked thoughtful. "You have my word for the rest of today and tonight. We have to work anyway. We can renegotiate in the morning after you tell me what you've found."

Cross' eyes turned black, but before I could panic, they shifted back to amber.

He nodded to Vena and looked at me. "You should be safe for now. Come nightfall, I'll be nearby."

"Nearby?" I asked. "You mean here? Or are you following us to work?" After Anchor's reaction to smelling him here, I didn't think it would be wise for Cross to walk into Blur.

"I will be here, awaiting your return. Stop for no one on your way home. Understood?"

I nodded.

"Hold tight," Vena said. "I'll find you something to wear so you don't have to wait for your clothes." She was already heading for our front door.

Glancing at Cross, I found him watching me. Why did he have to look so tempting in that towel? I needed a distraction.

"Have you had a chance to watch any television yet?" I asked.

"Not yet."

"It might help educate you."

Vena returned fifteen minutes later, which had given me enough time to introduce Cross to our favorite reality show.

"It's ridiculous that this is how werewolves managed to gain the acceptance of polite society," Cross said. "For centuries, they were nothing but backwoods mongrels, not fit for a drawing room."

"Polite society? Drawing room?" Vena said, closing the door behind her. "You're making yourself sound like eighty when you only look thirty. Tops. If you want to blend, you can't look or sound old." She punctuated the statement by tossing him a bundle of clothes.

"Those are trendy as of this year. No trick." She paused for a moment, growing serious. "Please find my brother."

Cross rose with the clothes in his arms.

"I will do my best."

I stood as he walked away.

"I'm going to go blow dry my hair so it doesn't dry funny for work," I said. "Don't forget Shepard wants us there early."

"We still have hours, Ev," she said as I walked away.

By the time I left my bedroom with silky smooth and golden dry hair, the bathroom was open.

Cross' prowl of the dining room paused when I entered. Vena shook her head and waved a hand at him.

"Will you please tell him how he looks?"

My gaze slid over him, taking in the relaxed jeans and very snug t-shirt. The man could probably wear a sack and look delicious. But what he had on now was tempting enough that I'd offer to buy him a drink if Vena and I were out clubbing.

"These trousers are ridiculous. What man of refinement would wear this coarse cloth?" he demanded, glaring at Vena.

"I told you," she said. "They aren't trousers because you

aren't eighty. They're jeans. They're what men who look your age wear when they're going into a strip club."

He curled his lip at her.

"It isn't a strip club. It's a feeding den."

"Well, those clothes are what my neighbor would sell me for forty bucks, and they're in fashion. I'm doing my best here, Cross."

"You look amazing, Cross," I said quickly to stop the fight. "Very attractive. Those are the kind of clothes that will make women interested in you. Trust me when I say you would get a lot of offers."

His gaze shifted to me, and his eyes flared black.

"Are you offering?" he asked, his voice silky.

"No hitting on Everly," Vena said. "You both have work to do. You're going to save my brother so Everly doesn't risk another bra malfunction, and we're going to serve drinks tonight so I can reimburse myself for the clothes I bought an ungrateful friend."

Cross' head swung toward her. "I am not your friend."

She crooked a grin at him. "I like how you didn't correct the ungrateful part."

He snorted and started for the door. "I will see you when you return this evening. Do not leave this house until it is time for you to work."

"Wait," I called when he opened the door. "You need a key. We can't afford more broken or unlatched locks." I dug my key out of my purse and handed it to him. "Thank you for helping."

His gaze swept over my face, and he caught my hand to bring it to his mouth. The way his lips brushed over my knuckles flushed my cheeks and set my pulse racing.

"For you, anything," he said.

Vena waited until he was gone to mock him.

"For you, Everly, anything," she said in a deep voice. "You're asking him for the damn ring next time."

"I can't ask him after he just killed people for us. Be grateful we're alive, and get a copy of your key made so I have one again."

I returned to the kitchen to make us both something to eat for lunch. After the morning we had, it felt great to sit and watch mindless television for several hours. I groaned when I saw the time and grudgingly stood.

Vena turned off the TV and made a sympathetic sad face.

"I am sorry about this morning."

"I know you are. You'll be even more sorry if Shepard sees the cut on my hand so soon after the cut on my face. My 'taking one for the team' quota's been met today, and I'm putting the blame right where it's due."

She made another face and carried our lunch plates to the kitchen, giving me a chance to steal the bathroom first.

After we had arrived home from Juicy, I had washed away the heavy makeup and the blood then placed a new, small strip of medical tape over the healing cut on my cheek. I did the same now for my palm.

As I stared down at it, wondering if Shepard would notice, I realized I had no chance of hiding it. Anchor had smelled the scrotum on Vena's hand after she'd washed. So, the likelihood of Anchor smelling blood on me was probably a given.

The real question was if Shepard would believe I ended up on the wrong end of a friendly knife.

Vena was ready and waiting at the front door by the time I finished dressing.

"Ready to flirt with men and get paid for it?" Her face lit with a sudden thought. "We really *are* women of ill repute by Cross' standards, aren't we?"

I snorted and shouldered my purse. "Ready to deal with Shepard?"

"What's to deal with? The man's just as in love with you as Cross."

"And he's about to be as *un*-in-love with you."

She frowned as she followed me out to the car.

"Why?"

I held up my cut hand to remind her, and she made a face.

"Why can't I have an overprotective hunk hovering over me?"

"Pfft. At the first sign of attachment, you boot them."

She slid into her seat. "I'm too young to settle down. I'm not done sampling the selections yet."

We both knew it had nothing to do with her age and everything to do with her lifestyle. She feared having yet another person worrying about her treasure hunting who might try to hold her back from what she loved.

Something told me Anchor could give Vena a run for her money, though. He was the kind of guy she fell hard for and wasn't overbearing. At least, not that I'd seen. He always kept his cool and discreetly asked if I wanted him instead of jumping in without invitation.

If anyone could take Vena off the market, I'd bet it'd be him.

CHAPTER FIFTEEN

WE MADE IT TO BLUR WELL BEFORE THE START OF OUR SHIFT AND stowed our things in the lockers. Neither of us clocked in, though.

"Come with me," I said, grabbing Vena's arm.

"Where?"

"Shepard is going to have questions, and you're going to confirm it was an accident. He's not going to believe I'm unlucky enough to have two injuries in a row."

She rolled her eyes. "Or he can stop playing the alpha man role and see that it's just a boo-boo."

I pulled her with me, only pausing long enough for her to wink at Anchor and for his cheeks to flush under her pointed gaze. Maybe he wouldn't survive with Vena after all.

When we reached Shepard's office, I lifted my hand to knock on the closed door. Inside, I heard someone say, "I'm sorry. It won't happen again."

I hesitated.

"Three murders under our watch," Shepard growled. "If

you're late for rounds again, you'll be out. It's our responsibility to keep Blur and everyone here safe. Go!"

Gunther opened the door and paused when he saw us. I quickly dropped my hand to my side.

"Everly, come in," Shepard said.

I awkwardly switched places with Gunther as he made his retreat. Shepard's furrowed brows smoothed until I lifted my hand and showed him my taped palm.

"Another accident?" he asked slowly.

I pulled Vena inside. "She can verify it."

Shepard eyed Vena as she nodded.

"She needs bubble wrap and a change in careers. A baker is obviously going to be too dangerous for her. So, um, did I hear right? Another person died?"

I almost cringed at Vena's obvious change in topics. But Shepard didn't even bat an eye at it. He let out a deep sigh and nodded.

"Three nights in a row. I'm sending Anchor home to stay with you again tonight."

"Uh, we'll be fine," I quickly said, knowing Cross wouldn't like Anchor on the couch for a second night.

Shepard stood and walked around his desk, stopping in front of me. He leaned in and inhaled slowly.

"Why do you smell like vampire, Everly?"

"What?" Eyes wide, I glanced at Vena for help.

"Huh," she said with a frown. "Keen sense of smell." She lifted a finger. "Aversion to vampires." She lifted a second one. "Strong. Tends to stick to . . . packs." She added a third and fourth finger as she raised a brow at Shepard. "Working here just got a whole lot more interesting."

Shepard glanced at me nervously.

"She'll be a pest about it, but she won't say anything," I said.

He leaned against the desk and tilted his head at me. "And you?"

"I've kept quiet this long."

"You knew?" he asked at the same time as Vena.

"I suspected but chose to remain ignorant until I couldn't anymore," I said.

"And you're not afraid?" he asked.

I shook my head. "As you said, everyone here is like family."

He held my gaze for a long moment. I couldn't tell if he was okay with me acknowledging him as werewolf and as family.

"Okay," he said finally. "Now tell me why you smell like—"

"Boss!" Doc shouted from the VIP lounge. "We got one!"

Shepard went from a relaxed lean against his desk to out the door.

"Got one what?" Vena asked, already running to follow.

I raced after them down the stairs and out to the back parking lot. Arriving winded and with a side cramp, I watched Shepard join Anchor and Buzz.

"Where?" Shepard demanded.

"It was a block away. I tracked the scent as far as I could," Buzz said. "But I only got this thing hiding in the garbage."

In his hands was a black cat who looked as though it was grinning.

"Does that cat look familiar?" Vena whispered to me.

It *did* look familiar. What were the chances that the cat from Juicy would show up where we worked?

I shared an uneasy glance with Vena as the gate to the parking lot opened and Sierra pulled in. Her gaze passed over everyone standing in the lot as she parked in her usual spot.

"Well, this is new," she said, exiting the car. "I didn't think I was worthy of getting an escort to and from my car."

Her gaze flicked to the cat Buzz was still holding by the scruff of its neck. She had her phone out and snapped a picture.

"With all the humans dying around here, adding animal cruelty to the list seems a bit much." She gave Buzz an angry look. "I happen to like cats. Wonder what your patrons would think about this."

She waggled her phone, showing the image of Buzz holding the cat, with the Blur building visible in the background. I couldn't believe the size of her lady balls.

Buzz immediately set the cat down, and it bolted, hiding under Sierra's car.

"It's not abuse, Sierra," Shepard said. "Buzz pulled the cat out of the garbage. And he's allergic. He wouldn't be able to work his shift if he cuddled up to it now, would he?" Shepard crossed his arms. "Make sure you know what you're talking about before you try to threaten me. And that's your last strike. Next one, you're out of here. Am I clear?"

She looked a little sick as she put her phone away.

"Crystal."

"Inside, ladies. As Sierra pointed out, it's not safe out here."

I stood back, letting her go first, and glanced back at the cat. It was watching us all with an avid interest that seemed very un-cat-like.

Shepard motioned for us to follow him while Sierra put away her things. Back in Shepard's office, he asked Vena and me to take a seat.

"There's a lot going on right now," he said, moving to the glass wall that overlooked the main floor. He clasped his hands behind his back, stretching his button-up shirt over his broad shoulders.

"People are dying, and the police can't do a thing about the killer." He turned to look at us. "But my pack can. I'm asking for your discretion so we can do what we do best."

"And what's that?" Vena asked.

"Protect the places we call home and the people who live there against vampires."

"I appreciate the public service," Vena said.

Shepard gave her a hard stare.

"Seriously, I'm not going to say anything to anyone," she said. "But I'm probably going to have some questions. Mind if I ask Anchor tonight?"

He lifted a hand to rub over his mouth. I couldn't tell if he was trying to hide a smile or a frown.

"I'll let Anchor know you're curious. You should know, Vena. My kind doesn't do casual relationships well."

Her smirk vanished.

"I will absolutely keep that in mind. Thanks for the warning."

He nodded and looked at me.

"You have nothing to worry about from me," I reiterated. "I meant what I said. You're like family to me."

A slight frown pulled at his brows before quickly disappearing.

"Then maybe you can help me understand why you smell like something we've sworn to kill?"

"Uh…"

Vena came to my rescue.

"We're trying to save up for the next semester and heard there might be daytime openings at Juicy," Vena said. "For servers, not strippers. But when we got there, this creepy guy locked us in a room filled with syringes and tubes. You know… the kind for taking blood.

"Everly cut herself when we were trying to jimmy the door

with my knife, which is why she's wearing a new bandage. Seriously, pure accident. Don't trust her with sharp objects.

"Anyway, when we got out, everyone in Juicy was already dead. But, I think that syringe room is why she smells like a vampire."

Shepard's arms fell loosely to his sides, and he stared at both of us for a long minute. "You got locked into a room at a strip club, and everyone was dead when you got out?"

"We didn't kill them. Promise. Everly hyperventilates at the sight of blood. Not a murderer bone in her body," Vena said.

Shepard leveled her with an unamused gaze before yelling for Anchor. I jumped. Shepard glanced at me, his expression bordering on anger. For the first time, it felt like it might be directed at me.

Anchor appeared in the doorway and glanced questioningly at us.

"Take Buzz and go to Juicy," Shepard said. "It might be a vampire den. I want as much info as you can get before we open tonight."

Anchor gave a nod and retreated. Shepard's gaze remained on the empty doorway for several seconds. After a deep, calming breath, he looked at us again.

"Can you two stay out of trouble until we open?" Shepard asked.

I nodded quickly, knowing any sarcastic comment from Vena might push Shepard over the edge. Even now, the veins along his neck throbbed.

"Since you need extra work, clock in and help Gunther and Griz in the kitchen, or clean the main areas. Some of the chrome work needs polishing."

"No problem," I said, taking Vena with me as I escaped from the office.

"Since Sierra's early, make sure she has something to do, too," Shepard called after us.

As we headed downstairs, I whispered, "Do you think the bodies are still at Juicy?"

"Probably not. If the house mother is still alive, she'd probably send out for a cleaning crew. It's bad business to keep bodies lying around."

We fell quiet for a beat, likely both thinking of the bloody aftermath.

Vena hadn't said anything after we escaped Juicy, but she had to know that her lead on Miles might be among the dead. Hell, *Miles* might be among the dead as well. I rubbed my stomach as it twisted in uncertainty.

"I hope Anchor and Buzz will be okay going there."

"You're afraid for the big, strong werewolves?" Vena asked.

"Of course I am." After seeing how much damage Cross had done, I feared what would happen to Buzz and Anchor if they ran into a vampire.

We headed into the kitchen to find Sierra. We found her leaning against a wall, her thumbs typing madly on her phone.

"Shepard wants us to clock in and either start cleaning in the main room or help in the kitchen."

Sierra paused her typing to glare at me. "Where will you be?"

"Probably in the main room."

"Then I'll help Gunther. What's with Anchor and Buzz leaving so quickly?"

I shrugged. "Shepard needed something."

Sierra raised a brow and resumed typing. I wasn't about to babysit her to make sure she helped Gunther. If she wanted to press her luck with Shepard, she was on her own.

Grabbing the polish and rags, Vena and I went to the bar

area. We spent our time cleaning until Anchor and Buzz returned. They veered past us and went straight up to Shepard's office.

"Ev, I think some chrome up there needs to be polished." Vena took her rag and jogged up the stairs.

So that she didn't bust her way into the office, I followed. I had to admit that I was curious to know what happened. Neither man was bloody, but both wore a strained expression.

The office door was closed, and Vena busied herself by lightly polishing a nameplate hung on the wall nearby.

I stayed in the VIP area, peeking at Vena as she paused to lean her head toward the door.

After a few minutes, Vena scrambled out of the hall. The door opened behind her, and Shepard and the others walked out. He took one look at us and raised a brow as we polished a potted fern.

"If you're going to eavesdrop, have a better cover."

"Well?" Vena asked. "What happened? What did you find?"

Her tone told me she was hoping for news that might lead to her brother.

"That you were out of your depth, and I don't know how you got out of there alive. It wasn't just a vampire den. That room in back, the one they kept you in, had more than transfusion supplies and tourniquets. There was also a refrigerator filled with stored blood."

A full-body tremor ran through him, and he took a deep breath.

"While I'm grateful we're aware of this change in their feeding habits, I'm not happy how we came by this information."

"That doesn't make any sense," Vena said, and I knew she

was thinking about how a vampire den would be related to Miles.

"Which part?" Shepard demanded angrily. "The part where you and Everly almost died by whatever killed everything in there, or the part where vampires are now smart enough that they would have kept you and Everly alive indefinitely as donors? Do you understand what kind of hellish existence that would have been? You were this close–" He held up his thumb and index finger indicating less than an inch.

"Shepard," Anchor said softly.

Did he think Shepard was saying too much? Because I didn't think he was saying enough.

"Hellish existence?" I questioned before I could stop myself. "I thought vampires created a bond with their donors."

Shepard shook his head at me. "No. Historically, vampires leave a trail of bodies in their wake. That's what made an infestation easier to spot. This level of forethought makes our job harder."

"Were there donors there?" Fear and worry painted Vena's face.

"Yeah. The dead dancers and guards you saw when you left. Based on the marks we found on their bodies, they had been there for a while."

I could see Vena's mind racing. She didn't disappoint with the questions that poured out of her mouth.

"You said den. Does that mean there was more than one vampire there? Did you kill them?"

"There were none there," Anchor said. "I could smell at least a dozen, but most of those were older. Three scents were fresh."

A dozen vampires roaming around D.C. didn't sound like a good thing.

"What now?" I asked.

"Now you get ready for your shift and forget that you ever went to that place. And you are never going back again. Am I clear? If you need more money, don't look for another job. Come to me. I take care of my own."

I nodded, more than ready for this conversation to be over so I could forget this day ever happened.

"What about Juicy?" Vena asked. "Are you going to let them keep doing business as usual?"

"No. We'll take care of it tonight. It's nothing you need to worry about."

Vena's brows went up, and she glanced at me. "Was that a 'don't worry your pretty little head about anything' talk down?"

I grabbed her by the arm.

"We'll stay out of it. Thank you, Shepard," I said in a rush as I pulled her toward the stairs.

"Do I look like I'm incapable?" she asked me.

"You did get us locked in a blood farm disguised as a night club, so yeah. Maybe you do," I said in a hissed whisper as we descended the stairs. "We're lucky all we got was a condescending tone."

I stopped us at the bottom and turned toward her.

"You know that too, don't you?" I demanded.

Her expression fell, and she pulled me into a hug.

"I am sorry, Ev. Really. I didn't mean for any of this to happen."

I hugged her back. "I know. Just...no more risks, okay? We're no use to anyone locked in a room or drained of blood."

"Okay. You're right."

She stepped back from me and grinned a little. "But not everything today was a loss. Some good came out of it. Books, bath towels, and bras. Am I right?"

I snorted, understanding her references all too well. And also, thanks to our stunt at the club, we officially had Cross' help.

Once the shift began, Vena and I settled into a routine. Vena didn't need more training, so we split my section. While that meant I didn't get as much money at the end of the night, I was still content that she was safe with me at Blur.

Shepard had assigned us upper stage left, right by the kitchens and overwatched by his office above. It was also the farthest section from Anchor, which meant Vena had a harder time flirting with him. Even across a crowded nightclub, though, when she bent down to pick up a fork off the ground, Anchor's full blush had her grinning.

"Stop that!" I whispered as she winked at him. "You heard what Shepard said. Anchor doesn't do casual."

"I know. But I can't help it. He's so damn cute when he does that."

"Well, start helping it. Because Anchor's coming home with us again."

As we cleaned our section for the night, I glanced over to find Sierra walking out from the kitchen. Her phone was in her hands as she typed on it.

"How has she not been fired yet?" Vena asked. "I swear that's the fifth time I've seen her on her phone."

"I don't know. But I'm not bringing it up. Shepard's been cranky all night."

If Vena felt guilty over the part she played in Shepard's mood, she didn't show it. Not that I expected her to.

With the two of us working together, we finished our clean-up quickly. Anchor was at the door, waiting for us when we clocked out.

This time, he had a backpack with him. He slung it over his shoulder as he walked us to the car.

"I'll be right behind you," he said. "Wait for me before you go into the house."

Vena smirked. "I hate waiting. But I'll make an exception for you."

I stifled an eye roll as I got into the car and started it. Anchor waited until our doors were locked before he hopped into his truck.

"What if Cross is at home?" I asked once we were on the road and knew Anchor wouldn't hear.

"Then we'll see a vampire and werewolf pissing match."

"I'm serious. I don't want either of them to get hurt."

Vena laughed. "Only you would be concerned about a vampire and werewolf getting hurt. But don't worry. Cross is cautious. He won't be chilling on our couch and downing potato chips."

I supposed that was true. But I was still nervous.

By the time we arrived at the house, my hands were strangling the steering wheel.

Anchor parked his truck behind us and hopped out with his bag. I rolled down my window when he walked toward my side of the car.

"Let me check the house first."

I nodded, and we watched him walk to the house. Vena frowned with me as he unlocked the door.

"How does he have a key?" she asked.

"He installed the lock. Maybe he kept a spare, knowing he was going to be on babysitting duty?"

"Locks come with two keys. I have one and–" She gave me a look, still not happy Cross had the other. "I'm not sure how I feel about my coworker having a key. Now if he were my side piece, I wouldn't mind so much."

"Please stop talking," I said.

She grinned at me.

Anchor waved us into the house a moment later.

As Vena and I headed inside, I was both relieved and let down that Cross wasn't there, which made me pause. Since when did I miss him?

Anchor had dropped his bag near the couch and was already double-checking that the windows were locked when I shut the door behind us.

Part of the kitchen curtain had been jostled to the side. As I shifted it back into place, movement beyond the tracks caught my attention.

Cross stood in the shadows near the rail line, his hands tucked into the pockets of his relaxed jeans. The dark color of his t-shirt made him blend even more with the background but didn't hide the chiseled expanse of his chest. His eyes reflected a hint of light as he nodded at me.

I started to smile in return until he suddenly disappeared.

"What has you smiling like that?" Anchor asked from nearby. "I think that's the first real smile I've ever seen."

My brows rose, and I turned to face him.

"What do you mean? I'm smiling all the time at work."

"Right. All the time. That's your work smile. Your 'here's another drink, sir' smile. That's not the same smile you had right now."

"Wow, Anchor," Vena said, emerging from her bedroom. "That's a lot of personal detail there. Makes a girl wonder why you've been paying her best friend any level of attention. Do you have feelings for Everly?"

Heat flooded my face, and I glared at her. "Vena, cut it out."

"No, it's okay," Anchor said, looking surprisingly

collected. "I pay attention because it's my job to make sure Everly is safe. I notice every little detail so I know if she's distressed and needs my help. Her scent. Her body language. The words she uses. I don't only use my eyes, ears, and nose. I use my brain, Vena, to know when I'm needed and when I'm not."

The steady way he held her gaze for that last line had her looking away uncomfortably.

"So, no personal interest then?" she asked.

"There's absolutely interest," he said before clearing his throat. "Everly is like my sister. Mine to protect but not to control."

"You like control?" Vena asked.

"Nope! Stop. We are not going to treat Everly like she isn't in the room," I said, speaking of myself in the third person to make a point.

I turned to Anchor and jabbed a finger at him. "Do not tell her you have control issues. She'll try handcuffing you at some point just to test it."

I started for my bedroom.

"You're both going to drive me insane. And, Vena, I'm officially instating the roommate clause."

The roommate clause was a pact Vena and I had made when we'd first moved in together. On any given night, when evoked, there was nothing but silence from the other roommate. No shenanigans. No drinking and watching *The Other House* at full blast after a failed date (that one was me) or knife throwing at a target setup with a range buzzer (that one was Vena). Nothing but silence.

"Aw! Ev, don't–"

"Goodnight!" I slammed my door on her objections and stripped out of my work clothes, safe in the knowledge that I would *not* wake up to the sounds of those two going at it like rabbits.

After changing into my pajamas, I ducked into the bathroom to wash my face. Being a good hostess, I checked on Anchor one last time once I was done.

"Sorry about that," he said quietly from his place on the couch. "She has a way of getting under my skin."

I snorted.

"She has that ability with a lot of people." I gave him a sad smile. "Just protect your heart, Anchor. I've never had a big brother and wouldn't mind keeping you around."

He flashed a smile at me.

"I'll do my best. Night."

"Night."

It felt like I'd barely closed my eyes when I heard a light tap on my partially closed door.

"Everly? You awake?" Anchor whispered.

I groaned and rolled to my back. The sun was barely starting to brighten the sky beyond my curtain.

"No," I mumbled. "Go away."

He chuckled. "I'm heading out. You should be safe now. Call if you need anything, okay?"

I grunted at him. He laughed again, and I heard the front door close a few seconds later.

Dreams of dwarves with big wallets dedicated to tipping filled my mind, and I happily sank into a deeper sleep.

The next disturbance only tickled at my consciousness until I heard Vena's softly spoken threat.

"If she doesn't kill you, I will. Get out of her bed."

"Go away, Vena," Cross murmured nearby. "Your presence is neither required nor wanted."

"You can't even give an insult without sounding like there's a stick up your ass. Let me swap that stick for a stake, m-kay?"

"You want to impale my ass with a stake? You are a deeply troubled woman."

Vena sputtered, and I grudgingly opened my eyes to prevent Cross' murder.

CHAPTER SIXTEEN

V<small>ENA GLARED FROM MY BEDROOM DOOR. B</small>UT<small> SHE WASN'T GLARING</small> at me.

Turning my head, I blinked at an up-close view of Cross' perfectly sculpted face only inches from mine. He lay on his side, watching me sleep.

His soft brown gaze swept over my face. Was it me, or was there a flicker of affection in their depths? If so, I wasn't sure what I'd done to warrant it...or his presence stretched out beside me.

"Why are you in my bed?" I asked calmly.

He frowned slightly, any hint of affection disappearing.

"It's a lot more comfortable than where I've been sleeping. But don't worry. I'm not here to despoil your womanhood. We're due at the pawnshop soon, and we need to have a serious discussion about the club in which you two nearly died."

"Fine, but I'm getting coffee first," I said as I sat up. "And a shower."

I crawled over him to get out of bed and saw his eyes

darken. Swallowing hard, I scrambled off and tried to deny my awareness of how his body had felt underneath mine.

"Vena, you're on coffee duty," I said as I fled to the bathroom without a backward glance.

Once I closed the door, I heard their squabbling begin again. Thankfully, the shower drowned out most of what they said.

I wasn't sure what to think about waking up with Cross in my bed. Hell, I still wasn't sure what to think about *Cross.* Shepard said vampires were murderers. But then again, Grandpa Barnaby's book said werewolves were murderers, too. I preferred to form an opinion of a person based on how they acted. And both Shepard and Cross acted like decent people. A little rigid about some things, sure, but still both decent.

Who cared what they were? I knew Shepard was a werewolf and was willing to work for him. Why should I treat Cross any differently because he was a vampire?

Or was I telling myself this because I found Cross extremely good-looking and wanted to justify my attraction to a person who fed on blood to live?

Making a face at my thoughts, I stuck my head under the spray to rinse and not think.

I was toweling off when I heard the doorbell ring. Curious about who would be at our door so early, I wrapped myself in the towel and crept into the dining room to peek around the corner.

A woman who looked like my doppelganger, from the shoulder-length blonde hair to the grey eyes and generous curves, stood in the living room right inside the door. The sultry smile on her lips was aimed at Cross, who stood beside her.

From her place by the couch, Vena crossed her arms and glared at the pair.

"Who are you?" she asked.

"I'm a gift and peace offering," the woman said to Cross. "Yours to feed upon whenever you wish."

"To feed upon?" Vena demanded, echoing my shock. "What the hell, Cross? Did you order delivery?"

"I don't know this woman," he said, not looking away from the blonde. "Who sent you?"

"My employer," the woman said.

"Who is your employer?" Vena asked.

Before the woman could respond, Cross escorted her out the door. "Tell your employer I'm not interested." He closed the door in her face.

"Why in the hell did that peace offering look like Everly?" Vena asked.

"That's what I was going to ask," I said, stepping into the dining room so they could both see me.

Cross' gaze silently raked over me. When he took a step in my direction, I fought the urge to retreat a step and lost. Then I felt guilty when I saw he meant to go to the couch, not me. He tugged at the jean material on his legs as he sat.

"We might as well speak of the club now." He glanced at my towel-wrapped body again. "Unless you'd like to dress, Everly."

I tucked the towel tighter under my arm and boldly moved forward to perch on the arm of the couch.

"No. I want to know what's going on and why self-proclaimed food that looked way too much like me showed up on our doorstep. It seems to me that someone knows who you're hanging around with. Am I in more danger because of you? Because frankly, Vena's tendency to go off half-cocked already fills my danger quota."

Cross looked uncomfortable, and Vena gave me an apologetic, guilty look.

"I promise I will make these last few days up to you as soon as we find Miles," Vena said.

Cross sighed. "As I said before, you are out of your leagues. You're lucky to be alive. When I left here yesterday, I returned to the club to investigate further and came across the scent of an old acquaintance. She's not someone you want to cross."

"She?" Vena asked.

"Did you believe all vampires were male?" he asked.

"Of course not. But exactly what kind of an acquaintance was she?"

"One that I have no desire to talk about."

Vena's expression lit with interest. "An old lover?"

Cross narrowed his eyes at her. "Call her what you wish, but I'm serious when I say you don't want to provoke her. She has a long memory. So if you wish not to have her as an enemy for the rest of your mortal life, I suggest staying away from the club."

"What about my brother?" Vena asked.

"We'll have to find him a different way. It is not worth risking Everly's life by forcing the issue at the club."

"Only Everly's life?" Vena asked.

He ignored her. "Regardless of my desire for you to avoid my old acquaintance, the club would still be a dead end. Your werewolf friends saw to that yesterday when they ensured it would not open for business again in the near future." Cross inhaled deeply and frowned. "I hate the scent of the wolves on you."

"I just showered."

"It's probably the couch," Vena said helpfully. "Give your backside a little wiggle to really work it in." Her smirk died quickly. "Wait, is Anchor going to be able to smell that you were on the couch after he was on the couch?"

It was Cross' turn to smirk. "Perhaps you have far too many male callers."

"First, no one uses the term 'callers' anymore. Second, he–"

"Hold up," I said, stopping a fight before it could start. "Can we focus on the bigger issue here? Why would an old acquaintance you just warned us to stay away from send you a feeder that looks exactly like me to my door and call it a peace offering *after* werewolves destroyed their club?"

Cross sighed and pinched the bridge of his nose.

"There are several possible scenarios. The first, and most likely, is that she sensed me when I woke and has been following me. Sending the feeder was to gain information and test my bond with you.

"The second, less likely option is that she realized you belonged to me after I killed everyone in the establishment and sent the feeder as a sincere apology. The club had cameras that might have recorded me there.

"The third and least likely option is that she somehow managed to taste your blood before the werewolves destroyed the club and sensed my bond with you. Since she is unable to walk in daylight like I am, that is highly improbable."

I briefly thought of the blood smeared on the back of the door Cross had ripped off its hinges. Nope, not going there.

"Okay, that doesn't answer either of my questions. Why me, and am I in danger?"

"She knows me well, Everly. I often have many feeders to prevent weakening any of them, but I only stay close to my favorites. I won't let anything happen to you. You have my vow."

My thoughts almost snagged on the fact that he considered me his favorite. But I heard the deeper message too, thankfully.

His promise to keep me safe meant I was in danger.

"Wait, are you saying Everly is your flavor of the month?" Vena asked, sounding a little offended.

"Based on my close interactions with Everly, that's what my acquaintance would believe. Which is also why she provided another woman who looks very similar to Everly. Meanwhile, the three of us understand that this is a business relationship. As such, I believe it's time for Everly to dress and for us to be on our way to our meeting. Wouldn't you agree, Everly?"

I nodded but didn't move.

"How much danger am I in now that some other vampire knows about me?"

"None so long as you stay away from the places you do not belong."

"Such as?" Vena pressed.

"Such as feeder dens. Much has changed since I was last awake. My kind used to feed and kill. A few like me grew smarter and realized that, if we wanted to remain hidden and thrive, we needed a better way. I stopped killing centuries before I chose to sleep."

"Damn. Way to clarify that it wasn't a choice out of some growth of consciousness."

I shot Vena a warning look.

"It would seem the rest of my kind came to the same conclusion and started gathering feeders of their own. I believe they...shared them."

The complete disgust in his tone almost made me smile.

"Orphia knows I don't share. She will stay away from you so long as you do not place yourself directly in her path. Even then, she may hesitate." As he spoke, he ran his thumb over the ring on his first finger thoughtfully.

"She better stay away, or I'm holding you responsible," Vena said before looking at me. "Your coffee is in the kitchen when you're ready. Extra whipped cream and chocolate shavings on top. After the pawn shop, we need to get Cross a phone so he can text you instead of slinking into your bed at dawn."

"I did not slink; I let myself in through your front door."

I left them to bicker and hurried to dress so I could enjoy my Vena-venti before the whipped cream melted.

Fifteen minutes later, we were all on the way to the pawn shop.

Like the previous time, the door was locked, and we had to wait for Stan. Unlike the last time, he wasn't alone. He led us to a back room where Mr. Davies was seated at a scuffed conference table.

"Mr. Cross," Mr. Davies said, standing to offer his hand. "It's great to meet you in person."

"The pleasure is mine." Cross shook his hand, releasing it quickly. Davies wasn't offended. He turned to greet both Vena and me politely. Before I could take Mr. Davies' hand, Cross stepped between us.

"I apologize, but I'm a bit pressed for time. I thought this would be a simple exchange and made arrangements accordingly."

"Of course," Mr. Davies said. "Please. Sit. We can start on the paperwork while I examine the coin in person."

Cross slid his hand into his right pocket and withdrew the coin between his first two fingers. Davies' eyes lit up, and he indicated to set the coin on the soft cloth in front of his chair. A scale and a magnifying glass sat next to it.

"Where did you say you got this?" Davies asked, picking up the magnifying glass.

"It's an heirloom, kept by my line for centuries."

"Amazing. The markings are correct." He transferred the coin to the scale and watched the numbers. "Correct weight, too. I sent the picture to a friend of mine. She said it's authentic if the weight checks out. Do you agree to our negotiated price of two point four million?"

"I agree."

Davies pulled out his phone as Stan started filling out a form.

"Name?" Stan asked.

"I would prefer to remain anonymous," Cross said smoothly. "It prevents unwanted inquiries regarding other antiquities I might have in the family home."

Stan glanced at Davies.

"Fair enough," Davies said. "Where should I wire the money?"

I was surprised he was so willing after the quick examination. Then again, we were in a pawn shop.

Cross glanced at me.

"Um. Can you wire to a personal account?" I asked.

"Of course."

"Do I need to let my bank know it's coming? Honestly, I've never had more than ten thousand in there. There's not some kind of cap, is there? There's always those warnings on bank sites about being insured up to a certain limit."

Davies smiled at me. "You'll be fine. Personally, I wouldn't keep it there. Make your money work for you and invest."

"Great advice. We'll deal with that later," Vena said, nudging me.

Once I gave Davies my information, he sent a text.

"It will take a few minutes for the wire to go through. My assistant is taking care of the matter now."

My balance updated five minutes later, and I nearly passed out seeing all those zeros.

"Got it," I said faintly.

He slipped the coin into a protective pouch and placed it in his briefcase.

"It was a pleasure doing business with you. Let me know if you have any other family treasure you want to part with."

"I will," Cross said. "Thank you."

Vena had a very pronounced bounce to her step as we left the shop.

"Please tell me we're going to do something fun now. We should buy you a car."

"Not until he can legally drive." I glanced at the time. "Let's start with something more practical. We have some time to buy you clothes if you want, Cross."

Vena frowned. "Clothes shopping? That's not fun. I want to go home and research before our shift, but I don't want to leave you with Cross. He crawled into bed with you like he belonged there."

"You know I can hear you, right?" Cross said dryly.

Vena arched a brow at him.

"And he saved our asses yesterday, Vena. Don't forget that he's had plenty of opportunities to bite us and hasn't. Considering the trouble finding us lately, I think he's as safe as it's going to get. Anyway, we're in public."

"So was the grocery store employee before Cross lured him away."

I sighed. "Cross, do you promise not to lure me away?"

"I promise not to lure you in any way...today." His expression was a combination of playfulness and something with a bit more steam.

My eyes went wide, and he grinned.

"See?" Vena said. "Flavor of the month."

"I'll be fine," I said. "Today."

He chuckled low, and Vena tsked but then nodded.

"I'll hire a ride home. But I want regular check-ins." She leaned in to whisper, "And pick up a new TV while you're out. He owes us that much."

"Did you forget the part where he saved our lives?"

"Fine. We can keep watching *The Other House* on our poverty TV. But don't complain when it does its twitchy thing again."

"I promise I won't."

Once Vena hired her ride, Cross and I walked to my car.

"What kind of clothes do you want?"

"Not these," he said, looking down at his T-shirt and jeans. "I prefer a finer cut of luxury linens."

"Just how rich were you?"

"Rich enough."

I supposed that meant he had lived like a king. He would again, based on the value of all the coins he had tucked in his pocket.

Driving a few miles to a store that had an onsite tailor, I parked and asked, "Do you want me to get you a phone while you look for clothes?"

"I prefer you by my side, Everly."

"Okay. Then clothes first and a phone later."

We walked in and were immediately given the once over by a snooty salesman. Based on his tepid hello, we obviously didn't look like his normal clientele.

"Please feel free to browse the rack. Clearance items are in back."

"Clearance?" Cross asked.

"He means the stuff that's on sale."

"Why would I care if it's in the back?" Cross asked.

I shushed him and pulled him away from the salesman's judgmental stare.

Cross glanced at a few shirts. "They have the scent of other men on them."

"People are allowed to try them on before they buy."

He crinkled his nose. "It's distasteful."

"Stop being a snob and try something. But keep in mind that nearly everything in this store will have to be dry cleaned." Before he could ask what that meant, I pointed to a mannequin wearing a crisp suit. "What about something like that?"

"I admire the cut. And…" He sniffed it. "It hasn't been worn yet. It could work."

I paused my browsing to look at him. This wasn't the first time his nose had provided him with useful information. He'd smelled Anchor. He'd smelled his ex-girlfriend. Now, he was sorting through clothes.

"Just how powerful is your sense of smell?"

"Powerful enough to know who you've been around. Who touches you. I can smell if you are bleeding or on your womanly flow."

I snorted while he continued, "I know the shampoo and body wash you use. Your feminine products."

I held up my hand to stop him. "I get it. So, if I brought you somewhere, would you also be able to tell me what type of creatures had been there last?"

"If the scents aren't too old, perhaps."

Absently lifting my hand to wave over the salesman, I considered what Cross might find at Miles' apartment. Knowing the species that took Miles would help narrow down the list.

"Can I help you?" the salesman said again.

"My friend would like to try on a suit, please. And these shirts." I indicated the two that Cross had selected.

"What type of suit are you looking for?" the salesman asked Cross.

"Something comfortable, not like these coarse jeans."

The distaste on Cross' face was almost comical, but it was like his words had touched the salesman's soul.

The guy smiled at Cross and indicated another section of the store. This one had comfy-looking chairs and a half-body mannequin.

"I'm certain we can fit you with the perfect suit. Come this way."

Cross and I were seated and sipping tea within minutes while the salesman laid out some cloth swatches for Cross to feel.

"Considering your coloring, I kept with the blues."

Cross touched several but went back to a deep blue one.

"What do you think of this one, Everly?"

I glanced from the cloth to him.

"I think it's going to look great on you. But it might be a bit dressy for everyday wear."

The salesman was already shaking his head. "Not in the capitol."

"Right. He'll fit in where the businessmen are, but what about nightclubs and the grocery store?"

The salesman gave Cross a considering look. "I think I have the perfect solution."

It took another hour for the guy to find Cross the right "casual" pants, several shirt-and-tie options that Cross liked, and measurements for two suits. The suits wouldn't be ready for a week, and the pants would need to be altered but would be ready the next day. However, Cross could take home the shirts and ties.

The price tag for all of that made my heart hurt. The total

equaled three months of busting my butt at Blur. However, since I would be using Cross' money, I handed over my credit card, willing to benefit from the reward points his purchase would earn me.

"Let's drop off this bag in my car, and we can get a phone," I said as we left the store.

"We've done enough shopping today. Let's revisit the phone tomorrow."

I agreed. After the early wake-up and the extensive shopping, I was exhausted. Plus, it meant more time alone with Cross and his keen sense of smell. While Vena might agree to Cross sniffing out Miles' apartment, she'd also get her hopes up. And I didn't want to do that to her.

As I drove to the apartment, I distracted Cross from our route change with some not-so-idle chit-chat.

"So, do I have to worry about your ex sending more feeders to our house?"

"Leave her to me."

"She must still love you since she sent you an actual human." I wanted to know what level of obsessiveness I was dealing with in his stalker ex.

"She does not love. Vampires are proprietary. She wants what she used to have."

Okay. Definitely code-red stalker level.

I glanced at Cross, wondering how he felt about her. He sounded detached right then, but was it because he didn't care or because he'd anticipated his ex would send him a feeder?

And if she didn't love, why had she been his lover at one point? Or did he leave her because he'd found out she couldn't love? Could Cross love?

I had a lot of questions that I was too chicken to ask. Mostly, I didn't want to know the answers. Cross was growing on me.

When I parked in front of Miles' apartment, I scanned the area for the fairy I had "accidentally" whacked.

"Where are we?" Cross asked.

"Vena's brother lives here. You don't want Vena to pull me into more danger, which I agree with, by the way, and the only way to do that is to figure out what happened to her brother. With your sharp sense of smell, I'm hoping you'll look around and pick up a scent."

"I'm not a dog. You have half a dozen mutts at Blur you could choose from."

"Would you rather I ask them?" I asked, a little surprised given his previous distaste.

He opened the door. "No."

Fighting not to grin at his sulky answer and quick exit, I got out with him. We walked the path to Miles' door, and like the last time, that damn fairy flew out at me from the bushes. I screeched and stepped behind Cross.

Using him as a shield, I clung to the back of the t-shirt he still wore.

"It's a blue-winged rodent." The amusement in Cross' tone wasn't lost on me. "Don't tell me you're afraid of it."

"One tried to kill me."

"I'd like to hear that story after we're done here. Perhaps over lunch?"

I felt him wave an arm at the fairy and waited for the movement to stop before I peeked around him.

"You are quite adorable, Everly," Cross said, twisting to look back at me. "I do wish I would have been awake when you realized you fell into a fairy den."

"No, you don't. It wasn't pretty." I straightened away from him and smoothed out the wrinkles I'd made in his shirt. He held still for me, and I understood why when I looked up and caught his black-eyed stare.

"Sorry," I mumbled, pulling out the key I still had for Miles' door.

As soon as we entered, Cross said, "The strongest scent is most likely the brother."

Heading to the kitchen, he stopped at the table that was still covered in research on vampires and picked up the vampire propaganda pamphlet.

"Amusing."

He dropped it back down and looked at some of the other research.

"Why was he researching vampires?"

"After we realized what we'd done by taking the ring, we panicked. I think he was trying to find a way to help."

"None of these would be helpful."

"We know."

He glanced at me. "Besides the vampire you mistakenly woke, are there any other creatures who might be looking for you, Everly?"

"Me? No. Well, maybe if the people who took Miles know we have the book."

"Then I will find them." He looked over to the refrigerator. "An unpleasant odor lingers here."

He opened the refrigerator and pulled out a half-eaten, half-mushed cake.

"Don't eat that," I said, rushing toward him.

He lifted it to his nose, sniffed, and grimaced.

"I smell you on it and something quite disturbing. Why would you eat cake made with sheep scrotum?"

I made a sad face, crossed my arms, and frowned at him. "I'm feeling very judged right now by a guy who eats people."

"Not people. Only their blood." He put the cake back where

he found it. "You seem to have a love for any type of confectionery."

"No, not any kind. I prefer the normal kind. The sheep scrotum was a horrible surprise that I'm probably going to have nightmares about for years."

Cross smiled slightly.

"My poor Everly. That will not do."

He inhaled deeply again, turning his attention to the rest of the apartment.

"There are other scents there. Older. Harder to distinguish. But there's a definite feminine one that is not you or Vena." He sniffed again and slowly walked to Miles' open bedroom door.

"Perfume," Cross said, going to the bed and leaning in. "Human."

I bit my lip at the implication. A human woman's scent concentrated on Miles' bed meant one thing. A booty call.

"That troubles you?" Cross asked, catching my disappointment.

"I just wish we'd found something. An actual lead."

Cross arched a brow at me.

"And the scent of a human female isn't a lead?"

"As a kidnapper? No. As a secret girlfriend that's going to upset Vena? Yes."

"Vena led me to believe that she and her brother didn't keep secrets."

"I mean, they don't usually."

"Then why would you think he would keep a love interest secret from her?"

"What are you saying? That a human woman kidnapped Miles?"

Cross approached me and pointed to the charm hidden under my shirt.

"If he was wearing one of these, a human with ill intentions is the only creature who would have been able to kidnap him, correct?"

Cross made a valid point. One I'd thought initially, too. But it was a worrying one.

"Do you know how many human females live in D.C.? Instead of narrowing down our suspect pool, it exploded. I wish he would have rigged cameras in here." I immediately wrinkled my nose. "No, scratch that. That is not footage either Vena or I would want to watch."

"I don't understand," Cross said as he looked thoughtful. "The knowledge I've acquired gives me conflicting information on what a camera is."

"There are a lot of different types of cameras, but the one almost everyone has is in their phone."

I pulled out my phone and showed him a picture of Vena and me the last time we'd gone out together.

"Lovely," Cross said, stroking a finger over the image and accidentally flipping it to the next one. The drunk selfie of me in a club bathroom showed way too much cleavage. I pulled the phone away and tucked it back into my pocket.

"My phone is my camera. I use it to capture images. If we knew what the woman looked like, that would at least give us a starting point."

Cross stared at my chest for a long moment. I told myself he was probably thinking about the wonders of technology and not staring at my boobs. Why did I feel a little disappointed when he turned away and headed for the main room, then?

"No screaming, Everly," he said as he pulled the front door open. "Please come inside."

A yip still squeaked out of me when the blue fairy zipped in, and Cross closed the door behind it. The fairy went right for the silver framed picture of Vena.

"I will gladly give you the frame if you answer a few questions for me," Cross said, halting its flight.

My mouth dropped open.

"It can understand you?"

CHAPTER SEVENTEEN

"The fairy understands us both," Cross said. "It simply chooses to ignore you."

"First, that's rude. Second, I assumed they didn't have any thoughts in their heads except finding shiny objects and stealing them."

"That might be their main focus, but they aren't mindless drones." He attracted the fairy's attention and held it. "Do you remember the woman who was here?"

The fairy pointed at me.

"Not her," Cross said. "The one with the perfume. What does she look like?"

"The fairy can talk?" I asked.

"No. But it has ways of communicating if you're patient enough."

The fairy began gesturing to itself and pointing to its back.

"Is it trying to say the woman was a fairy?"

Cross frowned. "It is not a fairy who lured Miles away. Please try again."

With a light huff, the fairy zipped over to me, which made

me screech and duck for Cross. He caught me in his arms, one hand cradling the back of my head as I hid against his chest. The way his fingers idly stroked over my hair sent a shiver through me, and I wasn't sure if I was safer with the fairy or Cross.

Cautiously lifting my head, I saw Cross wasn't focused on me but on the fairy who pointed to my lower back. Hovering in the air, it struck a pose with its arms and legs bent like it was on all fours but leaning on its elbows to thrust its butt in the air.

"I'm disturbed," I muttered.

"Hush," Cross said, watching the fairy intently as it gestured to itself then to my lower back again.

"Perhaps I understand," Cross said. "Women mark their flesh with tattoos now, correct?"

"Yes."

"I believe the fairy is trying to tell us the woman had a tattoo of a fairy on her backside."

The fairy straightened and nodded once.

I eased out of Cross' arms. "Oh. I guess that would make sense. But why a fairy tattoo?" I shuddered.

The fairy zipped forward, snatched a lock of my hair, and yanked hard.

"Hey," I snapped. "One of your kind tried to kill me for a stupid curling iron. Don't tempt me to retaliate."

The fairy flew away and picked up the heavy silver frame. It bobbed in the air as it flew to the door and waited for Cross to open it. I was glad when it was gone.

"If not many people would want a fairy tattoo, then finding this woman should be simple," Cross said.

"Simple? Do you know how many tattoo artists are in the D.C. area alone?"

"I do not."

"Neither do I. But I know it's a lot. Do you smell anything else that might help?"

"No. But I insist you throw away the cake. I will buy you better confectionery."

I took the cake, threw it in the garbage, and cinched the bag closed. "Someday, I want to own a bakery."

"You do?"

"I'm going to school for business management and taking any culinary-type classes they offer."

"You would resign yourself willingly to the servant class?"

His tone had me grinning.

"It's not like that anymore. Jobs that were once for servants are now for those who find passion in it."

"Passion," he echoed as his eyes scanned my face and rested on my lips. "This new world tempts with its possibilities."

I fought not to flush and cleared my throat.

"Do you have any passions?"

He smirked. "A few."

Ignoring his darkening gaze, I headed to the door with the garbage bag.

"Times have changed greatly since I last walked among humans," Cross commented as he followed. "Servants used to remove the trash, and women did not live alone."

"I'm not alone. I have Vena. And if you want to carry the scrotum-cake trash, I'll let you."

He made a noncommittal sound as I set the bag down outside and locked the door. When I finished, he held the trash.

"If I want to blend, I will need your assistance procuring a residence. Although preferably something nicer than this and closer to your home."

"There aren't nicer houses close to mine," I said, leading him toward the car. "And with the way you want to dress, you're going to need fancy. Maybe even something with a doorman."

I opened the trunk for him to stow the garbage. He surprised me by walking with me to the driver's side door and opening it for me.

"In my time, a gentleman showed a woman every courtesy," he explained when he caught my stare.

"I'm pretty sure I remember you calling me a hooker the first time you saw me."

His lips twitched. "True. *Almost* every woman then."

I snorted and shook my head at him as I sat and he closed the door for me.

"Guys still do nice things for girls," I said as soon as he settled into his seat. "They're usually dating, though."

"Interesting."

I pulled away from the curb and merged with traffic.

"Take me to a bakery you enjoy," he said. "You can dine and tell me your fairy story."

I glanced at the clock. There was still plenty of time before I needed to be home for my shift, and he was offering bakery.

An hour later, I sat back and grinned as Cross laughed at my expense.

"I now understand your fears. Hopefully, the sweets helped soothe your nerves."

The two empty plates that had held my decadent "sweets" were scraped clean on the table in front of me. One chocolate cake and a red velvet bonbon. I'd ordered the bonbon for Cross, but he'd insisted I eat it since he preferred the kind that I made.

"The sweets did their job. Thank you."

He stood and did that chair thing that guys sometimes did, and I absolutely loved it. A girl could get used to this kind of attention.

He burst my bubble outside, though, when he led me around to the passenger side of the car and opened the door for me.

"What are you doing?" I asked.

"I would like to attempt to drive."

"In the city? Do you see all the cars?"

"I do. I've been paying attention as well. It seems like a simple task."

"Cross, I can't afford a new car or the medical bills I'll rack up if you crash us. I'm human and breakable."

He smiled at me. "Give me your trust, Everly. You will not be disappointed."

"I'm pretty sure that's what Vena said right before I found myself dressed up like a real hooker and walking into Juicy."

Cross' eyes flashed black. "I am not Vena."

"No, you're not. She's trouble I can handle. I'm pretty sure I can't handle your level of trouble."

He leaned closer to me, our gazes locked, and I watched his slowly shift back to amber.

"Perhaps you can," he said softly. Then he stepped away from me.

"The choice is yours. I would prefer my first attempt to drive under your guidance, but I can ask another."

I sighed and got into the passenger seat.

"Don't make me regret this."

"Never," he said before he closed the door.

He got in, buckled, and started the car before I could say anything. Then he surprised me further by smoothly pulling out into traffic. The distance he kept between my car and the car in front of us was perfect. Same with his lane alignment. His acceleration and braking were both smooth, too.

"There is no way you are this good the first time driving."

He flashed a grin at me.

"I'm very observant, Everly. Plus, I have a few additional memories."

"Ah. That's right. The grocery boy?"

"No. I only feed on the same human once a week. I've acquired a few others since then."

"Wow. That's impressive." I wasn't impressed, though. I was a little...disappointed? Jealous? I wasn't sure what the feeling was, but I didn't like it.

As soon as Cross parked in front of my house, I got out.

"If it's all right with you, I don't think you should come in. My boss is worried about the killings happening around work and has been sending one of the guys home with us to ensure we're safe at night. He's got a good nose."

Cross nodded and handed me the keys to my car.

I popped the trunk and was going to take out the garbage when he swept in and removed it for me.

"Thank you," I said, wondering at the change in his behavior. Was he merely being polite in return for all the help we'd given him? Doubtful. If that were the case, he'd offer the same courtesies to Vena. No, he had a definite preference for me. Why else had he been in my bed this morning?

I studied Cross as he tossed the garbage into the bin at the side of the house. He was deliciously handsome. Almost decadent. Something that was mesmerizing to look at but intimidating to be close to.

He caught my head-to-toe scan of him.

"I will leave my things with you for now, Everly, if that's okay."

I nodded. "We can pick up the altered trousers and your phone tomorrow."

"Then I will see you tomorrow." After a feather-light caress along my cheek, he motioned for me to go inside.

The door was already unlocked, and as soon as I closed it behind me, I peeked through the window to see that he was gone.

"It's about time you got home," Vena said from the couch. "I was about to text you. Where's money bags?"

"His name is Cross."

Vena raised a brow. "Did someone get a sugar daddy?"

I collapsed onto the couch next to her. "No. And you should be nice to him because he just got us one step closer to finding Miles."

Vena sat up. "How? When?"

"I realized that Cross has a really good sense of smell, so we went to Miles' apartment. Cross detected a woman's perfume. He also spoke to the fairy that's been hanging around outside Miles' door. Do you know those things can communicate? It pantomimed that the woman had a tattoo of a fairy on her lower back."

Vena frowned at the news. "Did you say a fairy tattoo on her lower back?"

"Yes. Why? Do you know of someone who has a tattoo like that?"

She frowned and shook her head. "Probably not." She pulled out her phone. "We'll need to start canvassing all the tattoo parlors in D.C."

"That's a lot of places. Would they even remember a woman asking for a fairy tattoo?"

"Doesn't hurt to ask around. We can bring Cross to compel people to talk."

"He already took off for today. But we agreed that I'll bring him to the store to pick up his clothes tomorrow and get his phone."

"That's fine. It'll give us time to come up with a list of places. I'll map it out so we're not driving the city ten times over."

"Deal."

The rest of the time before our shift was dominated by creating the list. D.C. catered to everyone, human and creature alike. So we needed to weed out the places designated for specific creatures.

Since we trusted Cross' nose, we stuck to the human ones.

After the list was compiled, we scarfed down sandwiches I'd thrown together then changed for work.

"Do you think I'll be in my own section tonight?" Vena asked.

"You'll have your own section once Shepard posts the new schedule. Otherwise, all the sections are filled."

Vena and I ended up splitting the bigger section near Anchor. She winked at him every time she passed with a drink order. He didn't help the situation when he kept blushing. The man was begging for her attention, and without a full load of tables, she had plenty of time to give it.

It was midway into the night when she dropped a napkin near the last table and bent at the waist, ass toward Anchor. He looked everywhere but at her, but I knew from the shade of red creeping up his neck that he wasn't oblivious.

When I saw her going toward the bar with another order, I hurried to follow her. She paused when she caught me power-walking in her direction. I kept my smile bright just in case Shepard was somewhere watching.

"Knock it off," I said close to her ear. "You're going to get yourself fired."

She snorted.

"Or maybe I'll get one hell of a raise." She nudged me as if I needed help understanding her double meaning.

"You're impossible. Behave."

"Don't I always?"

She was slipping her arm through mine with a huge grin on her face when there was a burst of yelling at the door. Standing as we were, between the door, the bar, and the tables, we had a clear view of the men who rushed Army, the current bouncer at the door. Seven of them surged forward, using their combined weight and momentum to bring Army down.

"Holy shit," Vena said as more came rushing through the now unguarded opening.

They grabbed the nearest patrons and attacked them. Hitting. Kicking. Biting.

Buzz jumped over the bar and moved incredibly fast to pull one off of a woman.

"Vena! Everly! Move!" Anchor yelled as he rushed past us.

Vena dragged me back as men poured through the opening. We hurried toward the stairs. The DJ killed the music, and everyone in the bar realized something bad was happening.

The place morphed into chaos and panic in an instant.

While some people were smart enough to run for the stage exit at the back of the building, Vena and I raced up toward the VIP area. People jogged down the stairs, and we had to fight against the flow of panic. Women screamed. Men shouted.

I looked over the railing as Anchor grabbed one guy by the collar and smashed his forehead into the guy's face. Blood poured from the guy's nose, and his eyes rolled back in his head. Before he even hit the floor, Anchor was already reaching for the next one.

Vena pulled my arm to keep me with her.

My damn heels and lack of cardio were going to kill me.

Winded, I reached the top, one step behind Vena. With the crowd cleared, we raced to Shepard's office. Vena barricaded the door while I went to the glass wall to watch the scene below.

Sierra struggled against a man. She was surprisingly agile as she twisted out of his hold and ducked under his swing. Her shirt wasn't so agile, and buttons went flying.

"We should be helping," I said.

"How? You want to throw a cupcake at them?"

"Hey!" I glanced back at Vena where she was watching the door.

"Sorry," she said without looking away. "That was mean. But you're not a fighter, Everly. This is the safest place for you."

"But not for you. Is it?"

"This is exactly where I need to be. We stick together."

I faced the glass wall and saw Thomas hit the guy attacking Sierra over the head with a drink tray. The guy went down, out cold, and Sierra bent down to pick up her own tray.

Her shirt, untucked and askew, rode up her back, showing a tattoo of a fairy. I stared in disbelief. What were the odds?

Sierra was a bitch, but a kidnapper? No way.

I opened my mouth to tell Vena what I'd seen, but a loud bang on the office door wiped away all thoughts of Miles. Pivoting, I saw Vena racing toward me.

"Help me with the desk," she said.

Kicking off my heels, I put everything I had into pushing Shepard's solid wood desk toward the door. The latch gave out when we were still a few inches away, and the door hit the desk.

An eye peered through the crack at us.

"You will suffer," the man yelled.

He wedged his fingers through the door.

"Mistake number one," Vena said. "Push, Ev."

I closed my eyes and pushed.

His screams of pain rang in my ears, and I fought not to gag.

"Puppies and kittens," I said under my breath. "Puppies and kittens."

"Cute kittens," Vena said immediately, catching on. "Grey with a stripe of white running under their bellies. Tiny. Maybe two weeks old. Young enough that they still walk like they're drunk. You still with me, Ev?"

I nodded and continued to keep pressure on the desk.

"Keep talking," I said. "What do the puppies look like?"

"Little Shepards."

My eyes popped open, and I shot her a look. "Now?"

"Don't you like German Shepherds?" she asked innocently but with a mischievous grin. "Let up."

I immediately did. The guy's hand disappeared.

"Push."

We closed the door with the table. No one tried the door again.

"Go check," she said, keeping her weight against the table.

I ran to the window.

A crowd of men still fought against Shepard, Anchor, Doc, Buzz, Griz, Army, Detroit, and Boulder. A stream of liquid shot out from the bar area underneath us, dousing everyone. It wasn't stopping the fighting, but whoever had the hose wasn't letting up. It didn't matter, though. The Blur crew was methodically taking out the fighters and leaving bodies on the floor.

"It looks like the fight's dying down," I said. "Let's wait to leave until someone comes for us."

"Exactly what I was thinking," Vena said from her place against the desk.

Below us, Shepard got hit with more water and said something to whoever was wielding it. The stream immediately vanished.

The last man fell, and Shepard shook his head, sending water everywhere. It felt like I'd turned on an old romance movie when he tugged his shirt off and used it to wipe his face because every inch of that man's chest was chiseled in muscled perfection.

All thoughts of how he was my boss and absolutely off limits fled as I took in the view. His gloriously mounded pecs created a valley deep enough for the charm or whatever he was wearing around his neck to call home. Below that, golden abs for days greeted his delicious happy trail.

"I think I just got pregnant," I said softly.

"What? What do you mean?" Vena asked.

Shepard looked up at me then, catching me staring. The sudden, knowing smile on his face had my face heating scarlet. He motioned for me to wait then said something to Buzz.

I hurried away from the wall to fan my face and give Vena an explanation.

"I just saw Shepard without a shirt, and I think he heard me."

Vena laughed like an insane person, which she apparently was.

"It's not funny," I said.

"It's *so* funny."

Something pushed at the door, moving Vena and the desk a few inches. We both scrambled to brace it.

"It's me," Shepard said from the other side. "You're safe."

Face still flaming, I stepped away, and we watched Shepard easily muscle the desk back using the door.

"Are you both all right?" he asked as soon as he walked in. I tried not to stare at his chest, but it was difficult.

His gaze swept over Vena then locked on me. "Everly?"

I nodded, and he exhaled like my answer meant everything to him.

"Good. You were smart to come up here," he said as he moved to the shirt pile and took a dry one for himself. "I told Buzz to gather the rest of the staff and get them up here with you. Keep them busy while we look around. I'm sure someone called the police by now, and you'll need to answer their questions."

I was a little sad to see the pec display put away, and he caught my stare.

"I didn't know you wore a necklace," I said, hoping to play it off.

"Family keepsake. Stay up here."

The next hour passed in a partial haze.

After the wait staff joined us, we learned it had been Pam who had wielded the hose. She had a black eye, and Thomas had a sprained wrist from his handy tray skills. Doc had given Sierra his shirt since hers wouldn't close. He'd been the only one to escape Pam's spraying.

We all spoke with the police, answering their questions as they hauled away the men, some of whom were already starting to come around. I overheard one of the officers mention that the attackers didn't know where they were or how they'd gotten there.

Once we'd given our statements, the police said we could

go. Vena and I weren't as fast to hurry down the stairs as the others. Mostly because I had to put my shoes back on.

When we reached the bar area, Shepard told everyone that the bar would be closed the next day.

"I hope it's paid time off," Sierra said under her breath.

"It will be. And I'll cover any medical bills, too."

"And ruined clothes?"

He stiffly nodded to her. "I'll take care of everything."

"I'll walk you out," Doc said.

The others quickly jumped on the escort to their cars even though a few police cars were still parked outside. By unspoken agreement, Vena and I hung back.

The bar was an absolute mess. The floor was soaked, and broken glass was everywhere. Partially eaten food was sitting at the tables, and I could smell a hint of smoke coming from the kitchen.

Shepard pulled out his phone to send a message.

Knowing that everyone was safe for now, my adrenaline crashed, and I began shaking. He looked up from his phone and noticed. Of course he did.

Before I could tell him I was fine, he pulled me into a hug that had my face pressed against his chest. After everything, it felt too good to pass up. I wilted into him as he rubbed my back.

"Go with Anchor, and check in with me tomorrow," he murmured. "I have things I need to do now."

"Like what?" Vena asked.

"Nothing for either of you to worry about."

Reluctantly, I detached myself from his chest. "I overheard one of the officers. Some of the attackers couldn't remember how they'd gotten here. He used the word compelled. Vampires were controlling those people, weren't they?"

He nodded. "It was retaliation for destroying Juicy. I should have been more careful. I'm sorry you got caught in the crossfire. It won't happen again. I promise."

"You can't promise that," I said.

His jaw clenched for a moment before he said, "I can, and I did. I protect the people I care about, Everly. They'll learn the consequences of bringing the war to my door. There is no room for them in my city."

"Them? The vampires or the regular people they sent to fight for them?"

"Not regular people," Anchor said. "Feeders. I've never seen anything like it before. They had identical tattoos to cover up bite marks on their necks and needle tracks on their inner arms. The ones at Juicy had the same."

"Did you take a picture of these vamp stamps?" Vena asked.

Anchor nodded but glanced at Shepard.

"Show it to them when you get to their house. They'll be safer if they know what to watch for."

Shepard looked at me.

"I won't harm a compelled human if I can help it. Killing the vampires that control them will fix the problem. Don't worry, we'll find and eliminate the vampires. Until then, get used to seeing Anchor on your couch."

CHAPTER EIGHTEEN

"What about Pam and everyone else?" I asked. "Will they have someone to stay with them, too?"

"Don't worry," Shepard said. "Everyone will have an extra set of eyes on them at night until we resolve this. But you're the only two who will know it. Understand?"

I nodded quickly then followed Anchor as he escorted us to our car. Once Vena started the engine, he hopped into his truck.

I waited until Vena pulled out of the lot to ask, "Did you see the vamp stamps?"

"I saw a neck tattoo on the guy trying to get into the office, but I was too focused on trying not to get killed to study it. What about you?"

"I was too freaked out to see any details. But I saw a fairy tattoo on Sierra's lower back after her shirt got torn."

Vena nodded thoughtfully, not looking nearly as shocked as I'd thought she would be.

"You knew?"

"I glimpsed her tattoo when we were in the employee room the other day, but I couldn't remember the exact design. I saw it again when Doc gave her his shirt. She has to be the one who was in Miles' apartment, but why?"

"We don't know for sure it was her. Did Miles even know her?"

"That's what we need to find out. I say we pay her a visit tonight and ask."

"First, I don't know where she lives, do you? Second, you heard Shepard. She's got a bodyguard, and so do we. If we go tonight, there will be a ton of questions."

"Fine, we'll wait until first thing in the morning and bring Cross. He can sniff her perfume and tell us if it matches."

"I don't remember smelling perfume on her."

"It might not be actual perfume. When she walked by the other night, I did smell something citrusy. Cross might have assumed it was perfume and not body wash or lotion."

"I suppose. He'll be able to confirm it tomorrow, either way."

Vena smirked at me.

"What?" I asked.

"Don't think that I'm going to ignore the hug Shepard gave you. Why do you get to have two beasts at your beck and call, and I'm here all alone?"

"They're not at my beck and call. And you have Anchor drooling over you."

She made a pouty face. "But you won't let me have any fun."

"You heard Shepard's warning. Wolves don't do casual. If you want Anchor around for the long haul, go for it. I bet he'd be one hell of a ride. But if you think I don't like your treasure hunting, what do you think an overprotective wolf will be like?"

That wiped the eagerness off her face, and she shifted uncomfortably. "Way to kill the mood."

"Something needed to cool you down."

"You doused me with the perfect ice bucket."

"Good."

We parked and waited in the car while Anchor searched the house. It didn't take him long to give us the all-clear signal.

Before we left the car, I patted Vena's shoulder. "Find a human to harass."

When we entered, Anchor was by the couch, frowning at the blankets he'd used the night before.

"Everything okay?" I asked.

"Yeah. It's fine. There's a smell here that hasn't faded like I would have thought."

Vena smirked at him. "What exactly have you been doing on our couch that you don't want us to smell? Did it involve lotion?"

"Vena." I thrust a finger toward her room.

She huffed a sigh but didn't argue.

I waited until her door closed behind her to look at Anchor, who was staring at the hallway like he was thinking about following her.

"Don't do it," I said. "She's still at the love-'em-and-leave-'em phase of her life."

"What about you?" he asked, looking at me.

"I'm trying to focus on a career and keeping Vena out of trouble. It's more than enough for now." I took in Anchor's wrinkled shirt and still-damp jeans. There were blood splotches —probably not his own—in a few places.

"Do you want to use our shower? I can throw your clothes in the wash while you're in there."

"Maybe once the sun's up," he said.

"Don't be silly. We'll be fine for five minutes, and you can keep the door open if you want—so you can hear everything."

He glanced at the front door then the hallway.

"You know what? I think I will."

He only glanced at Vena's door once on the way to the bathroom.

Too late, I wondered if Anchor would be able to smell Cross in the shower, and I mentally kicked myself. But Anchor didn't say anything as I showed him where the towels were.

"Toss the clothes into the hallway, and I'll grab them."

"I really appreciate this, Everly."

"Any time."

I closed myself into my bedroom and changed out of my uniform. A wad of tip money fell out of my apron, a reminder of how wrong the whole night had gone. No tips counted and divided with the bartenders. No tabs closed out. How much money had Shepard lost tonight? And all because Vena and I had been dumb enough to go into Juicy.

Weighed down by guilt, I opened my door and picked up Anchor's clothes. Vena's door was open again, but she wasn't in there. She wasn't in the bathroom either. I peeked.

I found her by the washer, leaning against it with a grin on her face.

"You're such a good friend, Everly. I'm going to buy you breakfast tomorrow."

I gave her a narrow-eyed stare.

"What are you up to?"

"Nothing. Just showing the person I love most some appreciation."

"I don't trust you."

She watched me put Anchor's clothes into the washer.

"Notice something missing?" she asked.

"No?"

"That fine specimen of man in our shower goes commando."

"Or he kept them on for protection," I whispered to her. "Behave."

She gave me an innocent look. But when the shower turned off, she straightened away from the washer, and excitement danced in her eyes.

"This one's for me," she said softly.

I opened my mouth to ask what she meant.

"Everly?" Anchor called before I could.

"Yeah?"

"Did you move my bag? I had a change of clothes in it."

I shot Vena a disbelieving look. She smirked at me and started for the living room.

"What did it look like?" Vena asked.

I hurried after her and was only two steps behind her when she turned the corner to the living room. If not for her lead, I would have crashed into her. As it was, it was just enough of a delay to watch her face plant into Anchor's very naked chest. One of his arms went around her waist to catch her, and the other held onto the ends of the towel that was too small to close around his waist fully.

"Are you okay?" Anchor asked, looking down at her in shock.

She didn't lift her head.

"So good," she breathed from between his enormous pecs.

"Okay," I said, grabbing her by the ponytail and hauling her back.

She was grinning like an idiot, and Anchor looked like he was two seconds from throwing her over his shoulder.

"I'll...wait in the bathroom," he said. He took one slow, deep breath then turned on his heel and closed himself inside.

"What are you doing?" I mouthed at Vena, who was no longer smiling.

She used her phone to write out: *I'm trying to make him run. I saw Cross lurking around outside. If Anchor leaves, we can go check out Sierra's tonight.*

I grabbed the phone from her and typed out: *We don't even know where she lives,* then handed it back to her.

"Find his bag and go to bed, Vena. It's been a very long day with too many close calls, don't you think?"

I loved Miles, but I knew he would not be okay with how reckless Vena was with our safety. And she knew it, too.

She gave me a sad look and nodded.

Opening the closet door, she took out Anchor's bag and gave it to me.

"I guess it's better if you give it to him."

I was tempted to add a snarky, "That's what she said." But refrained since Anchor was likely listening.

Once she was back in her room, I knocked on the bathroom door.

"Anchor, I have your bag."

He cracked open the door and looked past me to Vena's closed door.

"Sorry," I mumbled.

He shook his head as if to clear it. "It's okay. Thank you for finding it."

While he dressed, I went into the kitchen and made him a sandwich. I added enough meat and cheese to take his mind off Vena. Hopefully.

By the time I was done, Anchor had found his way to the kitchen. He eyed the sandwich as if afraid to ask for it.

"Double the meat and mayo on both pieces of bread," I said. "Want mustard?"

"It's for me?" he asked.

"Yep. For having to sleep on the couch and saving our butts at Blur. Did you get hurt?"

He shook his head. "Nothing to worry about."

"Are you sure? I have a stocked first aid kit."

"Why am I not surprised?"

I grinned at his teasing and pulled out chips to pile on the plate next to the sandwich.

"What do you want to drink?"

"Water is fine."

"I have beer."

"No. I'm on duty."

"Are you ever off duty?" I asked as I poured him a glass of water.

"Not when you have Shepard as a boss."

"You don't sound upset about it."

"I'm not. We stick together."

I took the plate and water and set them on the coffee table for him. He eased down onto the couch, and I caught a slight wince.

"You *are* hurt," I said.

"I'll be fine by tomorrow. The sandwich will help." He gave me a small smile that made me feel guiltier.

"I'm sorry, Anchor. Everything that happened tonight was because of Vena and me. If we hadn't been at Juicy, there wouldn't have been any retaliation on Blur."

"Don't feel guilty. You brought a vampire's den to our attention. We might never have found it without you, and countless people like you and Vena would have been hurt because of it."

"Shepard said you took care of the den at Juicy. What happened there?"

"We wrecked it so there's no easy way to reopen. Since it's in our territory, they'd be stupid to come back."

"Do you think there will be more retaliation?" I asked.

He looked thoughtful for a moment. "Maybe. Shepard will put the heat on the vampires. They'll either move on or—"

"Or?" I prompted.

"Or they'll get the war they've been itching for." He frowned. "Don't tell Shepard I told you that. He's protective when it comes to his employees. He's going to tell you everything will be okay. And it will be. The next move is ours." A wolfish grin followed. "They'll be hurting far worse than us."

I took a breath. "I'd prefer you don't get hurt at all."

"Don't worry. I don't go down easy. That's why Shepard assigned me to you."

"Because you're the best?"

He grinned. "You know it."

I gave a small laugh. "Then I'm glad you're here." I was about to say goodnight, but I paused.

"Got something else on your mind?" he asked as he took a large bite of the sandwich and groaned. "So good."

"I was just wondering…if we get the best, who does Sierra get?"

"Gunther."

"Oh. I suppose that's good. I think they're sort of friends, right?"

He raised a brow.

"Or maybe not," I said quickly. "It's not like Sierra's really a person who befriends others." Still, I had seen her talking to Gunther a few times, which was more than she spoke to anyone else without snark or animosity.

"G'night, Anchor. Thank you."

"Night. Do you want me to wake you when I leave?"

"Please."

Not that I had any intention of sleeping in. Anchor got hurt because of me, and he was at least going to get breakfast out of it.

Before I went to bed, I peeked out my bedroom window to see if Cross was outside. If he was, I couldn't see him.

Disappointed, I rolled into bed and pulled the covers up over my head.

The next morning, I woke early to the alarm I'd set, knowing Anchor would leave as soon as the sun rose. I quickly dressed, trying to be as quiet as possible, and tiptoed into the kitchen. After a night of fighting and sleeping on the couch, Anchor deserved a very large breakfast.

Using the stovetop light so I wouldn't wake Anchor with the bright overhead light, I pulled what I needed from the cupboards. Stealthily, I mixed together enough pancake batter for an army of werewolves. I also whipped up eggs for omelets, shredded potatoes for hash browns, and laid strips of bacon on the pan.

By the time it sizzled, I sensed Anchor behind me.

"What are you doing?" he asked.

"Making breakfast?"

He peeked around me at the pans of food cooking. "How many people are coming over?"

"It's just us."

"It smells good, but I think you made too much."

"You were hurt, and you need fuel to heal."

"Not that much fuel."

"Put your clothes in the dryer, and feel free to use the bathroom. I'll have food ready soon."

Anchor returned in a few minutes, and I pulled down three plates.

"What do you want to drink? There's coffee, water, and orange juice."

"Coffee is good."

After handing Anchor a heaping plate of food and a large mug of coffee, I went to Vena's room and knocked on the door before I peeked inside. Even though the sun had begun filtering through the rest of the house, her black-out shade made her room feel like a tomb. It wasn't like her to sleep in like this.

"Vena," I whispered.

She groaned. "It's too early. Unless Anchor is standing naked at my door, I have no reason to get out of bed yet."

I heard Anchor choke.

"Breakfast is ready. But if you don't want any, I'll wrap some up for you to heat later."

She groaned again, and I heard the rustling of fabric. "I swear it feels like I just fell asleep. Give me a few minutes, and I'll be out."

I closed her door and returned to the kitchen to find Anchor had shoveled the rest of the food into his mouth.

He handed me the plate, gave me an awkward kiss on the top of my head, and then said, "I'll be back tonight. Keep my clothes for me."

He grabbed his bag and was gone.

Vena shuffled out right when his truck roared past the house.

"Where's the food?" she asked.

"On the counter. You scared off Anchor. He practically choked himself to eat and leave before you came out."

"He'll be back."

"Yeah, under Shepard's orders."

Vena smiled sleepily. "I think I'm going to get Shepard a gift basket. What do you think werewolves like?"

"They like to mate for life."

She tsked. "You're in a mood. This is way too early for you to be awake. But that's okay. We'll harness your attitude for the greater good today. I stayed up last night and did some digging. I found Sierra's address, and I'm going to need you to bring out the Queen Bitch when we get there."

While she grabbed some bacon, I glanced outside for Cross and wondered how long we would need to wait for him. Considering the pace at which Vena was wolfing down her food, I didn't think she would be willing to delay for very long.

"Go get dressed," she said as if reading my mind. "I'll clean this up so we can head out."

"We agreed we need Cross with us."

"Go check your bed. Maybe he's waiting for you."

"Ha-ha. Very funny."

She grinned at me and shooed me from the kitchen.

Unfortunately, Cross wasn't in my bed. Not that I expected him to be there. Or wanted him to be. (I was a liar like that.) I only hoped he would show up before Vena insisted we leave. I did not want to go snooping around without backup.

I threw my hair into a ponytail and grabbed a pair of jean shorts and an off-the-shoulder shirt. By the time I was finished, there still wasn't any sign of Cross.

And as I'd anticipated, Vena didn't want to wait. She had her shoes on and was already by the door.

"She's human, Everly. All we're going to do is ask her a few questions. Like where she got the tattoo. And if you happen to use her bathroom while we're there and peek into a few rooms, it's no big deal. It's not like we're walking into another strip club without a clue."

"It's like you enjoy handing the universe a challenge it can't refuse, don't you?"

"Miles has been missing for five days. Each minute is killing me a little more. Because it's Miles, and I know he's smart and can take care of himself, I've been listening to you and trying to be careful. I don't want you to get hurt. I don't. But, Ev, if it were you, I would have torn this city apart on day one. I wouldn't have waited, and Miles would have been right there with me."

"Ouch," I said softly.

She gripped my shoulders. "That wasn't a guilt trip. Open and honest, right? That's our deal. I'm only letting you into my head so you can decide if you'd rather stay here or not."

"I hate when you do this."

She gave me a sad smile. "Me, too. But she's human, Ev. We'll be fine."

I slipped on my shoes and waved her out the door.

It didn't take us long to find Sierra's place. Vena drove by the modest single-story home and parked the next block over.

"Isn't that Gunther's truck?" Vena asked, pointing to the red pickup across the street and two houses down from Sierra's.

"Yeah. I wonder why he's still here. I thought the lookouts were only at night."

She and I both looked around for Anchor's truck.

"If he tailed us, he'd be at our car asking what we were doing by now," Vena said.

"Agreed. But why is Gunther still here then?" I asked.

"Playing find the fairy?" She shrugged. "I mean, I wouldn't touch Sierra, but dudes tend to be less picky."

"Whatever his reasons, we can't exactly ask her about your brother in front of Gunther."

"Says who? Let's see what he's doing."

Vena got out before I could respond, and I scrambled after her.

She was already halfway to Gunther's truck when I caught up. We saw him slumped in his seat at the same time.

"Shit. Is he dead?" I whispered in horror.

Vena jogged across the road and went up to his window. Frozen, I stood on the other sidewalk and watched her pause, shake her head, and walk back to me.

"He's breathing, and there's an empty bottle of whiskey next to him. Some guard."

I glanced at Sierra's house and mentally cringed.

"What if—"

"Nope, we're not playing that game. Our only lead is not dead. Fate wouldn't be cruel enough to take another one of my family members without a trace."

"I was thinking it's another trap like the one at Juicy," I said with a guilty glance at Vena.

"That's not happening either. We're knocking on her door in the middle of the day. We'll be fine."

"The vampires sent compelled people into Blur. What if they did the same here? Daylight won't save us from that. You saw how insane they were."

"Fine. I'll listen to your anxiety-fueled voice of reason. What do you want to do? Should we call Shepard and tell him that his guy is passed out so he can grill us about why we're here and then tell us that my missing brother isn't something we should be worrying about like everyone else? Or should we call Cross on the cell phone you got him yesterday?"

"I'm supposed to get him the cell phone today." I scowled at her. "And I don't like you when you don't get enough sleep."

She sighed and looked at Sierra's house, partially obscured by a pine.

"Everly, I know Miles was looking into something big and that he might go quiet for a while. But after everything that has happened, my gut is telling me that's not what this is. It's like there's an invisible clock ticking in my head." She frowned. "Did you see that? The curtain moved."

I watched the front of Sierra's house and saw the curtain twitch.

With her phone pressed to her ear, Sierra peeked out her window. Her expression was a mix of fear and anger. The anger wasn't new. General pissiness seemed to be part of her personality chart. The fear *was* new, though.

"She looks like she's freaking out. Why? About last night?" I asked softly.

"Or that Gunther is still here."

The curtain fell back into place, and Vena strode forward.

"What are you doing?" I hissed even as I hurried to keep up with her. I hated let's-wing-it Vena.

My heart was in my throat when Vena rapped on Sierra's door with all the force of a jackhammer. I shot her a side glare.

"Keep it casual," I warned.

A moment later, Sierra cracked open the door. "What are you doing here?"

Her face, while in its normal bitchy scrunch, was also a little pale. The blue tint under her eyes made me suspect she was either sleep-deprived or possibly sick.

"We're just here to check on you for Shepard," Vena said. "Can we come in?"

"If I barely tolerate you at work, why would I want you at my home?" She didn't wait for a response. "Tell Shepard I'm not fine, and he'll have to cough up more than a lousy day off of work."

Sierra went to close the door in our faces, and Vena stuck her booted foot into the opening to block her.

"What the hell is your problem?" Sierra demanded.

Vena added her weight to the door as Sierra stomped on her foot.

"All we want to do is ask you a few questions," Vena said.

"I'm not talking to you, or Shepard, or anyone. Get the hell off my property."

"My brother's fairy neighbor told us about a woman with a fairy tattoo, and I know you have one. I have questions."

Sierra's expression changed to one of panic a second before she kicked Vena in the shin. Vena hopped back in pain, and Sierra lunged to close the door.

I charged at it. I might not have been a fighter, but with my slightly more voluptuous frame, I managed to keep Sierra from closing it. Vena shoved at the door, too.

Sierra's footing slid on the floor, and she toppled back. The door flew wide open, and Vena and I fell to the floor next to Sierra.

I groaned and pushed at Vena, who'd landed on top of me.

"You okay, Ev?" she asked, carefully getting off.

Sierra swore under her breath, and I heard her scramble away from us.

"Fine," I said, accepting Vena's assistance.

"Get out!" Sierra yelled as I stood.

I looked at her right as she threw a vase.

Vena batted it aside.

"This would be a lot easier if you cooperated," she said angrily.

With a battle cry, she ran at Sierra.

CHAPTER NINETEEN

I HURRIED TO CLOSE THE DOOR SO THE NEIGHBORS WOULDN'T witness anything. Vena only used the battle cry if she was intent on serious ass-kicking, and the last thing we needed was for someone to call the cops.

When I turned around, Vena had Sierra pinned to the ground face first with an arm twisted up between her shoulder blades. It was a move she'd tried teaching me over and over when we'd been sixteen, even though we both knew I wasn't a fighter. I could never manage the level of aggression Vena could.

"What do you know about my brother?" Vena demanded. "A woman with your tattoo was at his house when he disappeared."

"Do you know how many people have tattoos, you psycho?" Sierra panted, wincing at Vena's hold.

"Of a rat with wings?" I scoffed. "No one wants a fairy tattoo these days, Sierra."

"Maybe not a Miss Perfect like you."

Sierra surprised the hell out of me when she reached back with her free hand to claw at Vena.

Vena jerked back to avoid her nails. I saw her hold loosen on Sierra's arm. That was all the freedom she needed to buck Vena off and scramble to her feet. Vena was a beat behind her as she dashed for the kitchen. She tried to grab Sierra again but missed and skidded into a long breakfast bar.

On the other side, Sierra grabbed two knives, holding one in each hand.

I couldn't see Vena's face since she had her back to me, but I saw how she inched back a step.

"Why'd you run, Sierra?" Vena asked. "Are we hitting too close to the mark? What do you know about Miles?"

"I'll show how I hit too close to the mark."

She whipped a knife at Vena, but Vena was fast and ducked to the side.

In slow motion, I saw it continue straight at me. My eyes went wide. I opened my mouth. The fearful squeal I emitted morphed into a choked cry of pain as the blade sunk into my upper arm.

Blood ran down my skin.

Pitiful wounded sounds tore from my throat.

I staggered back a step and stared at the blade sticking an inch into my skin. The handle's weight slowly pulled it down until the blade slid free. Then the blood started to pour.

The outer edges of my vision blurred.

"Why me?" I whispered as panic magnified my disbelief.

Was this really the way Vena finally killed me? I was okay with death by chocolate, but not bitchy Sierra's kitchen knife that still had remnants of food on it.

"Put pressure on it, Ev!" Vena yelled.

The scuffling sounds finally registered, and I tore my gaze from my arm.

Vena grappled with Sierra, who was going for Vena's eyes with her nails. With a shove, she sent Sierra back a step. Lunging forward, Sierra wrapped her hands around Vena's neck.

Vena looped her arm through Sierra's and broke her stranglehold. A second later, Vena threw an old-school punch to Sierra's face. My soon-to-be-former coworker looked like the blow barely registered. She drew her lips back in a silent snarl and went for Vena again.

The tickle on my arm drew my attention back to my wound. Dazed, I belatedly remembered Vena's instructions and clapped a hand over it. A whimper escaped at how much putting pressure on it hurt.

We needed help.

Thinking of Gunther, I turned toward the door.

Before I could take more than one shuffling step toward it, it crashed open. An enraged vampire dressed in loose-fitting jeans and a dark t-shirt filled the lit opening. I stifled a squeal and met Cross' black gaze.

Tears filled my eyes. If I wasn't so afraid of bleeding more, I would have hugged him.

"Everly." He said my name like a relieved prayer as his gaze raked over my face then down to the hand I had clapped over my bleeding arm.

"Vena needs your help," I said.

His gaze went from my arm to Vena and Sierra. He disappeared around me in a blur.

I turned and saw him standing between the two women, staring into Sierra's eyes.

"You will cease struggling and sit on the couch until I tell you to move."

All the anger left her expression, and she made her way toward the couch.

Cross blurred and stood in front of me once more. He breathed in deeply, his black gaze dipping to the hand clasped over my cut. The dark veins appeared around his eyes with an intensity I'd never seen before.

My pulse skipped even as I took a step back.

"Please, Everly. Allow me to care for you," he said. "I will never harm you. I only want to help."

His smooth tone wrapped around me, encouraging me to agree. I wasn't sure if I could trust that urge, though, and glanced at Vena.

She was giving Cross the same oh-shit look I had been. Her gaze met mine, but after a brief hesitation, she nodded.

When I looked at him again, his eyes were the same–black surrounded by an intense network of slightly pulsating veins. He should have scared me. I should have wanted to run, but something about Cross made me believe that he only wanted to help.

Now and always.

"Are you using mind control on me?" I asked.

"I will never use mind control on you. You have my word."

"Ev, you're bleeding a lot," Vena said softly.

"I can make it stop," he said. "Please. Trust me."

When I nodded, he gently took my hand and lifted it away. The veins around his eyes pulsed a little faster as he brought my arm to his mouth. The feel of his lips on my skin sent a jolt of awareness through me. As did the gentle suction over my wound.

"Are you feeding?" Vena demanded, hurrying around the counter. "You said you'd help."

He tore his mouth from my skin and turned his head toward her. I couldn't see his expression, but whatever Vena saw had her stopping in her tracks with wide eyes.

His mouth returned to my skin, and I felt that gentle suction again.

What had he said about feedings? That donors often found it euphoric? I could see why. His fingers caressed my skin as he gently held my arm. Add to that the way his head was bent near mine, it felt like a lover's embrace. I lifted my other hand to run my fingers through his hair until I saw the blood on them.

Another whimper escaped me, but the feel of his tongue swiping over my cut distracted me. It stung the first time, but each stroke after hurt a little less until it felt like he was only licking my skin.

When he finished, he took my hand and licked the blood from that too.

I watched the black slowly fade from his eyes as he collected every last drop. My skin tingled once he finally released me, and I finally understood why feeders didn't run away from their vampires. The experience was seductive, and having Cross' singular attention made me crave more. What would it feel like to be fully possessed by him? To allow him to feed from me, knowing I would be marked as his forever?

A shaky exhale escaped me.

"Did you feed from me?" I asked, knowing I was heading down a complicated path.

"I only took enough to be able to heal you," he said.

"Okay," I managed. "Thank you."

"It was my pleasure."

"Does that mean I can move now?" Vena asked angrily.

Cross turned toward her, and she immediately marched over to him and hit him in the face. Not some girly slap but a wicked punch years of training had honed. Cross moved from the force of the blow, but there wasn't a hint of injury as he looked at her.

"Vena!" I grabbed her arm and pulled her away from him with a worried glance at him.

"He fucking controlled me."

"I do apologize for the use of force, Vena. However, I believe the situation warranted it. Why did you risk Everly after promising me you wouldn't?" The deadly warning in his voice extinguished her indignation, and she flushed a deep red.

"Blur was attacked last night," I said. "During the chaos, I saw Sierra's fairy tattoo. It matched the one the fairy at Miles' apartment described."

"We came over here to ask her about it, but she flipped out and started throwing knives," Vena said. "We didn't think we needed you in order to question a human."

"But now we know we do," I said with a nudge at Vena.

She nodded and mumbled an apology. I wasn't sure if it was meant for me or Cross.

Either way, he exhaled heavily and turned toward Sierra.

"Do you have any information regarding the whereabouts of Vena's brother Miles?" he asked.

"Yes," Sierra immediately answered.

"Are you fucking kidding me?" Vena snapped, taking a threatening step toward Sierra.

"Vena, stop. Let Cross do his thing," I warned.

Sierra's gaze shifted to Cross, and I saw a flicker of fear there.

"I hate vampires," she whispered.

"Tell us everything you know about Miles' disappearance and vampires," Cross commanded.

Sierra's expression glazed over, and she started talking.

"A month ago, I went to a club and met a man. He was handsome and had an obsession with wearing cat ears. I never learned his real name, but I got his number. He called me a few times and came over. In the bedroom, he liked to be called Master. Sometimes, he brought a friend who he called Pet." She frowned slightly like she was trying to remember. "I think Master and I had sex while Pet watched, but I'm not sure. It's hazy."

Vena and I shared a glance. I was all for a woman embracing her sexuality, but Sierra didn't strike me as the threesome type. She didn't even strike me as a twosome type. Men usually avoided homicidal crazy chicks.

"I mean, with names like Master and Pet, they had to have some fetishes. Maybe they're less picky," Vena said, seeming to read my mind.

Cross went to Sierra and tugged back the collar of her polo, revealing a tribal-looking tattoo with a swirl in the middle on the base of her neck.

"She's a feeder," he said. "Likely, they changed her memories of their time here. Continue, Sierra."

"Master told me to get a job at Blur. He wanted to know things about the werewolves. Like how many of them worked there. Their names. If they had mates. He wanted to know what kind of jewelry they all wore and who was in charge of their pack."

Cross frowned and glanced at us.

"Is it common knowledge that werewolves work at Blur?" I asked. "We just found out this week."

"Seems to be," Vena said, her tone reflecting her impatience. "Can we get to the part about my brother? Where is he?"

When Cross nodded to Sierra, she said, "In the spare room."

It took Vena and me a second to process what she meant. I'd thought she would give us another clue, not tell us he was in the house.

Vena dashed down the hall and cursed moments later.

"It's locked. Cross, break it open." Frustration and anger laced her words.

He glanced at Sierra. "Stay as you are until I tell you otherwise."

Not wanting to stay with her, I followed him to the room where Vena was twisting the knob ineffectively.

With a single thrust of his hand, Cross hit the door, and the frame splintered, allowing Vena to push her way inside.

The curtains over the small bedroom's single window blocked almost all the light, making it hard to see until Vena turned on the light.

Miles sat on a kitchen chair in the middle of the room. His familiar dark head of hair hung forward as his chin rested on his chest. His arms were tied behind him, and his ankles were zip-tied to the chair's legs.

"Miles!" Vena bolted into the room and fell to her knees beside the chair.

He didn't respond as she shook him, trying to wake him.

"What did she do to him?" she demanded.

"Sierra, come," Cross called.

Sierra appeared in the doorway a moment later. If Sierra felt any guilt over Miles' condition, she didn't look like it under Cross' control.

"What's wrong with him?" Cross asked.

"I gave him a sedative. He needs another dose soon. It should begin to wear off in the next thirty minutes."

"Why did you sedate him?"

"To control him and keep him quiet," Sierra said.

Vena focused on Miles, gently tapping his cheek. Cross stalked around to the back of the chair and snapped the zip ties binding Miles while Vena spoke gently to her brother. Miles groaned and moved his head a little, but his chin returned to his chest, and he didn't move again.

"Perhaps he would be more comfortable on the bed," Cross said, already nudging Vena aside and picking him up.

Vena didn't protest. She held Miles' hand as Cross moved him. Then she sat on the edge of the mattress.

Cross looked at Sierra and gestured to the chair.

"Sit."

She did as she was told.

"Why did your master want to know about the werewolves?" he asked.

"He didn't say," she said.

"Did he ask you to kidnap Miles?"

"Yes."

"Why?"

"He didn't say."

"What does your master look like?"

Her expression turned a little dreamy. "Master has black hair, short in back and long in front. He looks emo but without any makeup. Just thick black lashes around his dark eyes, and he has the cutest ears.

"Pet was like you. Tall, about your height. Long dark hair. Dark eyes. He wore dress pants and a button-up shirt. He didn't button it, though. Master told me to lick Pet's skin."

I made a face, and she noticed.

"Fuck off," she said with a little heat.

"Focus," Cross said.

Her expression immediately mellowed again.

"That's not much of a description," I said softly to Cross.

He nodded and opened his mouth like he was going to give her another order, but then he whipped his head toward the open doorway. I heard someone yell outside.

Cross closed the distance between us and clasped my arms.

"The wolves are here. Tell them everything she said. I will return to you soon."

He brushed his lips across my forehead. The touch was there and gone in less than a heartbeat, and so was he.

Vena and I looked at each other and then at Sierra. She didn't try anything, though. She continued to sit there calmly, looking at us.

A few seconds later, Shepard appeared in the doorway. He inhaled deeply, his worried gaze sweeping over everyone in the room then landing on me.

"I smell vampire and your blood. Where are you hurt?"

I looked at the vibrant scar on my arm. "It's fine."

His gaze turned sad as he looked at the new mark. Then, he wrapped me in his arms, holding me tight as he stroked his hand over the back of my head.

"Sweetheart, it's not fine. A vampire fed on you. Until he's dead, he'll continue to call to you. I'm so sorry this happened. But don't worry." He pulled back to look me in the eyes. "I'll take care of it."

"It wasn't like that," I said quickly. "I was cut, and he healed it. That was all."

Shepard studied me for a moment, kissed my forehead, and hugged me again. I knew he didn't believe me, but convincing him of Cross' innocence would only make me look more crazy. And why wouldn't it? Vampires were dangerous. I knew that too. So, I settled on trying to reassure Shepard and maybe comforting myself a little by hugging him back.

After the morning I had, it felt really nice,

"Can you tell me what happened and who the man on the bed is?" he asked.

I eased out of Shepard's hold and looked at Vena. When it came to telling half-truths, she was our group expert.

"This is Miles, my brother," she said, still holding his hand. "He went missing five days ago. It turns out that vampires compelled Sierra to kidnap him, but she doesn't know why."

"She's a feeder who was just following orders," I said. "She was also compelled to work at Blur and provide her vampire friend information about all of you. She doesn't know why or his name."

Shepard growled and turned toward the door where Anchor stood, his gaze locked on Vena.

"Take Sierra," Shepard said. "We need to figure out what she was doing."

Anchor tore his gaze from Vena and tossed Sierra over his shoulder like a bag of sand.

"I'll be back," he said before disappearing as Cross had.

"Whoa. Are you all that fast?" I asked.

"Yes. We're as fast as our prey," Shepard said.

I glanced at Vena, worried about Cross.

"How did you know to come here?" Vena asked.

"Gunther didn't report in. It smells like his bottles were spiked with something." He moved closer to Miles and sniffed. "Same stuff she's been giving him, I think. It would be better if we didn't involve any authorities, but if you'd like to take him to the hospital, I'll drive you there."

Vena looked down at Miles and slowly shook her head.

"Sierra said the sedative she gave him should be wearing off soon."

Miles moved his head again, rolling it toward the sound of Vena's voice.

"Let's give it a few more minutes then," Shepard said. "Gunther was already waking up, too. How did you know to come here to look for your brother?"

"It turns out that fairies aren't the mindless trash diggers we thought they were," Vena said. "The one that lives in the shrubs outside of Miles' apartment pantomimed that a woman with a fairy tattoo had come for Miles. Guess whose fairy tattoo I saw during last night's fight?"

"Why didn't you come to me?" he asked, looking at her then me.

I felt the weight of his disappointment in that single glance.

"Would you have believed me if I'd marched into your office and said that I suspected Sierra kidnapped my brother? Because I wouldn't have believed me. She had no reason to. Honestly, I thought we were just going to find out where she got her tattoo and go there to start asking questions. I didn't think she'd have him tied to her chair in her spare room."

I could tell by Shepard's expression that he believed Vena, and he didn't like it.

"From now on, come to me. No matter how unbelievable it might be, I'll do my best to believe you."

Rather than make any promises we both knew she wouldn't keep, she turned to look at Miles.

"What are you going to do with Sierra?" I asked, hoping to distract Shepard from the fact that Vena hadn't given her word.

"We'll keep her somewhere safe. Vampires are proprietary about their feeders, and I'm hoping hers will come looking for her. Until then, we're calling in backup. D.C. isn't as clean as it should be, and we need to do something about it before it gets worse. If we kill the vampire controlling her, Sierra will be free to go. Until then, we'll keep taking care of her."

"Shit," Vena breathed. "Look at his neck."

She pulled back Miles' collar, and I moved closer to look at the twin holes there.

"Is someone controlling him, too?" I asked.

Shepard studied Miles for a quiet moment. "It's hard to say. A single feeding doesn't necessarily mean a vampire has control. We'll need to keep an eye on him for a while."

"I wish I understood why Sierra kidnapped him in the first place," Vena said.

"Research," Miles breathed. "Tired."

Vena gave a shout of joy when he spoke. She hugged him hard.

"I think it's safe to move him now," Shepard said. "Let's get you home."

CHAPTER TWENTY

MILES SAT AT OUR DINING ROOM TABLE AS I FINISHED PREPARING soup. He looked like he'd lost ten pounds since I last saw him. His unhealthy pale skin accentuated the dark circles under his eyes.

"Soup?" Fully lucid, Miles made a face as I set a bowl in front of him.

I sat across from him and gave him my no-nonsense stare.

"You said Sierra kept you drugged the entire time and can only remember being fed twice." He didn't remember being fed on, but I didn't bring that up. "Yes, soup. You've lost a lot of weight and are probably starving for something substantial, but your stomach won't know what to do with it, and you'll make yourself sick. So, eat the soup."

He looked to Vena for support, but she shook her head. "Everly's soup is a cure-all. Trust her. Trust the process. You're still pale, and listening to you heave will break my heart."

He grumbled but dipped the spoon into the soup. We waited until he was finished eating before asking more questions.

A few had already been answered before we left Sierra's

place, like where his car had gone. Shepard's guys had found it in Sierra's garage, which Vena used to drive Miles to our house. But we still didn't know how Sierra had managed to kidnap him in the first place.

Vena and I needed answers, especially after what we had been through to find him.

"How do you even know Sierra?" Vena asked.

"I don't know her. Not really. Before you came home with that ring, I'd gotten a lead on some research I was doing. Spawn connected me with Sierra. Since she's human, I thought she was relatively safe enough, so we scheduled to meet at my place."

"I remember opening the door for her and then…" He shook his head. "Next thing I knew, I was drugged and tied to a chair."

"Spawn connected you?" Vena bristled at the information. "I *asked* him if he knew anything."

"What happens at the Shadow Market stays at the Shadow Market." Miles gave a weary grin. "You know not to trust any of them. I'd grown too comfortable with Spawn and forgot that lesson. A vampire must have paid him really well for him to stab me in the back like that."

Vena got up from the table to pace.

"I hate vampires!" she fumed.

I gave her a warning look. While she may hate *most* vampires, she had no cause to hate Cross when he was the reason Miles was home again.

Thinking of Cross, I took Miles' empty bowl to the sink and looked out the kitchen window. The tracks were empty.

After Shepard had taken away Sierra, he'd ordered Doc and a team to track the vampire they could smell. I was worried something might happen to Cross and Doc.

Both sides had made it clear they had no love for the other.

Truthfully, the werewolves seemed to hate the vampires a little more deeply.

I could empathize if the majority of vampires were going around brainwashing and kidnapping people.

"So you don't know why Sierra kidnapped you or why she kept you tied to a chair for days," I asked, returning to the table.

"It's obviously not some crush gone wrong since you were also fed on," Vena said.

Miles lifted his hand to touch the twin, raised bumps on the base of his neck.

"I'm going to kill Spawn," she said under her breath before she disappeared into her room.

"When we talked to Spawn and showed him the ring we'd found, he freaked out," I explained. "He didn't want anything to do with us. He said that we needed to stop looking into things or more family would go missing. Why would he warn us but sell you out?"

Vena emerged from her bedroom and dropped the skin map on the table next to Miles. "Does your kidnapping have something to do with this?"

"What the hell, Vena?" I scolded.

Vena shrugged and looked at her brother. "Well, does it?"

Miles' gaze lit with excitement, and he pulled the map toward him. "You got it open?"

"She fondled it for days, Miles," I said. "On my coffee table. On my counters. Even at work. And why would you put it in a delicious piece of cake? I ate some of that cake, Miles. It was in my mouth."

He gave an absent laugh as he studied it with interest.

"I knew if something happened to me, you'd find it."

"That's not okay. Never do that again. Wait. Please tell me this nasty sheep scrotum isn't the reason you were abducted."

He didn't say anything.

Vena narrowed her eyes at him. "I want information. Whatever you know. Spill it."

Miles rubbed his forehead like he was trying to rid himself of a headache.

"You're not going to like the answers, Vena. Spawn was right. What I'm looking into is dangerous."

"Let me guess," she said. "Following old leads? We followed your breadcrumbs, Miles. The map in the cake. The picture of the book Grandpa Barnaby checked out of the archives before he and Grandma disappeared on an expedition. The stupid vampire strip club someone texted you."

He looked surprised by that, and Vena suddenly seemed very tired. "Our parents have been trying to find leads for years, Miles. They asked us to leave it alone. They didn't want to lose us, either. Yet, you…*you* disregarded their wishes, put yourself in danger, and almost disappeared forever, too."

I frowned. "Even if you found information regarding your grandparents' research, why would Sierra's vampire friend care enough to kidnap you?"

Miles shook his head. "I don't know. Maybe my research intersected with someone else's? That book our grandparents had was supposedly a key for this map."

Vena and I glanced uneasily at each other, knowing we had the missing piece. I had a bad feeling that combining them would make my already stressful life a hundred times worse.

Miles noticed our shared glance. "What aren't you saying?"

Vena went back to her room and returned with the book.

"Where did you find that?"

Miles stood and reached for it, but Vena held it out of his way.

"I found it with a little help," she said. "And if these are why you were taken, I'm hiding them again."

Miles was about to argue, so I leaned over and pressed hard on his fang marks.

He winced. "Fine. Hide them."

"Good," she said.

"How about more soup?" I asked.

He groaned. "No more soup. I want a cheeseburger. Pizza. Anything but soup."

"It'll make you sick," I warned.

He turned to Vena. "Can I please go home now? I've eaten the soup, and you've taken away my research. I just want to shower and go to bed."

"Do you promise to stop all research until Mom and Dad are back?"

"I promise."

Vena wasn't dumb. She knew her brother as well as I did. And I knew he wasn't going to sit at home and watch TV for more than a few days. Yet, she knew when to push and when to give in.

"Fine," she said grudgingly.

She handed Miles his phone, which she'd kept with her since the beginning.

"You will respond to all texts within fifteen minutes and send proof-of-life pictures to me without prompting every three hours. Those are my conditions for your temporary freedom."

"Agreed," he said quickly. "After being held captive and drugged for five days, I'm open to heavy monitoring. Would you like to find a vet to tag me?"

"Don't tempt me," Vena said.

I wasn't entirely sure Miles was kidding. I supposed if I had

BLOOD AND BONBONS

been held captive and fed on, I'd want someone monitoring me, too. Cross came to mind. So did Shepard.

Uneasy over how they were both becoming major players in my life, I refocused on Miles.

"I'll bring you home. Vena and I can drop your car off tomorrow." I glanced at her, and she nodded. "Let me pack some soup for you to eat until tomorrow."

He whined a little, and Vena patted him on the back. "If you didn't do stupid things that got you into trouble, you wouldn't be force-fed soup. Remember that."

She followed me to the kitchen and whispered, "While you're dropping off Miles, I'm going to my parents to hide the book and map. I don't think we should keep them here."

"Are you sure you want to keep them at all after all of this?"

She nodded. "For now. I'll figure out what to do with this stuff later. Right now, I just want it out of here."

Since I wasn't sad to see either go, I agreed.

"After I drop off Miles, I'm going to stop for that new phone I've been meaning to pick up. Then I'll head to Blur to see if Shepard needs help with the cleanup."

Vena smirked at me. "Look at you juggling two sets of *balls*. So proud of you."

I made a face at her. "Make sure you're home in time to let Anchor in. He'll be here to claim his spot on the couch before dark."

She paused. "We'll be alone?"

"Maybe for a little while. I'll be right on your heels, though."

"So, a little playtime."

"I think you both deserve it. But, Vena, be careful. Don't hurt him."

"Yeah, I know." For once, Vena looked serious when she spoke about Anchor. "I get that he has to find his mate and all that. I'll be somewhat good." She grinned. "Starting after playtime."

She hugged Miles tightly, told him he was rank and needed a shower, then waved goodbye at the door as he and I left. His steps were a little slow, but he didn't need my assistance to get to my car.

"Are you sure you don't want to see a doctor?" I asked.

"And tell them what? That I was drugged for five days by a crazy woman who manhandled my junk so I could pee in a bottle and fed me broth and pudding so I wouldn't die?"

I looked down at the soup in my hands.

"Miles, I'm so sorry."

"Hey, don't worry about it. And don't make a big deal about it in front of Vena. I don't want her to worry more than she already is, or I'll have to send proof of life photos every fifteen minutes."

I helped him into the car and hurried around to my side.

"I have some questions now that she's not here," he said as I closed my door. "How did you really find me if Spawn didn't talk?"

My phone chimed with an incoming text that I quickly read as I buckled.

Shepard: Boulder told me you're leaving with the brother. Where are you going?

I looked up and scanned the street but didn't see anything.

Me: Why am I being watched? Did I do something wrong?

"Everly?" Miles asked, probably wondering why we were just sitting there.

"Sorry," I said, glancing at him and saw Vena still standing at the door.

I waved and gave her a thumbs-up as I answered Miles.

"The story of how Vena and I found you is a little crazy." My phone chimed again. "Give me a second to take care of this."

Shepard: You've done nothing wrong. But a vampire that can survive sunlight fed on you. I'm not letting you out of my sight until he's dead.

I groaned.

Me: I'm taking Miles home, and Vena is running to her parents' house outside of town.

Shepard: Addresses.

I sent them then sent a text to Vena.

Me: We're being watched. Shepard wants to know where I'm going. I let him know you're going to your parents and gave him the address.

Shepard: Someone will be at Miles' place in five. No side trips.

I tossed my phone into the center console and started the car.

"You want to know how we found you? It all started with that dumb cave and the vampire we woke up."

As I drove, I gave a cliff-notes explanation to Miles about how we'd found him gone at the same time Vena discovered the vampire was missing. How we'd gone to the market to ask Spawn and received a text with the strip club's coordinates. How we'd gone to their parents' house that night to look for clues, and the vampire had found us and the deal I'd struck.

"Wait. Are you saying you've been helping this vampire?"

"No," I said, signaling for a turn. "I'm saying we've been helping each other." I recapped the events from finding the book to pawning the coin.

"Hold up. You're a millionaire right now?"

"It's like you're the boy version of Vena. No. That's Cross' money. I'm only holding it until we can figure out how to get him papers. If you have any connections for that sort of thing, let me know."

Miles snorted, and I continued with the mystery text asking to swap the ring for information about him at the club, the dead end it had led to, and how Cross had saved us.

"Vena has a death wish," Miles muttered.

"Must run in the family."

Finally, I finished with the retaliation at Blur–inadvertently revealing werewolves ran it–and how the attack the night before had led to seeing Sierra's tattoo.

"So, you owe your rescue to Vena's persistence, Cross' knowledge, the fairy that hides in your bush, and the werewolves," I concluded.

"I can't believe you're on good terms with a vampire."

"He seems to be unique in that regard. I wouldn't trust any other vampires. All the wolves are nice, though."

He sighed and nodded. "Thank you for telling me, and I'm sorry you got wrapped up in this, Everly. As soon as I'm on my feet again, I'm hand delivering you sweets for a month."

I grinned. "Take your time. Vena's already committed to a week of waking up to dazzling confectionery delights and one hot date at Enticed."

"The fancy fae place downtown that's booked out for weeks?" he asked in disbelief.

"Yep. If I space out both your apology treats, I'll live like a queen the rest of this summer."

He chuckled, but the humor died quickly. "Wolves hunt vampires, Ev. I've read that again and again in my research. Aren't you worried you're going to get caught in the crossfire between Cross and Shepard?"

"I'm hoping I'll be able to convince Shepard that Cross is not controlling me."

"How do you know he's not?"

"The people I've seen acted weird. If I start acting weird, Vena will say something."

Miles made a thoughtful sound and tapped on the soup container in his lap as we pulled up to his house. Part of me wanted to tell him that the wolves would be watching him and not to worry. But I didn't. I wasn't sure hearing that would help him feel better.

There was a truck parked in front of Miles' apartment. The big guy within looked at us then looked down again.

"Is it just me, or is that guy giving you uh-oh vibes?" Miles asked, making no move to get out of the car.

My phone chimed a second later.

Shepard: That's Gator in the truck. He's going to watch over Miles for a bit.

Gator looked up and nodded at us.

"He's one of Shepard's guys. He's going to hang out for a bit to make sure you don't get kidnapped again," I said.

Miles reached up and touched the protection charm under his shirt. It had been one of the first things Vena had returned to him.

"This thing had been useless against Sierra. It's good to know I have backups against vampire-controlled humans," he said. "I think I might invest in some better wards."

"Wouldn't hurt," I said, getting out of the car.

Miles let himself out, and we moved up his walk together.

"And it wouldn't hurt to befriend that fairy," I said when the tiny blue monstrosity flew out from the bush at me. "It's the reason we figured out how to find you."

The fairy stopped in its tracks and glared at me with its arms crossed.

I reached into my pocket and removed the dime I'd tucked in there.

The fairy darted forward and stole the coin from between my fingers.

"I thought you hated fairies," Miles said.

"Not a fan of how they fly at my face, but maybe they aren't completely horrible." A small twig hit the side of my head as I unlocked the door, and I hurried inside.

The place was a chaotic mess, just as we'd left it. Miles sighed and started straightening the papers on the table.

Knowing that he was safe and under Shepard's protective watch, I left him to his mess, knowing it would keep him occupied for a while, and headed back to the car. As I walked, I sent Shepard another message.

Me: Miles is safely home. Thanks for watching over him. How's Sierra?

Shepard: Angry. She's talking a little more. It seems that her friend is the reason there were so many deaths around Blur.

Me: At least we know now.

I got into the car and debated my next move, not entirely sure I wouldn't be followed once I left Miles. While I appreciated Cross could be at my side in an instant if I bled, I'd rather *call* him when I was in trouble. However, I wasn't sure I'd get away with a new phone purchase if I had a tail following me.

Debating for only a minute, I dialed Shepard.

He answered with an edgy, "Are you in trouble?"

I smiled slightly. "No. Do you have a minute?"

"I do."

"I know you're busy with everything that's going on. Gunther. Sierra. The vampires. Blur," I said, listing what I knew.

"You're making me nervous, Everly."

"Sorry. That's the opposite of what I intended. My point is that I know you feel responsible for Miles, Vena, and me on top of everything already on your plate, and I don't want you to spread yourself or your men thin, trying to take care of everyone.

"So, I'd like to propose a compromise that will allow you to put your focus where it matters most. I'll add you to my tracking app so you can see where I am at any given time. I use it to keep track of Vena when she goes treasure hunting, and it makes me feel better. Maybe it would give you some peace of mind without sacrificing one of the guys to follow me around?"

Shepard was so quiet on the other side that I looked at my phone to make sure the call hadn't dropped. It hadn't.

"It was just a thought," I said quickly. "I didn't mean to insinuate that I expected you to keep track of me or anything. I only meant it–"

"Everly," Shepard said, cutting me off. "I *am* putting my focus where it matters most. You matter. I do like the idea of being able to see where you are at any given time without having to rely on someone else. I'll send my info so you can add me."

I could feel the heat flooding my face. Was I reading into what he'd said, or did I actually matter to him?

"Okay. I better let you go. Bye."

I hung up and wondered if I'd made things awkward in my attempt to make my life easier. Then I wanted to shake my head at myself. How many times had he said we were like family? Of course family mattered. I really needed to stop letting Vena get into my head.

My phone pinged with an incoming text from Shepard, and I added him as a valid contact in my tracking app.

Having my boss be able to track me was a little odd, but I knew I could turn off the tracking feature if I needed to.

Feeling a little better, I texted him.

Me: You're all set up. I'm heading downtown to the phone store and plan to stop at Blur after to help clean up.

Shepard: What's wrong with your phone?

Me: I dropped mine at Juicy and want to replace the screen protector. Nothing for you to add to your plate.

When the phone didn't ping again, I set it in its holder, waved to Gator, and pulled away from the curb.

I found a parking spot almost right in front of the store.

Inside, I struggled with financial sensibilities and what I knew of Cross' expensive tastes. Acknowledging I wasn't spending my money but his, I forked over way too much on a high-end phone and left with a new line added to my plan.

Cross was outside, leaning on my car in the midday sun.

Fitted slacks molded to his muscled legs as he watched my approach with a sexy smirk. Relieved and glad to see him, I smiled back.

"Do you know how many wolves are following you around like love-sick pups? It's going to be a lot harder to speak to you now."

I handed him the phone.

"You'll need to start using today's technology then. Gain any knowledge about it lately?"

"A bit," he said, taking the phone from me.

Then he surprised me by pulling me into his arms and kissing my forehead.

"I'm sorry for leaving you as I did," he said against my hair. "I knew the wolves wouldn't hurt you, but…are you all right?"

"I'm fine," I assured him, hugging him back.

And I was.

Miles was finally safely back home.

Sure, I had a best friend who liked causing trouble, but now I also had a vampire willing to save me and a wolf family to watch over us all. What more could I want?

"I saw a dessert shop down the way," Cross said, releasing me. "My treat."

He truly spoke my love language.

Yep, life was good again.

Thank you for reading Blood and Bonbons, book 1! If you want to find out what happens next for Everly and Vena, check out Fangs and Fudge, book 2.

AUTHOR NOTE

Thank you for reading! We truly hope you loved Blood and Bonbons as much as we loved writing it.

Just in case you didn't know, Melissa Nicole is an amazing writing team of two extremely creative and funny minds. Melissa is romance-obsessed with a heavy preference toward paranormal, and Nicole is the queen of humorous cozy mysteries. After countless lunches together, Melissa asked Nicole the fateful question, "Will you be my partner?"

And you just read the proof that Nicole didn't reject Melissa's advances.

Blood and Bonbons is only the beginning. We have so much planned for this world...and a lot of it was inspired by real-life conversations. Especially the opening line of this book, which Nicole said after Melissa uttered a very unhelpful comment. It was so giggle-worthy to Melissa that she insisted it go in the book. Nicole has jokingly fired Melissa as a friend at least a dozen times. And Melissa keeps luring Nicole back for more.

Their friendship is a little like Vena and Everly. We won't say who is who, though. (*Cough* Melissa has more Vena tendencies than Nicole).

The friends were entertaining to write. The whole cast was, actually. We can't quite decide who we like more between Cross and Shepard for Everly, but we're shipping Anchor for Vena pretty hard. So is she!

We can't wait to see how she deals with falling for a werewolf.

Speaking of werewolves…poor Gunther! We have a whole backstory for him that didn't quite make it onto the pages. He lost his mate previously which is why he's drinking. Drinking for werewolves doesn't work like it does for normal people, which means he drinks heavily and all the time. That's how Sierra managed to drug him. She spiked his bottle, and the alcohol covered the scent of the drug. Poor guy never knew what hit him.

And if you like that little bit of backstory, you're going to love hearing more about Cross' origins. After you sign up for our newsletter at https://melissanicoleauthor.com/subscribe, we'll send you a link to our bonus content, including access to a short story from his point of view, detailing his arrival in America.

We don't give away why he left. At least, not yet. But it does tie into those mysterious stones that Vena and Everly discovered at the back of Vena's grandpa's book. Curious about those too? Keep reading for a peek at that page.

And don't forget that Melissa and Nicole write separately under many pen names if you're hungry for more books from them. (We've included a helpful list for you!)

Happy reading!

Melissa Nicole

MEET THE CREW AT BLUR!

Shepard

DOB - October 10th (33 years old)

Sex - Male

Hair - Dark blonde

Eyes - Light grey

Height - 6'4"

Weight - 260 - all muscle

Occupation - Owner of Blur

Hobbies - Doesn't have time for hobbies. Protects the city and his pack.

Quirks - Can't stand strong perfume, know-it-alls, or unreliable people. Respects loyalty.

Anchor

DOB - February 14th (27 years old)

Sex - Male

Hair - Dark brown

Eyes - Brown

Height - 6'3"

Weight - 273 - all muscle

Occupation - VIP bouncer

Hobbies - Protecting those who can't protect themselves. Watching Vena.

Quirks - Hasn't dated seriously before. Embarrasses fairly easily. Tugs on his earlobe when nervous.

Doc

DOB - November 17th (45 years old)

Sex - Male

Hair - Brown with sliver streaks (mostly silver)

Eyes - light blue

Height - 6'2.5"

Weight - 255

Occupation - Blur's second in command.

Hobbies - Working with the younger guys to train them. Stopping violence before it starts. Kicking back with a glass of bourbon.

Quirks - Doesn't take kindly to disrespectful people. Hates violence but has to use it more often than he would like.

Gunther

DOB - March 21st (39 years old)

Sex - Male

Hair - Black

Eyes - Unknown. Doesn't make a lot of eye contact.

Height - 6'2"

Weight - 195

Occupation - Dishwasher at Blur.

Hobbies - None. He lost the joy of living after his wife recently passed away from cancer.

Quirks - Drinks heavily.

Buzz

DOB - August 3rd (29 years old)

Sex - Male

Hair - Blonde

Eyes - Hazel

Height - 6'1"

Weight - 220

Occupation - Bar Manager

Hobbies - Showing off his muscles. Light flirting with bar patrons.

Quirks - Big romantic. Flirts but is waiting for Mrs. Right. A big softy who can't stand the sound of a growling stomach.

Boulder

DOB - June 21st (25 years old)

Sex - Male

Hair - Auburn

Eyes - Mossy green

Height - 6'3"

Weight - 290

Occupation - Bartender

Hobbies - Playing any kind of full-contact sport, especially if he can pound his twin brother.

Quirks - Hates when people confuse him with Tank. They're twins but not 100% identical. Loves eating anything Grizz or Gator makes.

Tank

DOB - June 21st (25 years old)

Sex - Male

Hair - Auburn

Eyes - Mossy green

Height - 6'4"

Weight - 290

Occupation - Bartender

Hobbies - Beating his twin brother at EVERYTHING.

Quirks - Loves to steal food from Boulder while he's not looking, bonus if that food is made by Grizz and Gator. Doesn't mind when people confuse him with Boulder, especially if he's in trouble.

Griz

DOB - December 25th (30 years old)

Sex - Male

Hair - Brown

Eyes - Brown

Height - 6'5"

Weight - 320 - (90% muscle)

Occupation - Head chef

Hobbies - Loves a good book and smooth whiskey.

Quirks - Don't mess with his kitchen. Annoyed easily by people who send back perfectly executed food.

Army

DOB - November 3rd (32 years old)

Sex - Male

Hair - light brown (but it's cut so close to his head you can't see much of it)

Eyes - Green

Height - 6'1.5"

Weight - 225

Occupation - Front door bouncer

Hobbies - Loves the gym.

Quirks - Will pretend to be any woman's BF while at Blur to help deter unwanted attention. Most women want to keep him after. Won't raise his voice in front of a woman.

Detroit

DOB - July 11th (28 years old)

Sex - Yes, please.

Hair - Dark and always styled

Eyes - Golden brown

Height - 6'2"

Weight - 230

Occupation - VIP Bartender

Hobbies - Picking on Everly's shortness. Self improvement. Hitting the gym with Army.

Quirks - Loves to tease and flirt. A cocktail slinging god.

Gator

DOB - August 19th (24 years old)

Sex - Male

Hair - Sandy brown

Eyes - Hazel

Height - 6'6"

Weight - 280

Occupation - Sous-chef and muscle man as needed.

Hobbies - Food fusion. Loves combining recipes. Finds old cookbooks and recreates them with modern style.

Quirks - Likes being in the back of Blur where there are less people and noise . . . unless Grizz is yelling.

Gunner

DOB - July 30th (22 years old)

Sex - Male

Hair - Super blonde

Eyes - Arctic blue eyes

Height - 6'7"

Weight - 275

Occupation - Works wherever Shepard needs him.

Hobbies - Running long distances with the pack.

Quirks - Hates being the "baby" of the crew, especially since he is the tallest. Likes to cause mischief when he's off duty.

Never forget
Our protection is fleeting

Green

Matched
to the
dwarves

Red
(as is fitting)

Matched
to the
vampires

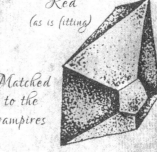

All color
and none

Matched
to the
fae

Blue

Matched
to the
werewolves

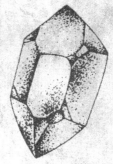

FANGS AND FUDGE

BY MELISSA NICOLE

Not all fur is friendly.

When one of the toughest shifters in D.C. disappears, Everly knows the vampire infestation is serious. To find her best friend's love interest and prevent her from going rogue and making things worse, Everly enlists Cross's help. After all, who better to rescue a wolf from vampires than the deliciously handsome vampire who loves kissing her forehead and waking her in bed?

Cross is more than willing to intercede on Everly's behalf, especially if doing so annoys Shepard. However, both must put their competitive feelings aside when they realize the vampires aren't just looking for their next meal. They're starting a war, and only by working together will the group be able to stop what's coming.

With centuries of deep-seated hatred, cooperating won't come easy.

Join the D.C. crew as Vena once again does what she's not supposed to in her quest to find Anchor, and Everly has to be rescued by not one, but two epic heroes.

A BLACK MOON MYSTERY
BY NICOLETTE PIERCE

Wanted: Paranormal Tracker

Late nights, low pay, dangerous assignments, and a cranky boss (werewolf, actually). Apply in person. If wolf is in bad mood, run.

As an untrained witch arriving in the town of Forgotten Falls, I must fight to become a paranormal tracker. Getting the irritable police chief to hire me is a challenge I'm willing to take in order to leave my old life behind. But in a wolf dominated profession, I must prove I can do the job.

Stumbling upon a dead body, I leave the case in the police's hands, knowing my subpar witch skills are better off tracking than sleuthing. But as I settle into my new town, clues emerge. The killer is on a mission and more people will die. After I receive a threatening message, I know I must act before it's too late.

To make matters worse, the only room available to rent comes with an occupant. Thinking Niles is just an obstinate talking cat, I find I'm wrong. Niles has secrets of his own. In the hidden town of Forgotten Falls, where witches and paranormal creatures live, anything is possible.

If you like humorous mystery adventures with mischievous creatures, wonky magic, giant donuts, treacherous traps, and awkward piggyback rides, you'll love Whiskers and Warrants.

FURY FRAYED

OF FATES AND FURIES
BY MELISSA HAAG

Griffins, Werewolves, Succubi...Oh-my! Norse and Greek mythology collide in this action-packed urban fantasy where shifters and romance abound.

I have no idea what I am, but I know I'm not human.

Megan's temper lands her in a town of misfit supernatural creatures. It's the one place she should be able to fit in, but she can't. Instead, she itches to punch the smug sheriff in his face, pull the hair from a pack of territorial blondes, and kiss the smile off the shy boy's face. Unfortunately, she can't do any of that, either, because humans are dying and all clues point to her.

With Megan's temper flaring, time to find the real killer and clear her name is running out. As much as she wants to return to her own life, she needs to embrace who and what she is. It's the only way to find and punish the creature responsible.

Made in the USA
Monee, IL
25 August 2025

23096462R00184